P9-DMK-111

Ghetto Girls

Black Print Publishing
289 Livingston St
Brooklyn, NY

Ghetto Girls

Black Print Publishing
289 Livingston St
Brooklyn, NY

Black Print Publishing
289 Livingston St
Brooklyn, NY 11217

Copyright © 2002 Anthony Whyte

All rights reserved. No part of this book may be reproduced in any form or by any means without the prior consent of the Publisher, excepting brief quotes used in reviews.

ISBN 09722771-2-9

Printed in Canada

9 8 7 6 5 4 3 2

Acknowledgments

I would like to thank my friends and family who helped to make this dream a reality. Michelle Robinson AKA Coco, Sublime Visuals creative director Jason Clairborne. Silky Black Sho Biz, Dexter Braithwaite the President of Black Print, and Carl Weber it's publisher.

CHAPTER 1

NO DRUGS OR ALCOHOL ALLOWED read the sign outside the club.

"Yo! You girls can't stand here. You're gonna have to move it on," the doorman yelled, pointing down the block.

"I hate this shit," Coco sighed. "But you know what? One day I'm gonna own this fucking club, and then I'll probably be doing the same shit."

Coco and her friends, Danielle and Josephine, Da Crew as she called them, started to walk. They had just been tossed from Broadway City, the teen club on 42nd Street and Broadway for smoking a blunt. Now they stood around outside, enviously checking out all the happenings. A lot of people were stepping into the club, some they knew and some they didn't.

"Yo, check out that fat Benz," Coco shouted. They all made tracks for the corner to see the sleek black whip.

"Damn! Now that shit is P-H-A-T. I could see jackin' a nigga for sump'n like that." Coco's friend Danielle placed her hand under her shirt like she was gonna pull out a gun.

"Yo, can I get a light?" the driver, a tall, dark-skinned sister in a Tommy Girl dress, popped out of nowhere, scaring the shit outta the girls. Coco tried to size the woman up as she stepped toward her.

Is this bitch packing, or can she be jacked? Coco wondered. The woman appeared to be sixteen or seventeen, taller than Coco, but much thinner. If it came down to a fight, Coco was sure she could kick her ass.

"Yo, are you gonna give me a light, or what?" The girl stood about three feet from Coco, one hand on her hip and the other one holding out a cigarette.

"How much does a ride like that cost?" Coco demanded.

"Don't ask me," she replied, "it's my uncle's, and he's outta town, so I'm driving it this weekend."

"For real?" Coco replied. She took her cigarette out of her mouth and gave it to the newcomer. The girl used it to light hers.

"Yeah, but it ain't all that," the girl replied as she returned Coco's cigarette. "Have y'all been inside the club yet?"

"Yeah, it's ah'ight. But we ..." The conversation ended abruptly as a volley of shots erupted. The blast of the bullets rang out and all the girls hit the dirt, except for the newcomer. She was frozen to her spot. Coco yanked her down.

"If you wanna keep driving this weekend, you better get your black ass down here."

All the girls scrambled on their stomachs back to the Mercedes. Another volley went off as they raced to get inside the car, slamming the door.

"Shit! Is this thing bulletproof?" Coco asked.

"Nah," the newcomer replied.

"Well then I think we should be out," Danielle yelled.

"Yeah, we should definitely be leaving this spot," Coco agreed.

The driver put the car in gear and slammed on the accelerator, barely avoiding another car. She swerved wildly to the middle of the street.

"Damn, this thing can really fly," Coco exclaimed from her place riding shotgun. "Oh, um, I'm Coco, and that's Da Crew, Josephine and Danielle"

"I know who y'all is! I mean, I've seen y'all in L.'s last video."

"Yeah, we were in that joint, but we're coming out with our own style now."

"I'm Deedee."

"What's up, Deedee? You seem like cool peeps. Thanks for the ride. What kind of biz is your uncle into?"

"Music biz," Deedee smiled. "He's a music producer."

"That's ah'ight," Coco smirked, pointing at McDonalds. "Yo, make a left here, Deedee. I want me some fries."

"Yeah, I could go for some fries," Danielle added. "But what I really want is a chocolate shake."

"I'm with that." Deedee turned into McDonalds. "Y'all

wanna chill here or go to the drive-thru?"

"Drive-thru," Coco ordered as she checked out the restaurant. "Ain't no niggas sittin' up in there." Deedee pulled up to the drive-thru window.

"Welcome to McDonalds. May I take your order, please?"

"Yeah, let me get four orders of large fries and," Deedee looked back. "And four chocolate shakes?"

"Three chocolate shakes," Danielle answered.

Deedee reached for her wallet. "I got it, y'all," she said. She found a twenty-dollar bill and stuck it under the cup.

"Do you have twenty cents so I can give you back a ten?" Deedee asked the cashier.

"Nah. Take it out the twenty," Deedee yelled, trying to be hard.

En garde! I'll let you try my Wu-Tang style. Bring the ruckus, bring the muthafucking ruckus! The hook from the Wu-Tang Clan knocked, and the whole posse moved in time as the car shuddered from the heavy bass.

"It's not the Russian, it's the Wu-Tang crushing roulette. Slip up, you'll get crushed like Suzette...."

It was smiles all around. The fries and shakes had hit the spot.

"Wu-Tang has mad, mad flavas, yo," said Coco, demanding agreement. Da crew nodded, but Deedee didn't agree.

"Yeah, too many," Deedee said. Then her eyes met Coco's stare of indifference, and her voice trailed off for a second. But Deedee didn't blink. She continued, "There's too many emcees, and they all wanna let off their rhymes at once."

"Shame on a nigga who try to run a game on a nigga whose buck-wild wit' da trigga...."

The lyrics of the Wu vibrated from the car's speakers and Da Crew nodded their heads to the music. Coco stared at Deedee's manicured nails, resting on the wheel. Besides an occasional glance in the rearview mirror, Deedee kept her eyes on the road. Flashing lights went by. The sound of the police proceeded in opposite direction.

"D'ya know much about da business?" asked Coco

with that same stare. For a moment, Deedee thought of elaborating, but decided to wait.

Coco continued to stare. She checked out Deedee's features against her dark skin, and decided that Deedee was a pretty girl. The Mercedes came to a halt at a red light.

Ain't a damn thing change. Protect ya neck...

As the car speakers blared, blasting the hype lyrics of "Protect Ya Neck," Deedee lit another cigarette and checked the time. She felt some kind of weird alliance forming with this shotgun.

"What time is it?" asked Coco.

Deedee smiled. "One forty. It's still early. Anything y'all would like to do?"

"Yeah," replied Coco. "Let's rock`n' roll downtown, yo."

Deedee hesitated. "Don't worry about getting into the clubs. We're performers. We know all the bouncers, girlfriend." Josephine tapped her on the shoulder in a reassuring manner.

"Josepine is such a show off," said Danielle.

Deedee lifted her foot off the brake and slowly pressed on the gas. The sleek car began to move toward the downtown lane, the sound of the Wu-Tang Clan in tow. Deedee smiled, enjoying the sense of camaraderie. Coco stared straight ahead, visibly impressed.

CHAPTER 2

"Cheeba. Cheeba Coco puff ...." The rhythmic chant of the hoarse voice was followed by a dry cough.

"What's up, Deja?" Coco greeted the neighborhood weed dealer with a smile.

"I got some serious shit, Coco. It's all that. No lie. You wanna give it a try?" asked Deja in a melodious tone that brought sweet music to Coco's ear and a five-dollar bill out of her pocket. Deja shoved a small plastic bag in Coco's right hand. Coco examined the bag, and the smell of the skunkweed engulfed the interior of the car.

"Peace, Deja. It looks good." Coco grinned as Deedee hit the accelerator and the car screeched away. "Damn, I hope he buys some breath mints or see a dentist, yo. His breath is kickin'!"

"Hell, yeah! Why'd you let him get all up in your face, girl?" Josephine chimed in from the back seat. "We were all tryin'a hold our breath. His breath was lethal." They all laughed. Coco stared at the contents of the bag.

"Yeah, that's my nigga, though. He always come through with the serious shit." Suddenly, she startled Deedee by yelling. "Pull over! I've got to get a Philly for this. Y'all want something from the store?" Coco slammed the car door and hurried to the store when she didn't get a response.

A few minutes later, she strolled back to the car. Once inside, she slit a cigar and dumped the tobacco out the window. She replaced it with the weed. Coco deftly rolled and licked it smooth, her tongue snaking up and down the length of the blunt. Deedee stared in awe at Coco's performance. She had seen her uncle's attempts to roll a blunt, but never had she seen him execute it as skillfully as Coco.

"Did you guys see that?" Deedee marveled. Danielle nodded yawningly. She had seen the performance before. To her it was nothing out of the ordinary. But to Deedee it was new and she was amazed.

Coco had this effect on everyone who saw her in action, whether she was dancing, singing or just rolling a blunt. She always drew stares of amazement. Her survival was also amazing. Coco hailed from a family of three, including a father she had not seen since she was two years old, and a steadily boozing mother who was so drunk at times that she couldn't remember who Coco was.

"Who da fuck are you?" Rachel Harvey sometimes asked Coco. "What are y'all doing in my place? Y'all got to go. Gon' git da fuck out, and don't try to steal nutt'n," she would scream at Coco and her friends. It was embarrassing, but Coco never showed the embarrassment. Instead, the girls would race to another venue and continue their rehearsal. Coco's high-energy style of singing and dancing always lightened the mood after one of her mother's scenes.

Sometimes, Coco relaxed by wandering up to the roof, where she would spend hours, daydreaming and crying. Sometimes she would fall asleep up there. But after a decapitated body was discovered on the roof, Coco stopped using it.

At school, she coped, and received passing grades. But it was a hassle keeping the nosy guidance counselor out of her business.

"How's your mother doing, Coocoo? I haven't seen her recently. Is she working?" Coco would stare, trying to decide whether she disliked this woman more for not being able to pronounce her name correctly, or for being a little too damn nosy. In any case, her reaction would be the same. Coco would force a smile and reply:

"My mother has a job."

"Well, when is she off?"

"On the weekends," Coco would yell over her shoulder as she hurriedly walked away.

"Coocoo...Coocoo..." Mrs. Martinez would yell back, but Coco would be out of hearing, and on her way to rendezvous with Danielle James and Josephine Murray: Da Crew.

Both girls were recent transfers to the school, and they were also talented singers and dancers. Before they came, Coco reigned as the high school queen of song and dance. All the trophies were stored at her house.

On the rare occasions when her mother was sober and user friendly, she related tales of a "No-good, singing, traveling man." Coco decided he must have been her father. At times when her mother was not too drunk she would produce pictures and wonder out loud if Coco and the man in the photographs shared any resemblance. *Maybe there is a likeness*, Coco thought as she glanced at the old, tattered pictures. "Y'all both got the same lips," her mother would say teasingly. It was compassion enough, and Coco shared the loneliness.

Singing was Coco's escape. She fantasized about being there onstage, the audience loving her. One day, wandering through Central Park, Coco was daydreaming about being a pop star. She got so caught up in her fantasy, she forgot that she wasn't alone, so a park audience was treated to an exclusive, imaginary performance from Coco. Closing her eyes, she became engulfed with the energy she radiated in her routine of singing and dancing on an imaginary stage. She was captivating, shining like a star.

She lost her mind to an encore and a couple of spins, mingled with a few turns. Coco burst into a verse from 'I'm Coming Out.' She was Diana Ross for a minute, and a crowd gathered and cheered her on, giving her their strong support.

"You're gonna be a star one day, Coco. Keep at it," some kid said.

"Maybe one day we'll work together," said a fat, dark-skinned man. He gave her a business card that read *Busta, the talent promoter.*

Coco never stopped singing, and one day danced herself into a music video. It was the first time she had received money for her fantasy. She felt good, but it only served to whet her appetite.

Coco first met Danielle and Josephine at that video shoot. Although they had been attending the same school, they were not aware of each other's existence. Danielle and Josephine were locked into Coco's vibes after this first meeting. Coco had dreamt of being another Diana Ross, and now she had found her Supremes. In school, the girls hung together, allowing Coco the time to discover the family she had been longing for. The three talented teens formed Da Crew, with Coco at the helm.

Danielle's mother didn't mind her daughter being out so much, since she thought Danielle was in the library most of the time. The grades were good, but at home Danielle was the product of a wrecked marriage. Her white father moved out and left her black mother. Danielle was heartbroken. At home she dealt with a divorced mother who changed boyfriends with regularity, a parent who provided for Danielle but didn't know, or maybe didn't care that her talented daughter was usually in the streets, running with the clique.

So Danielle hung with Josephine and admired Coco. Danielle, light-skinned and beautiful, was easily mistaken for Spanish. It wasn't unusual for her to hear questions in Spanish directed at her, and most of the time she gladly accepted the extra attention her exotic looks brought her.

Josephine's parents were working professionals, and her family was the closest to what could be called a normal family. She just wanted to fit in. It was ecstasy once she hooked up with the other girls. Her parents were happy to see their daughter happy, so they always allowed her to participate freely in extracurricular activities. She was allowed the time for rehearsal. There was only one stipulation.

"I'm good as long as my school work's up to date," Josephine would say whenever the topic of rehearsal schedules was brought up.

The posse rehearsed their routine almost every evening after school and performed on weekends, usually Friday evenings, at different clubs. Each was loyal to the clique that had blossomed right under their families' noses.

*   *   *

Headlights bounced off the paved streets, causing tiny speckled beads of reflection. The girls made their way past three older women, sipping, standing around, and losing their souls in the bottle.

Coco gazed out the car window. "Why do these people keep holding on?" she wondered aloud.

"That's their salvation, drinking, I guess," said Deedee.

"That's...that spot!" yelled Coco, changing the subject to something less depressing.

"Yeah...yeah," replied Da Crew as they gazed at the nightclub *Genesis*.

"Let's check this scene, yo," demanded Coco.

"Okay, I hear you. But can I park first?" asked Deedee.

"Yeah, right over there. They're pulling out," Coco shouted.

Deedee guided the car with some difficulty into the vacant spot. The teens standing in line turned and stared in the direction of the car.

"Why's everyone all up in my biz?" asked Deedee, loud enough for anyone to hear. No one answered. Da Crew had performed at this club before, so Coco moved toward the front, motioning Da Crew and Deedee to follow. The girls felt like celebrities as they were escorted into the nightclub.

"Hey yo, check this out. We've got some honeys in da house," said an Afro-headed youth as he menacingly approached the girls, his hips gyrating and arms raised above his head.

"Yo, y'all wanna be swinging wit' Lil' Long, or what?" he asked. Coco stepped closer to him, pressing four fingertips in his chest.

"We're gonna swing wit' you later, Lil' Long. But for now, just cool it. We're gonna chill. And here's a spearmint, yo. You might need some more, but it's a start." She turned to Da Crew. "Why does every stinkin'-breath wanna get up all on top of me, all up in my face tonight?" she asked as she lit the blunt.

"You're gonna have to put that out," said a club security officer.

"Okay, okay," said Coco. She inhaled and then crushed the lit tip under her right boot.

"Bitch, that's some expensive-ass weave you're wearing, right?" asked a roughneck with dreads down to his shoulders.

"Yeah, it's your mammy's," shot back Deedee.

"Oohh," chorused a small crowd of club hoppers who gathered at the site.

Coco and Da Crew were wearing headgear, so Deedee figured the voice was directed at her. She had to reply.

"Yo, I'll slap--"

"Whassup, Deja? Yo chill. This is my friend, Deedee. She's real down-to-earth once you get to know her," said Coco. She hoped the situation wouldn't get physical.

"Well, as long as she recognize that I'm not here to represent da bullshit! I'm only representing da real. Then we ah'ight."

****

"Watch da soundman," was the chant from the deejay as he flipped the script, and the music transformed the club into a hip-hop mass.

"Booyakka ... Booyakka ... soundman lick some shots," yelled the crew in their reveling.

The groove converted the club into a swirling, bass-heavy, resonating grind. The volume sent a quiver up the spine of even the most relaxed wallflowers. Coco moved toward the bar, not stopping to join the party. Deedee, hot on her heels, finally caught up to her.

"Coco! Thanks for what you did back there. That was the second--"

"Keep your mouth shut and stop acting like you have bodyguards and there shouldn't be a third time. Unnerstan'?" growled Coco, nostrils flaring, eyes wide.

"But--" Deedee's face wore a baffled expression.

"Nah. No buts," Coco said. "You wanna be really cool, buy me a thank-you drink." Coco drifted toward the bar.

"I can't do that. I'm a minor."

"Save it, yo. You're right. You ain't old enough." Coco's voice trailed off. She whirled off to the bar and came back with a beer.

"Don't you think you've had enough of that stuff?" asked Deedee, wondering how she got the bartender to give her a drink.

"Okay? So you gave Da Crew and me a twirl in your uncle's rented car. Now you wanna tell me what to do?"

Coco asked without even looking at Deedee. For a moment, Deedee reflected on what exactly she should say. She wanted to say "fuck-off," but repressed the thought. Instead she pulled out her cigarettes, offering one to Coco, who quickly took it and lit it.

Deedee stared at Coco, cigarette dangling from her lips.

"You're not even gonna offer me a light, are you?"

Coco's face almost formed a smile, but she spotted Deja and his dreads, and the frown quickly reappeared.

"Ah yeah, ah yeah" shouted Deja, in a party mood, his eyes locked on Deedee.

"Yeah, yeah," replied Coco, pushing Deedee aside and confronting Deja.

"Yeah, so are you wit' it now?" he murmured with a smile.

"Ah'ight, yo. Let's ketch a wreck".

Deja grabbed Coco's hand and pulled her toward the gyrating pile on the dark floor. She was ready. After the blunt and the brew, Coco's senses welcomed the groove.

"Time to get busy, yo," Coco, yelled as she whisked by Da Crew. The girls turned around in unison, following Coco and Deja to the dance floor.

Deedee watched as the trio partied with Deja. Suddenly, it seemed as if they owned the floor. Coco started moving precise, like a ninja anticipating a blow. The other girls took their cue. Before Black Moon could "Enta da Stage," the girls had the spot rocking and the crowd shouting, "Go Coco, Go Coco." Da Crew moved in for the kill, but Coco was sharp. She was in her realm; this was her world.

"I'm taking a break, yo," said Coco, leaving the celebration on the dance floor. She made her way past people twisting, turning and bopping their heads rhythmically to the urging of the excited deejay.

"Yeah, party people, we're gonna ..."

"I hate when they do that shit, yo," said Coco.

"What shit?" asked Deedee, still visibly awed by the way Coco had dominated the floor.

"Wow, Coco. You are really some kinda dancer. Were you always--"

"No, the question is, can you dance, Ms. Cool One?" Deja interrupted the girls.

"Yeah. Are you ready for me now?" Chimed in Lil' Long, grabbing his crotch, hips still in motion, aimed at Coco.

"Need to play around some more before I get to ya. You look serious," Coco tossed back at the disgruntled face of the crotch-grabber.

"Later," Coco said as she headed away from him. "I need some air, yo."

"What about you?" quizzed Deja, swooping down on the defenseless Deedee. She had let him come too near. She could not back up, and did not want to push him out of her face. The introduction was still fresh in her mind. His breath was hot. It smelled awful, like burnt body parts.

"Ah'ight, let's dance," she said as she reached for his hand and directed her thoughts to the floor. Two or three times his hands made contact with her hips, waist or breasts. Each time, Deja pretended the contact was incidental. She didn't push it. She paid it no mind and the sounds took her away--the bass-line driving hard, ricocheting from her hips, moving her body to a pelvic grind.

"Ah'ight, party people, as we continue on wit' that rub-a-dub style..." came the voice of the deejay, colliding with Deedee's efforts on the floor.

"I hate those fucking deejays," she said, mimicking Coco. It was now her exit line.

"I gotta get some air, yo," Deedee said as she made her escape from the floor. Deja wore a jilted look.

"You know where to find me," he said, as he turned and bounced toward the celebration on the dance floor. The floor now belonged to Josephine and Danielle, moving in an encore of Coco's performance. Da Crew was clearly enjoying themselves.

"Another one?" asked Deedee when she encountered Coco holding a cigarette and glass.

"Another one what?" Coco showed contempt for Deedee's meddling. "Listen," she continued, adjusting her expression with a crooked smile. "I know my limitations," she declared, holding the last syllable slightly longer than normal. "I do this all the time. There's nothin' new to this. So don't sweat it."

"Well, I just don't think you should have another..."

"Da posse is still tearing shit up," burped Coco. Deedee stared at Coco's crooked grin, then she put a cigarette to her lips.

"Yeah, they doin' their thing. Gimme a light," said Deedee, attempting to absorb the situation without sounding sympathetic. Coco obliged. Her grin had gone awry, clinging to another corner of her mouth.

"The performance. Is it-- uh?" Deedee asked awkwardly.

"Is it what?" Coco replied.

"Is it your salvation?" Deedee replied too quickly.

"Never thought about it like that. Never really."

"That deejay..." chorused Da Crew walking toward the smoking duet.

"...Talks too muthafuckin' much," said all four girls.

"Save me some shorts," said Josephine.

"I'm gonna get a drink," yelled Danielle. "Whew, I'm hot and thirsty."

"I seen you bumping an' all up in Deja's face. I tell you wha' my mother always sez, don't get friendly too quickly, and don't trust no man," Coco sleepily mumbled. The alcohol had numbed her thoughts, but she was still in charge of Coco. This had been done before. Deedee stared at her and for a moment. She felt pity, then a tinge of nervousness as her eyes met Deja's stare.

"Why is he clocking you so hard? What'd ya do to homeboy? He's got that sick puppy look, trying to catch a new owner. He's open like 7-Eleven, girlfriend," Coco said giddily. She even managed a chuckle.

Deedee stared at Coco. She watched as the alcohol stimulated the meltdown of Coco's hard edge. It made her friendly and almost childlike.

"It must mean it's my turn," said the one who called himself Li'l Long. Coco grabbed his hand. She motioned to Da Crew. They turned and strutted back to the dance floor. Deedee marveled again at Coco's moves. She was startled as someone's hands brushed against her ass.

"Hey," she said, and whirled around to face Deja.

"Chill with that, please."

"With what?" asked Deja, his hands held high.

"With trying to cop a feel," said Deedee emphatically. "I don't like it," she continued. "You should be trying to buy me a drink, talking sexy to me, or somethin' besides trying to feel on my behind."

"You're a spoiled an' bossy bitch," said Deja, dejected. "That's because you think you're all this `n' that." His voice rose, competing with the bass.

"All right, party people. Yeah! Give it up for Coco and Da Crew. Young ghetto celebs, no doubt. Doing their thing-thing."

"Oh shit. Oh no- he didn't," Coco said. She smiled, acknowledging the onlookers.

"Let's get da fuck off this floor," said Josephine.

"You guys can really go, yo!" said Deedee, catching up to Coco. Da Crew kept walking toward a booth.

"We'll be back in a few," said Da Crew, as if on cue.

"They must've seen their boyfriends. Hey, don't get lost, girlies," said Coco.

"Do you have a boyfriend?" Deedee asked without warning, surprising herself and Coco. She had figured Coco wouldn't mind talking a little.

"Nah," replied Coco effortlessly. Deedee had been right. She delved further.

"Why not? Don't you want one?" asked Deedee.

"Men shouldn't be trusted. Men start out as boys. They love to beat up women, and take advantage of them, because they think you're weaker. But not me. I'm not gonna be nobody's house pet, know what I'm sayin'?" Coco reached for a light and fumbled to get the last cigarette from her pack.

"And boys are no good," she declared finally, shaking the thoughts out. Deedee thought she saw pain. She felt it. She thought of reaching out and giving Coco a hug, but decided against it. What difference would a hug make anyway, she reasoned.

****

"Stogie," said Josephine, hands showing nails, tipped and manicured. Coco passed her the burning cigarette. Deedee considered offering another cigarette, but Coco turned and walked away. She moved clumsily under Deedee's watchful eyes, found an empty chair and plopped down. Either due to the hour, 3:30 a.m., or the effect of the alcohol, Coco seemed tired and worn.

"Looking for me?" asked Deja.

"No, I'm ... yeah--what time do you have?" Deedee answered.

"I have all night and most of the morning. Got to get some shut-eye, know what I mean?"

"I'm talking about the time on your watch, Mr. McNasty--I mean Deja," Deedee quickly added when she saw Deja grimace.

"Its 3:30, bitch," said Deja. He limped away.

"I'm sorry to hurt your feelings. I didn't..." yelled Deedee, apologetically. "Oh well," she said, hurrying back in Coco's direction. But Coco's chair was empty. Where was she, Deedee wondered. Anxiety slowly crept in. Deedee felt uncomfortable. She wanted to leave. *Damn! Where are these girls*, she nearly said out loud, but checked herself. What a night, meeting Coco and her posse, the gunshots outside the other hangout, and now, feeling stalked by Deja for something she had said.

I'm leaving, she told herself.

"Where are you running to, babygirl? Still looking for me?" asked Deja.

"I'm looking for my friends, ah, Deja," she said, using his name correctly.

"Always looking for everyone else but me, huh?" asked Deja.

"They're in the blunt-smoking section. Over there in the VIP areas," he continued, motioning with a movement of his head.

"Thanks. Thanks a lot," Deedee said, overplaying the graciousness. She turned away. Deja grabbed her right hand. His grip was strong, her body jerked back from the motion.

"You'll need one of these if you're going over there," said Deja, offering Deedee a Phillies blunt cigar. "Have blunt will travel."

"No, I'm not into traveling high," said Deedee, faking a smile.

"Bitch!" Deja shouted, unable to control the anguish he felt.

"She's--ah, ah, fuck it," he said to any clubbies who were paying attention. Then he turned and watched as she moved away, black sweater clinging to her sensuous body, shapely legs crowned by tight, round buttocks. _Damn! She's nice_, thought Deja, enraptured by her graceful walk.

"Listen, I gotta go," said Deedee as she stood next to the table where Coco and some other kids were puffing on a blunt.

"Yeah I'm through my damn self," declared Coco, getting off her chair.

"This some good weed, yo," said Lil' Long, offering the lit blunt to Deedee.

"I don't do that. They let you smoke that on this side?" asked Deedee hesitantly.

"This is the VIP section, honey. You do whatever, yo." Coco walked as if a shoestring was loose. She struggled to gain her balance.

"Coco, are you all right?" Deedee asked, giving a hand to Coco.

"Yeah, yeah. I'm fine. Just gimme a second. I'll steady myself, thank you."

Coco needed more than a second. Deedee allowed her the time. She felt like walking away and leaving Coco, but then she turned around and put an arm across Coco's shoulder, to steady her walk. Coco offered no resistance, so Deedee held her tighter, guiding her through the maze of club kids.

"Where are the other girls? Do you--"

"I heard you," said Coco, not used to the friendly treatment. "They ah'ight. They hooked up with their boyfriends..."

"Oh, they're not--"

"What are you, some kind of a counselor? They be ah'ight, yo. Come on, Ms. Harriet Tubman. Lead the way. Take me home," said Coco as Deedee ushered her toward the ladies room.

"Yeah, yeah. I gotta go. Were you gonna give me a ride back uptown?"

"Sure, if you want me to. I--"

"Yeah, cool," said Coco as she held the door open for Deedee. *She's real cool*, thought Coco, staring as Deedee's backside disappeared into a stall. *She has a nice shape.* Coco pulled down her sagging jeans, revealing colorful boxers.

****

Deedee waited outside the bathroom for Coco. Both girls made their way to the exit. Coco, hands in pockets, bopped, staring at the reflections of the faces in the mirrors on the wall. Deedee, meantime, fumbled for the keys to the Mercedes. *What if the car isn't there*, she thought.

"Where'd you stash it, yo?" asked Coco, catching up.

"Somewhere close, I hope," said Deedee.

"Okay, but where?" Coco asked.

"Ah, there. This way," said Deedee as she found her bearings. She grabbed Coco's arm and pulled her to the left of the exit door.

"Yep, there it is," she confirmed as she spotted the car, radiant in the moonlight.

"It's such a dope whip, yo," said Coco. Deedee did not understand, and for the moment she didn't see the two figures lurking in the dark.

"What's a whip?" she asked Coco.

"Some dope shit like this. That's a whip."

"Yo, honey. Why y'all moving so fast, huh?" came a man's voice.

"Who dat? Is it..." Coco peered around and felt the blow to her face.

"It's this, bitch!" came the voice. The fist crashed the party. Coco reeled and blanked out immediately when her head hit the pavement.

"Where you running to, bitch? Get back here and get in da fucking whip. We wanna test ride da shit," said the man with a chuckle. Deedee shuddered as she felt cold steel pressed against the back of her neck.

"I sez git in da car, bitch," he growled.

Deedee had seen this at the movies, heard of it happening to others. But never had she imagined it happening to her. Her knees became weak as the sudden demand hit her, and her mind reeled into a world of fear.

"I said get in the muthafuckin' car, bitch," he repeated harshly. He brought the weapon to her face, and pushed the nozzle against her right temple.

"Please," she begged. "It's not my car. It's not mine. I...I--"

"Shuddafuckup." A second man grabbed the keys to the Mercedes and headed to the driver's side. He opened the door, got in the car and started the engine. Deedee ran, even though the guy with the gun was still close by. He caught up quickly and used his left hand to slap her face twice. Her cheeks stung. Then he brought the gun to her face. She pleaded with him. Terror engulfed her whole body, but he only seemed to enjoy her reaction.

"Please, please," cried Deedee.

"What're you trying to do, bitch? Just act normal and git in da fuckin' car and you won't get hurt."

Deedee was scared, but she got in the car. She tried to slither to the back but he pulled her onto his lap.

"I want you close. We can fuck around while my man drives," he threatened.

Deedee did not turn around. She didn't want to see his face. She squeezed her eyes tight shut. Deedee whispered a prayer. Her heartbeat was so loud, she couldn't think of anything to say. She wanted to plead for her life but the words stayed stuck in her mind. She thought she was close enough to reach for the door handle, press on it and jump. Deedee tried.

The man anticipated the move, and as she reached over, he blocked her with a twist of his body. Her eyes stayed shut. She wished it was a bad dream and she would wake soon. Between the roar of the engine and the heavy beating of her heart, Deedee could hear the laughter. He was mocking her. The move seemed to have excited him. His voice sounded familiar. Maybe from inside the club. Where? She couldn't ponder right now and gave up.

The car shot into the middle of traffic. The driver showed his unfamiliarity with the controls.

"Yo, watch where ya going. Turn on some fucking lights," yelled an angry pedestrian as the car hurtled by wildly.

"Yo, what's up? I thought you say you could drive this bad boy, yo."

"Yo man, I'm not too familiar wit' da shit. Gimme time. Why your ass brought da bitch, son? Put her out," said the driver as he searched for the headlight switch.

"I brought her to tell your dumb ass where the light switch is. Cutie, tell him how to turn on the lights." Deedee felt too nauseated to speak.

"Tell him!" commanded the passenger. Deedee managed to point.

"Yeah, cool," said the driver, flicking the switch.

"This shit can do 'bout a hun'ed and fitty, yo," he shouted, getting excited. The car raced toward the highway, piercing the morning mist. Deedee couldn't believe what was happening. Then she felt his hands touching her body. She quivered as tears rolled down the side of her face.

"Please, please, don't," she begged. It didn't matter. His hand continued to roam. She started to resist, but felt the pressure of a gun. She allowed it to happen, out of fear for her life. The driver was doing eighty or ninety by now.

Where are the damn police? Deedee thought.

Deedee felt afraid and started to scream. He slapped a hand over her mouth, and with his other hand he placed the gun's muzzle against her ear.

"Click," he said. Mentally, she was dead. Physically, she awoke with him on top of her, she kept her eyes shut tight; wishing this was all a nightmare. The passenger seat reclined all the way back and her black spandex pants were off. Her black sweater was dangling around her neck. Lil' Long was prying open her legs with his torso.

She resisted and tried to push him off, but he was strong, and after a couple of minutes of struggling, he mounted her. He slobbered over her body, bit her breast and raked her thighs. She screamed. He slapped her again and again. Blood trickled from her lips. Deedee sobbed as he viciously thrust himself into her flesh until he exploded. She scratched his face. He slapped her harder.

"Don't kill da bitch, yo. Lemme get a piece."

The car pulled over to the roadside. The nightmare ride was over, she thought. Then the driver grabbed her, slamming her against the hood of the car. He was inside her, raping her on the hood of the Mercedes. When he was spent, he slapped her to the ground and got back in the car. Lil' Long threw the rest of her clothes at her. Then he fired twice, both shots striking within inches. The explosion produced a fall-out of dirt that settled on Deedee's tear-soaked face. She laid there, not moving, wishing she had died. Her sobs grew louder until she could only cough. Laughter and music came from the car as it disappeared into the mist.

How did this all begin? Deedee wondered. Dazed and confused, she passed out from the pain. Her thoughts ceased.

****

Meanwhile, outside the club, Coco gathered herself. She felt her nose. Blood appeared on her fingers, and her eyes stung.

"Those muthafuckas. Fucking bastards," she thought aloud as she pulled off her headwear and dabbed it at her nose. The white do-rag was now stained red. She headed back to the club. Her head was pounding from the blow. The music from the club only served to exacerbate the pain. She went past the entrance and straight to the ladies room where she washed the cloth and stared at her bloodshot reflection.

After she left the restroom, she went to the pay phone and paged her girls. They responded in a flash, and the three girls left the club before saying anything. Once outside, they walked a few feet away, Coco still holding the headwear to her throbbing nose.

"Yo, you're letting your dreads fly. What's up?" asked Josephine.

"This whazzup." Coco removed the blood-soaked wrap from her face.

"Some niggas mush me and jacked da shit, yo. They must've took honey too, cuz I ain't seen her since. Y'all seen her?"

"Oh shit! Oh fucking shit. They didn't!" Da Crew stood in amazement.

"Who did it? You know?"

"I didn't really see who they were, yo. But the voice sounded kinda familiar. It was like... did any of you see Lil' Long leave?"

"Coco, you know we were both in da back booths. We didn't see them. They coulda left anytime, yo."

"Word," said Coco, nodding her throbbing head in agreement.

"All she wanted to do was drop me at da rest, yo. That's it. That shit is fucked up." Coco searched for cigarettes. There were none. Her head throbbed. She wondered about Deedee. The thought made her whole body shudder. Then Josephine said it. Maybe Da Crew was thinking it, but nobody wanted to say it.

"We've got to call five-o, yo." The words hung for awhile. Then the discussion began.

"Now, ya know them muthafuckas ain't gonna do shit," said Coco.

"I think we should call the cops," said Danielle.

"Ah'ight," said Coco. The girls walked to the phone on the corner.

"Police, 911..."

"Yo, some guys just mugged some girls and stole a car. They kidnapped one of the girls. They had guns and they were shootin' at everybody. It's crazy. Send your baddest peoples out here."

"Slow down, Miss. Where are you calling from?"

"At the corner of 49th and 3rd. Send the baddest cops." Click. The girls moved out.

"I'm out. Y'all stay and talk wit' da cops. I gotta take care of my nose, yo."

"Yo, Coco, wait up. You know what happened. Come on, you gotta stay."

"Ah'ight, I'll stay. But shit's not gonna be solved by talking all night wit' five-o. We don't even know if she stole da shit or if she had her license."

"Well, she said her uncle--"

"Her damn uncle could've stolen that shit," said Coco. The sirens sounded and the police arrived in a swarm. They came four cars deep, totaling nine officers. The cars moved slowly, red lights flashing as the dawn echoed an ominous air outside the club. Members of the baggy-clothes generation were still haunting their favorite hangout. The officers got out of their patrol cars and began to scrutinize the kids. What were they looking for? These kids didn't know. Each group gave a negative response to the police inquiries.

The much quieter club-goers filed by the officers in a hasty urban exit, oblivious to whatever had taken place outside the club. Suddenly, the officers saw the three girls standing under a broken-down lamppost.

"Here comes the tin badges," said Danielle.

"Did any of you happen to hear any gunshots being fired? Or have you seen anything unusual?" asked the first officer.

"I think it all happened over there," said Josephine, pointing to where the Mercedes was once parked. "Some kids jacked this girl and her car, and they took off, heading that way." Josephine pointed the officers to where the car-jackers were last seen.

"Do you know the girl? Her name?" asked the second officer.

"Well, she--"

"Nah, not really," interjected Coco. "That's all we know."

"Your nose looks bad. What happened?" the second officer asked, looking directly at Coco.

"A fight, yo. Someone messin' wit' my man, you know. Gotta defend mines. "

"Did any of you happen to see any faces, or anything that may help to identify someone?"

"A black Mercedes. A bad car, rims and all that," said Danielle. Her voice trailed off.

"That's it?" asked the officer. "Is that all you know?"

"Yeah, that's it. They jacked her right over there," said Josephine.

"They?" asked the first officer, zooming in on Josephine.

"How many were there?" he questioned, excitement in his voice. "Two, three, four? How many?" He was almost shouting.

"There were two of them," Coco said sternly.

"And they kidnapped a girl," cried Josephine. "That's all we know."

"Well, stay here, I'm gonna get an ambulance," commanded the first officer.

"Can you describe the girl? What was she wearing?"

"Black spandex and a black sweater," replied Danielle.

"Anything else?" The officer mumbled, and proceeded to put in the call for an ambulance.

"Just a black girl in black with a black car," said Coco, sarcastically.

"That's all we know," said Josephine. The officers huddled. The senior guy returned.

"Stay out of fights," he said directly to Coco. The rest of you best be getting home." Sirens pierced the air. The ambulance arrived. Coco was treated by the emergency medical technicians. When she alighted from the ambulance, Da Crew ran to meet her.

"Well, it's not broken, is it?" asked Josephine.

"No. Takes more than a little punch from a sucker to break something here, kid," bragged Coco. The girls embraced. This was the first time all three had shown any emotion, other than in their passion for singing. They hugged, and each thought about Deedee. A oneness enveloped the group, which came through in the tenderness of the moment. Coco, still a little woozy from the alcohol and the blow to her nose, was now able to speak.

"Wonder what's up wit' Dee. I hope she's ah'ight."

"Yeah, I hope she's okay," added Danielle.

"She was only looking out for me. I owe her some kinda due, ya know?" Coco searched for corroboration. The idea was still overwhelming to her. She had just met Deedee, didn't even know her last name, and was already feeling connected. "Deedee was looking out, yo," she said, quickly summing up the moment.

"Y'all could stay at my place. My parents won't mind," said Josephine. She did not look directly at her, but

Coco felt the last part was meant for her. After all, her mother would probably be drunk and would curse up a storm had they gone there. Josephine understood. And besides, she had her own room, and her home was always clean.

"I got some loot. Let's catch a cab, yo," said Coco.

"Yeah, let's do, that," agreed Da Crew. They hailed a cab, and it stopped. The girls looked at each other with surprise.

"Aw shit!" said Danielle. "This must be some kinda omen or something. Strange things happen in threes, and this taxi stopping for us makes two. No more car rides for the weekend, y'all." The girls ran to the cab.

"A hundred and twelfth and Lenox," said Josephine. The three girls huddled in the back seat of the taxi. The driver hesitated.

"What's the problem?" Josephine asked. She repeated the address. The driver glanced nervously at the rear-view mirror.

"Aw, c'mon. We ain't trying to jack your ass. See, we got loot," said Coco. She showed the driver a couple of ten-dollar bills.

"See money. Now drive," ordered Danielle.

"Yeah. Let's go already," screamed Josephine.

"Alright," said the cab driver. "I drive."

"Think we gonna disrespect your livelihood, yo, Mr. Cabbie?"

"We should," said Danielle. "Take his lootchie and all. Straight jackin'."

"Will you cut that out, Dani. Hello, we are tryin'a get somewhere," said Josephine. "She's sorry, Mr. Cabbie."

The car started moving, but the driver was still a bit uneasy. He kept glancing back as if he expected something. Nothing happened. The girls remained quiet. The taxi driver's voice crackled through the tension in the air. The girls sat glowering in the backseat. They did not heed or hear what he was saying.

"Uh, what did you say?" asked Coco, annoyed.

"I said, did you hear the news? The police found some girl along Route eighty-seven? It was on the radio..." His voice trailed off quickly.

Coco grabbed her bandaged nose as her heart sunk. It had been on her mind since she had recovered from the punch in the face. Everything seemed to hurt a little more as the driver continued with the second-hand news.

"What happened to her?" asked Josephine.

"What happened to who?" asked the driver.

"The girl," came the chorus.

"Oh yeah, that girl. The news said that she was raped and beaten," informed the driver.

"Wait up. What girl?" Coco awoke from her daze.

"Found her where? Is she dead? Oh man. Damn!" Things became a blur to Coco.

"They fucking did her, those muthafuckas," cried Danielle in anguish. Coco winced from the pain. She sat erect, her back slightly arched, and held her nose. No sound came. She had just met Deedee, but the pain she felt was deep. Her head started to pound again. This was real bad. They had jacked her and the car. Why didn't they just take the car? Coco rewound the memory of the voices outside the club prior to her getting hit. She tried to mentally sketch the faces with the voices. Her head hurt. She stopped.

"Is ... the girl dead?" asked Josephine.

"Nah, she's alive," said the driver. The girls sighed. "She was taken to some hospital," continued the driver. Hope returned. The girls held one another's hands tighter. "... According to the news. You know you can never believe the news. But they reported that she was badly beaten and raped. She's the niece of Eric Ascot, some famous music producer."

Eric Ascot! That's her uncle, thought Coco. The girls looked wide-eyed at each other. The mention of Eric Ascot's relationship to Deedee was a big surprise to them. Eric Ascot was one of the most popular producers in the music industry.

"Those muthas," said Coco. "I don't believe that shit. But that's city life for ya...man," she said, staring straight ahead.

"They fucking did her." The words were so final that they made the air go dead inside the taxi. The ride continued in virtual silence, until they reached the building where Josephine and her parents lived. Coco paid the fare, and the girls walked to the entrance of the huge building.

"Dammit. I don't have any cigarettes," said Coco after searching the pockets of her oversized jeans.

"We could get some off my parents," said Josephine.

She opened the door and the girls walked in. Coco gave an excuse for not calling home. She knew her mother would be asleep or drunk, probably both. Danielle called her mother. Josephine led the way to her room, and the girls followed in silence. Once inside the room, Josephine turned the television on. All three girls plopped down on the small bed. Josephine sprang up and tossed the remote to Coco, who began to scan the channels.

"Nothing but reruns," said Danielle. Coco continued scanning. Talk shows and religious programs. "Misty and overcast," said the weatherman. Josephine left the room and reappeared ten minutes later with milk, soda, water, cookies and cigarettes. Coco helped herself to a cigarette and soda. She lit up and took a drag.

"This was a fucked-up evening, yo!" she proclaimed, her thoughts disappearing in the cloud as she reminisced over the still-unsettling events. The girls sat around, nodding their heads in agreement.

"Yep," Danielle finally said. "This was more a fright night than any thriller could bring."

"Shit's foul," Coco said. She laid back and closed her eyes. The room seemed to grow smaller. Josephine had always liked to get away to this space. When she closed the door, all the world's trouble stayed on the other side--except for today. The dawn had already dragged something sinister across the threshold of her room.

CHAPTER 3

In the emergency room, Deedee lay on a stretcher. Her eyelids felt heavy, but she could not sleep. A nurse smiled down at her, sympathetic. Deedee had just retold the most horrifying saga in her young life. *It wasn't supposed to be like this*, she thought. *I was just trying to have some fun, but it turned out to be the worst.* She had to tell the story to the police, who had brought her here. They showed no compassion. They made her feel cheap. Then there were the doctors and nurses, who tried to get more information.

"Did they penetrate? Was it oral, anal or vaginal?"

Damn it, I was raped, Deedee wanted to scream. Then those fucking rape advocates, with their phony promises. Yeah sure, it will be forgotten. Deedee was lost in thought when the smiling nurse approached and began to speak.

"Feeling a little better? Can I get you some water?" The smile annoyed Deedee. She wanted to lash out at the next person in a white uniform. She wanted to yell, *I've been violated. I want my virginity back!* But she just lay on the stretcher. Finally, she sat up.

"Water please," she said.

"Oh sure," the nurse replied. She brought a cup of water to Deedee. "You may get dressed anytime you wish. The bruises will soon be gone," she added.

"I'm scarred for life," said Deedee. The words poured out in a soft cry.

"It will get better. It's going to take some time. You'll have to come back for a follow-up, or you may see your family doctor. Call this phone number for the results of your tests. Your uncle is here." The last words sent a chill through Deedee.

"My uncle is here?" she echoed, and took the card with the phone number.

Her mind lingered. How could she face him? Deedee felt ashamed and instinctively covered her body with the hospital robe. This was not enough. She glanced around the room. It seemed everyone was staring at her, or talking about her. They all knew. She could see it in their eyes, even though they were all in the hallway, and she had a screen around the stretcher.

"Nurse, where are my clothes?"

"Oh, I'm sorry. Here you are. Your uncle brought these," said the nurse, handing Deedee fresh clothing. Even though the clothes belonged to her, Deedee did not feel right getting in them.

"Thanks," said Deedee. She sat on the stretcher, and a younger woman in a dark suit approached. *Here we go again*, thought Deedee.

"Hi, I'm Maxine Singleton and I am a rape victim counselor." Her stare made Deedee uneasy. "Here's my card," the woman said. "Feel free to call me. I know you've had an awful and scary experience. You're going to need a lot of help. I can provide that. All you need to do is call the number on the card and I will call to check on you periodically. But you should call me whenever you need someone to talk to. Call me and I'll try to help," concluded the counselor. Deedee took the card and stared past the fast-talking counselor.

"May I leave now?" she asked.

"I think the police have some more questions. I'll stay with you if you don't mind."

As if on cue, a policeman and a woman came around the screen. Deedee's uneasiness returned. She lay back on the stretcher and crossed her legs.

"My name is Officer Brown. I'm from the District Attorney's office," said the woman. She was dressed in a blue suit with black shoes. She looked more like a lawyer than a cop. She even smelled like one. Her perfumed hand was highlighting every word.

"How're you feeling, young lady?" asked the male officer. Deedee mumbled inaudibly.

"I know you've been asked this over and over. I'm afraid I'll have to ask you again. Can you tell me what happened?"

"We know it's a very difficult thing for you to do, but please, you have to try and help us catch the men who did this evil thing to you."

Deedee was close to tears. The query made her go back to the ordeal, which she sought to escape. It assaulted her mind, and started an ache in her stomach that rose to her throat. She cried uncontrollably.

Her uncle, standing just outside the screen, dashed in and grabbed Deedee. She sobbed into his chest. He held her close, reluctant to let go. But Officer Brown interrupted.

"We need to find out what happened, sir. Who are you?"

Ascot kept hugging his niece. He ignored the officer.

"Uncle, uncle. I'm sorry," cried Deedee. "I'm so sorry," she said, and the tears continued to flow.

"It'll be alright," said Eric. He held Deedee, hoping she believed him. He wasn't sure, but the words seemed to fit the situation. He loved his niece. He had raised her since she was ten years old, after her father, his brother and partner, was killed and her mother had succumbed to a mean crack habit.

"Are you the uncle?" asked Officer Brown. I have a question about--"

"What's your question?" Eric interrupted her.

"Did you loan your niece the car tonight?"

There was a long pause. Ascot smelled the stench of the hospital and it brought back a rush of memories about his brother's death. The police had rejected Eric's argument that the killing took place during a robbery. His brother's death had been labeled a drug-related incident. There was no trial. The police didn't care enough to pursue it. Ascot did some research on his own; paid an informer for the information he needed, and then took the information to the police.

He was certain they would find and prosecute his brother's killers. But the authorities saw no reason to reopen the case, and Eric couldn't produce the informant he'd paid. So as far as the record stated, Dennis was just another dead drug dealer. Eric knew this was wrong. This was a dishonor to his brother's memory, and Eric felt cheated.

Fuck these cops, he thought.

"I am not answering any questions until I speak to my lawyer," he said.

"Listen," said the officer. "We're asking real simple questions here. Your niece was raped and beaten up, according to this report. We'd like to catch the bastards who did this sick thing, so it would be very nice if you would just cooperate."

"We don't have to do shit. As a matter of fact, we're not gonna do shit, because you guys have never done anything to help me," said Ascot. He turned to his niece who was staring at him, bewildered by what she had just witnessed. *My uncle never gets angry*, she thought.

"Let's go, baby." He grabbed Deedee by the left arm and stomped past the rape counselor.

"We're trying to conduct an investigation. A carjacking and rape. You can't let the scum who did this get away," pleaded the officer.

Ascot wasn't listening. He rushed out the doorway, into the hallway and out of the hospital, dragging Deedee along. They hurried to the parking lot. He quickly found the green Range Rover and helped Deedee into the passenger seat.

Eric Ascot drove, paying close attention to the morning traffic. He tapped his thumbs frantically on the steering column. Deedee heard him breathe loudly through his nostrils, but neither said anything. Her usually talkative uncle had secluded himself in the quiet of his thoughts. He didn't even look at her. Maybe he was ashamed of her. She shuddered and looked away.

Deedee pressed the window control and welcomed the swoosh of the wind. It drowned the unbearable silence, and brought the refreshing smell of fresh air to the car's interior. Deedee had longed for the feeling of freshness, which the morning's episode had erased. She recalled the hospital and the medical examinations. *Those damn tests*, she thought, *just like being raped all over again*. The goal of those doctors, police officers, nurses and rape advocates seemed to be to make her re-enact the whole ugly scene.

They were all so cold--perhaps with the exception of the advocates.

Then she heard music. Eric had turned on the stereo. She watched as he adjusted the volume. He always asked if the volume was "good." That had always been her chance to critique any of the new recording artists her uncle had recently worked with in the studio. More importantly, it gave her uncle a chance to share quality time with her. The moment he opened his mouth, Uncle E. would start bragging and really loosen up. She always felt he was trying to sell the new group or artist to her. Then the 'they're-gonna-blow-up' discussions would begin. She felt these types of conversations had also taken place between Eric and her father before he died.

But, this was not an ordinary drive home. There would be no discussion of recording artists. Deedee's thoughts forced her back to the present. *I was raped and he's just driving me home. Like he just picked me up after a fight at school or something.*

"Oh, I have to take these pills. They're like birth control pill. Morning after," she said. "Can we stop so I can get something to help me swallow them?" Deedee was seeking verbal reconciliation, but it was to no avail. Eric pulled the vehicle to the curb without saying anything. Then she started out the door. The move brought a reaction from Eric.

"Um, I'll get it," he said. He jumped from the van and ran across the street toward the store.

"Apple," she yelled. Deedee watched as her uncle disappeared into the store. Tears clouded her vision. "I'll take apple, uncle E." she said, softly. Then she cried.

Eric Ascot could not hear her. He was already across the street and in the store. As soon as he entered, he wiped his shirtsleeve across his eyes, determined to keep Deedee from seeing his tears.

Maybe he had let her down somehow, he thought, reaching for any juice. *She likes apple,* he recalled and grasped the bottle. After paying, he walked lazily out of the store. He stared in the direction of the green van. *She looks so much like my brother,* he thought, *and probably just as tough. No mother, no father, just me.*

Deedee watched him approach. It was hard to tell, but he looked angry.

Well, she reasoned, *I did take the car without his permission. He should be angry.*

"I'm sorry, Uncle E.," she said as he neared her side of the vehicle. But Eric had purposely walked around so he could apologize to her.

"Sorry for what, baby? You have no reason to be." He handed her the apple juice. He was so overcome with emotion, he couldn't say a word. He was afraid she'd see his tears.

Deedee swallowed the tablet and gulped the juice.

"Thanks, Uncle," she offered, her words tainted by a disheartened tone. Eric went around to the driver's side and leaned against the hood. Without thinking, he put a cigarette to his lips and lit it. Ascot stared fiercely across the street, desperately holding his tears, as he continued to puff on that "occasional" cigarette. The smoke could not hide the pain on his face.

Deedee saw his six-foot frame slouched against the car. She watched as her uncle crushed the cigarette against the side of the car. *He has to be mad*; she thought as he wrenched the door open and slammed it shut. He never treats his car, or any property, for that matter, this roughly. After a quick reverse, they moved forward and joined the traffic.

Deedee turned to watch as the hospital disappeared in the background. They made a left onto Main Street and then were on the familiar path home. The silence emphasized Ascot's heavy breathing. Deedee saw his nostrils flare in the corner of her eyes.

We could talk about it, Uncle E, she wanted to say. But the words remained in her thoughts.

Ascot turned up the stereo volume, and Deedee closed her eyes. She awoke to find her uncle slowing down and making a right, easing the car into the driveway. He parked the van and helped Deedee out of the vehicle. Deedee was tired and clung to her uncle's arm. Then she shook free and walked quickly toward the house.

"Uncle E., whenever you're ready, we can talk about it," she said. She didn't fully understand why she had said it.

"Well, maybe you should clean up. Uh, I mean, do you want to take a bath, get refreshed?" he muttered in a disjointed manner. Eric Ascot was not sure what to say.

Deedee stared up at him, confusion pasted on her youthful face.

"Yeah, I think I will ..." Her voice trailed off. "My mouth is getting sore from all this jawing." She was exhausted, and on entering the house, Deedee headed immediately to her room, slamming the door behind her.

"I'll come and see you soon," yelled Ascot, heading for the rear of the house and the kitchen. He checked his telephone messages. "Damn! Where the hell is Sophia?" he said aloud to the machine. There was no message from Sophia. He decided to call her. The phone rang twice.

"Sophia!" he said urgently. "They found Deedee. Yeah, yeah, she's alive, but listen. You've got to get here right away, honey. She was raped. I don't know what the hell to do. I'm not equipped for this situation. This is my niece."

"Are you--?"

"Yes, I'm serious," he cut her off. "Get here immediately."

****

Deedee stood in front of the oval mirror on the back of the door. She stared at her reflection. *This is what happens when you take something without permission. You have to pay. But why such a heavy price?* Tears welled in her eyes. Deedee's chest heaved uncontrollably; then she cried hard and loud. Her uncle heard, and froze to the spot where he stood in the kitchen.

"Where is Sophia? I need her now!" said Eric, looking up at the ceiling. "And Deedee's damn drugged-out mother. I don't even know where she is. Dammit. I swear on my brother's grave, whoever did this shit, I will personally take care of them. I want no help from those fucking police."

He heard the key turning in the door and the sound of Sophia's footsteps rapidly approaching. They embraced briefly.

"I could hear her from outside. What's wrong? Why is she crying so loud?" asked Sophia.

"Listen, I really don't know. She came in and went straight upstairs and locked her door. I didn't get a chance to talk to her."

"What? You haven't spoken to her? Well..."

"I didn't know what to say."

"She may have wanted to say something to you."

"Well, she had a chance when we were driving from the hospital and--"

"Get me two glasses of cold water."

"For what? I don't need to cool down."

"Who said anything about you? They're for me and Deedee."

Sophia took the first glass and drank a mouthful. She set both glasses on a tray and took her black pumps off, then made her way up the short stairway to Deedee's room.

"Dee? May I come in?" she asked as she knocked gently.

"Hold on. Just a second, Sophia," came the reply. Deedee opened the door and headed toward the bed.

"Hey, girlfriend," said Sophia, trying to sound up beat.

Deedee mumbled. Sophia ignored the inaudible response.

"I brought some water. Cold water, with a few ice cubes. Thought maybe you could use a little. I know I could."

"Sophia, have--well no, but--" Deedee looked down on the beige carpeted floor, and then continued. "Have you ever been raped?"

The blunt question caught Sophia off guard. Just for an instant, she wished she could say she had been raped.

"No," she replied. "I have never been raped, but I can imagine that it's a terrible thing." A brief pause followed. "Do you want the water now?" asked Sophia, sipping from her glass.

"It's bad. It's really, really awful," said Deedee. "Thanks," she said reaching for the glass.

Deedee gulped the water and felt it roll down her dry throat. A surprise burp caused her to look at Sophia, who had been standing in the middle of the room. They smiled. Deedee walked over and hugged Sophia. "Thanks," she said. "I'm sleepy, but could you stay with me until I fall asleep?"

"Sure, girl," said Sophia.

****

The sun illuminated the room. Deedee walked over to the picture window and stood in the first light to enter. She touched her stomach and thought of her mother, wondered if she were dead or alive. Sophia silently watched Deedee. Suddenly it was clear: Deedee was no longer an innocent child; she was the victim of a heinous crime. Sophia walked over to the window and pulled the draperies closed.

"Get some rest, Dee," she said

"Yeah, but will you stay?"

"Of course."

Deedee moved over to the bed and turned toward Sophia.

"I have to take a long bath," she said. "Thanks, Sophia." She went into the bathroom and closed the door. Sophia sat on the bed. Tears rolled down her cheeks.

Deedee undressed and stepped into the shower. The spray sent a sudden chill through her body. She stood under the shower, allowing the water to soak in. It didn't dampen her thought: *If I hadn't taken that car, none of this would've happened.* She cried a little. *Why such a heavy price?*

She thought of the last time she had seen her mother, Denise, who had gotten heavy into drugs after her father's death. Perhaps she couldn't handle his dying, or maybe it was the way he was killed. Whatever it was, Deedee remembered vividly that the last month or so before she was carried away, Denise was stealing to support her crack habit. She had lost a lot of weight and looked quite emaciated. Her clothing no longer fit. Deedee remembered feeling real hatred toward her mother.

Uncle E. had tried to explain, but Deedee couldn't understand, wouldn't listen. She changed her name on the school register by forging her mother's signature. Denise had been part of Deedee's name. She had been Denise D. Ascot, but changed it to Deedee. She despised her mother. During this period she often wished her dead.

Then one day, five years ago, the ambulance had carried her mother away on a stretcher. Denise had overdosed on crack-cocaine and heroin. Deedee felt some type of relief. She hoped her mother would never come back. After the overdose, Deedee never saw Denise again. She would miss her, but kept that a secret. Now she wanted her mother. Eric had assumed the role of her father, and now that he was contemplating marrying Sophia, well, maybe she would have a mother again.

Deedee toweled herself and put on her robe. Sophia rose from the bed so that Deedee could lie down. Deedee brushed her damp hair and fell asleep.

****

Sophia rejoined Eric downstairs. He had downed two beers and was working fast on the third.

"Hey, big guy, don't drink yourself silly. Save me some."

"That silliness is not a bad idea. As for the beer, there's plenty in the fridge."

"Thanks. Don't kill me with your kindness," said Sophia.

"Listen, my niece was ..."

"I know. Raped. A bad thing, which only turns out to be good if you overwhelm her with good--and goods."

"Like?"

"Like a shopping spree, getting clothes. Like sending her flowers. And more shopping. The idea here is to try to help her to forget. I have friends who can provide counseling and support services. In time, this horrible experience may be put to the back of her mind."

"Is that possible?" asked Eric. His eyes widened with the knowledge Sophia had just imparted.

"Yes. You won't be able to take it all away. But, hey, it certainly won't hurt to try," said Sophia between sips of the newly opened brew.

"Sophia, that shit really hurts me. I don't know..."

"Yeah, I understand. What did the police--?"

"Later for them assholes. They have never helped me. Never."

Sophia saw anger in Eric. The furrow in his brow became pronounced as he stared at a snapshot of himself and Dennis, his older brother. She knew where all the frustrations stemmed from. Eric's brother had been murdered not long before Sophia met Eric, so she was with him when he learned the truth about his brother's death. Something in Eric changed after that, and Sophia knew not to press the issue with him.

Men wearing ski masks had tried to mug his older brother, Eric was told. Dennis fired at them with his .38 Smith and Wesson, but one attacker got behind him and shot him dead. Eric knew Dennis had gone to an address given to him by `Xtrigaphan,' the hot rap group he wanted to sign. Dennis had taken $10,000 in cash with him to lure the group to sign. Eric knew his brother dabbled in cocaine, but also knew Dennis wasn't dealing. He knew that the cash was for the signing bonus. The police weren't interested in Eric's version of his brother's murder. Since then, his hatred of the police bordered on obsession. Sophia decided to try another approach.

"Well, have you spoken to Deedee, to find out what happened?"

"No."

"Do you know what happened?"

"Not entirely, except that she was raped and the car was stolen."

"By whom? Where?" queried Sophia.

"Look, the cops told me what happened. They called me and told me they found her badly beaten. Told me that she had been sexually assaulted."

"So you haven't spoken to Deedee about any of this?"

"I told you. No," said Eric. He was annoyed now.

Sophia Woods, with her lawyer's mind, suspended the questioning when she saw Eric's resentment. She tilted the beer upwards, looking at his reflection through the beer bottle. His face appeared contorted, and he looked fat with anger.

Eric Ascot turned his back. He was rehashing his brother's death.

"I didn't want to include the cops," he said, turning to face her. "Not after the way they treated my brother. They treated him like he was some unknown, drug dealing nigga. Now I'm gonna handle this shit the way it should be handled."

He turned away. Then he stopped. The pain showed on his face.

"Soph, whatever it takes to make her better. Please don't spare the cost. Get her the best. That's my niece laid up there." Sophia nodded.

CHAPTER 4

Deedee lay staring into a wall of nothingness. She remembered the Mercedes, sitting at the end of the driveway; she thought and drifted off to sleep.

Such a pretty car, she thinks. So black that it glows. The noise of the car alarm prompts her to get the keys and deactivate it. She gets in it. Maybe, I should move it closer. Or maybe I could take it around the block just one time. It won't hurt. But she has to go downtown. Maybe check out some spots, meet up with some friends--Coco and her crew. They'll love the ride. Everyone is happy; everything is fine. Her uncle won't be back until the following day. He'll never know. Pick up some cigarettes, and no drinking while driving. Her guide drank some, actually a lot. "Hey chill with the bottle, chill." Coco and Da Crew perform.They're fabulous, graceful, exciting. The club stops make her sloppy. She's trying to make it back to the car, with or without a guide. She is outside. It's a jungle. There are wild animals chasing each other. She barely sees the Mercedes now. There's something after her or the Mercedes. Deedee runs and screams. It's to no avail. Her throat acts as a barrier to the sound. The man-beast catches up with her.

"I want you and da fucking car," roars the beast. It has a face she barely recognizes.

"Back off, vultures!" Deedee tries to yell. There are no words coming. Just the beast.

Then the beast grabs her. She screams, but fright muffles the sound. The hand begins to maul her, she tries fighting back, but she is much too small, and her limbs won't respond. She is trying to scream, but there's no sound. The beast clutches her and pins her to the hood of the Mercedes. Then the thing growls and enters her. Deedee fights back with long vicious scratching, her nails strong as talons. The flesh of the beast begins to fall apart. She grows stronger, and the beast retreats. But out comes the man. It is Deja, from the club. She screams violently.

"Get away. Stay away," she yells. Her uncle and

Sophia burst through the door. "Don't hurt me anymore," she cries.

"Deedee it's me. I'm here baby. It will be alright, it'll be alright," said Eric, hugging the girl. "You were having a bad dream."

"I'll get her something to drink," said Sophia. She ran downstairs, to the kitchen. Eric and Deedeed are left alone in the room.

"Uncle E., Uncle E.," cried Deedee. "He was trying to rape me again."

"Who was gonna do that to you, baby?"

"This thing was chasing me and Deja was gonna rape me again."

"Deja?" asked her uncle, bewildered. "Who's Deja?"

Sophia carefully handed Deedee a glass of milk. Deedee gulped twice, then excused herself and went into the bathroom. She felt the scrutiny as two pairs of concerned eyes followed her there. Once inside, she washed her face and checked her body. The bruises and marks were quite visible. Deedee looked at her face close-up, and noticed all the welts and gashes under her nose and above her eyes. Scabs were already forming over the smaller wounds. She decided not to look anymore--each time she did so, more bruises seemed to appear. But Deedee knew that these smaller bruises didn't really matter. The biggest wound would not heal. It would last forever.

****

"Hey, what's up?" asked Da Crew when they met in the school hallway. They were happy to see each other. The weekend was finally over. All the girls had stayed with their families and spoken with each other on the phone. Danielle and Josephine used their parents' phones. Coco called from the phone on the corner.

"I've got a test, yo. Got to go. Catch up wit' y'all later."

"Coco," it was Mrs. Martinez.

"Yes, Mrs. Martinez."

"Girls, I heard a report of a carjacking and rape. It happened to a student I know in this school."

The girls stared at each other, revealing no surprise, but a lot of interest.

"It happened over the weekend," continued Mrs. Martinez. Then questions came. "Do you girls know anything about what happened?"

"No-o-o," came the chorus. The three girls walked away.

"Well, the police think you do." Mrs. Martinez had to shout to be heard.

"We told them everything," Coco shouted back.

"We've got to get to class," said Josephine, famous for her late excuses.

"Talk to y'all," repeated Coco. Her oversized denim jacket and blue jeans sagged, and the black knapsack on her back moved with a slight bop as Coco made her way to the classroom.

Damn, hope I can ace this test, she thought as she took her seat. She slipped off the knapsack and jacket with a single move. She was ready to begin the High School Regents Examination.

Coco finished the test in three hours flat. She had always been a good student, always read and did her homework, and her grades reflected that hard work. Schoolwork afforded her the perfect escape from her volatile mother.

"Good luck," said the examiner with a smile as Coco handed her the pile of test papers. Coco retrieved her jacket and knapsack and nodded as she headed for the door. She walked slowly down the hallway with her familiar bop.

"Peace," someone called after her.

"Peace," acknowledged Coco. She immediately reached for her cigarettes but put them away as she remembered the signs posted in the school's hallways: NO SMOKING ALLOWED.

Coco spotted Josephine and Danielle and motioned for them to join her.

"Think they got the report, yo?" Coco already knew the answer.

"Yep, most definitely," replied Josephine.

"How else would they know?" added Danielle.

"You know what, yo?" Coco continued. "We should

stay da fuck out of this."

"You mean mind our biz, shut our mouths? Cool by me," said Josephine with a wink.

"Can't even remember what she looked like," chuckled Coco.

"But weren't you the one who was pledging to do something for da sister?" asked Danielle.

"Okay, ah'ight. Y'all didn't have to go there, but you did. Ah'ight, I can vaguely remember some of it. I was caught up in the situation. I got emotional, so I flipped. I'm allowed to flip and talk shit, right? Okay, then that's it, yo. Listen. I've got these bad lyrics."

"Yeah right, let's hear them, then."

"Ah'ight, let's get busy," said Coco. "But let's get da fuck outta here."

The girls put their silver-rimmed dark shades on and made their way out of the school building as if paparazzi awaited them. Danielle waved and blew a kiss to someone. Coco put a cigarette to her lips and turned her back to the wind to light it. She took a drag and passed it to Danielle.

"Hold this, yo." She reached into her backpack and pulled out a carefully folded white sheet.

"Here's some of the dopest lyrics you're gonna hear anywhere," she announced.

The girls paused to listen.

"It's called 'You Played Yourself.' Coco began to half-hum, half-sing a slow-tempo song.

"Go ahead, girl," cried Da Crew. Coco continued more loudly now:

One day, one day
You're gonna fade away
And I won't need you
anyway, cause you'd have
been played like the sucker
punk you showed me you are.
That day when you
Played, played yourself
You have played yourself
You've played yourself
like dirty old Huggies
Boy, get off my set

I don't want you
fucking up my environment
now that all your muthafuckin'
money's spent.

"Yo, right there--right after 'muthafuckin' money's spent,'--y'all kick in like this, 'Huh.' " Coco explained to Da Crew.

"Wait up. Back up. All we say is, 'Huh?'"complained Josephine. "That's it? Well, the shit sounds like it had some potential. But we gotta be saying more than just 'huh.'"

"I agree. But it sounds like some kinda suicide song. Do you think people will start blaming us when they start jumping from buildings?" asked Danielle.

"I could see it now," Josephine deadpanned. "This just in--A trio of men leaped from a thirty- story apartment building in the city after listening to the lyrics of Coco's latest song."

"Oh, so y'all gonna bail out on the P.H. tip? Okay, cool."

"Now seriously, sis, it has potential, but it needs a little work," said Josephine, with mock-tenderness. "I don't think it will sell in today's market, anyway. All the songs that hitting are songs about lick me up and lick me down, bump and grind. Shit wit' sex on the platter. You know what I'm saying? See, you can't get a hit with something that is positive for the sisters."

"Uh- oh, here we go with the sister shit again. Here, smoke some more," said Danielle, passing the last half of the cigarette to Coco.

"Ah'ight yo, if y'all wanna just keep dancing and singing other people's old stuff, then we're a group of--"

"A group of what?" asked Danielle.

"Imitators. There's nothing original about our stuff."

"Yeah, everyone says we have some dope steps. Come on, we got a little something."

"Yeah, well I think we have more. Lots more skills than we're showing," said Coco.

"Well, it takes time to happen. We have to become more popular," said Josephine.

"I thought that's why we did the club gigs on the

weekends, the things at school. To make us more known." Coco took a drag before continuing.

"We need a record deal. We could sing and do our own videos. We wouldn't just be dancing in other people's videos. We would be starring in our own joints, yo. Think about it," said Coco. She took the last drag and flicked the butt away, over the heads of the other girls. They listened intently. "We need someone to make the beats for us, yo," said Coco.

"Yeah, and some lyrics," said Danielle.

"Get a brother who could rap, ghetto style, roughneck type, and we would be in it like that," said Josephine, snapping her fingers.

"Like this, yo," said Coco, high-fiving the girls.

"Who do we know like that, y'all?"

"Well, we know Eric Ascot's niece. You know, the one with the ride."

"Yo, let's not go there. Leave it alone," said Coco. But her plea seemed too weak, and didn't convince Josephine or Danielle. Neither said anything, yet somehow the discussion ended on an unsettling note.

"Let's go get something to eat and work on our steps, sis," suggested Coco. She turned away sharply, avoiding further discussion. She put the folded paper with her lyrics back in her pack, and headed for McDonald's, three hundred feet away. Then she stopped suddenly as if reconsidering, and said, "Let's make tracks to da chicken place, yo. I feel like chicken."

Both Josephine and Danielle had caught up with her. They watched Coco, who continued with her bop. She slowly reached for a cigarette and stepped into a doorway to light it. The wind was brisk on this bright and sunny Monday, blowing the litter around the sidewalk in a swirl. Each time a pile landed, the wind would blow again, and the litter would float once more, then settle again. The girls headed for the chicken place, hands in pockets, shades over their eyes, thoughts shrouded in silence. They ordered chicken and biscuits. Coco opted for honey with her chicken.

"Why do you always get honey with your chicken?" asked Josephine.

"This shit just taste a little bit better when it's sweetened. Anyways--" Before they could fully discuss honey and chicken, a schoolmate came by and asked about the upcoming talent show and contest.

"Yeah, yeah. It'll be on in about two weeks," said Josephine.

"Well, good luck," said the questioner. He rejoined a group from school.

"Thanks," said Josephine and Danielle. Coco looked up momentarily, but said nothing. She continued chewing and nodded at the questioner, who was leaving with both of his friends.

"Now you know, these scrubs were trying a thing, yo...Niggas." She stretched out the last syllable, then broke out laughing.

"They weren't bad looking though, were they?" asked Josephine.

"Yeah, but y'all attract `em like honey to a bee."

"Well, their pickup was kinda corny," said Josephine.

"Speaking of pickup, I need to pick up on my calc. The test is Wednesday."

"Aw c'mon, Coco, you know you don't have to study that hard. You're one good lyric away from being a musical genius and a couple of tests from being on scholarship," said Josephine.

"Just trying to be all I can be," answered Coco.

"Aw, listen to her," said Danielle. "Now you trying to be modest?" There was a touch of sarcasm in her voice.

"Not your usual 'we-gonna-get-mad-paid,'" joked Josephine.

"Yeah. Now she's all 'I'ma-do-sumthin'-for-da-sista,'" Danielle laughed.

"See, see, y'all are dead wrong. Y'all know I'm on the down low, yo," said Coco.

"Yeah, but up on stage you swear your ass is Diana Ross. You be playing it," said Danielle. She sounded half-critical of Coco's style of singing and dancing.

"That's not true. I just do my thing, yo. I just be getting mine."

"Yeah, and everyone else's," said Danielle.

Coco faced Danielle. She looked deep into her eyes.

Danielle and Coco locked stares for a moment.

"Are you for real?" Coco asked at last. Her tone was serious. Danielle immediately knew she had crossed a line, but she wouldn't back down. Josephine, in the middle, grew uneasy. The silence lengthened.

"This food sucks," said Josephine. "Maybe we should bounce."

"Now!" said Coco. "We are a group, rrright?" she purred like Eartha Kitt.

"Y'all gonna fight over some bullshit? C'mon," said Josephine, playing peacemaker.

"Right, yo?" Coco repeated.

"Yeah we're a group," said Danielle, "and everything should be equal--including time at lead."

"Well, that's good that you said it," said Coco. "Cuz I don't wanna be running around with peeps who suppose to be down wit' ya, yet keeping' shit behind ya back."

Josephine's half-smile faded. The tension was still humming. Coco's lips curled as if they were trying to touch her nose. Her reversed baseball cap made her look angry, street fierce, someone ready at will to kill any challenger--a bully, only a lot prettier than most.

Danielle was the hunted, caught but not fully captured. She was confident about the avenue of escape. With her light brown hair and cool dark eyes, Danielle appeared to be calm under Coco's intense pressure. In the group, Danielle moved with athletic grace on stage. Her body always invited the movements, the turns and the rhythms of dance. Her voice was always ready to shout and share the chorus. Now she wanted to lead, too, if she could weather the storm Coco looked ready to bring.

"But Coco is the lead," said Josephine. "We build off her. I mean we can't always change the lead. Have you ever witnessed a lead change in 'SWV'? They always have the same person singing, and they don't do so badly."

"Yeah, maybe she's the only one who can really sing," deadpanned Danielle.

"Okay, yo cool," said Coco, "if that's what it's all about...then we'll practice the routine with everyone at lead, ah'ight?"

"No, no. I'm cool. Someone has to follow. That's me. I'm not taking it personal," said Josephine.

"It's not a matter of taking it personal," Danielle was about to conclude, but Coco interrupted.

"You're taking it that way. Why else would we be sitting here arguing about this bullshit then, yo?"

"I'm just sayin'..."

"Just saying what, yo?" asked Coco.

Josephine stepped in. "You're just saying that you want to lead sometimes, and Coco said okay. Me, I say yeah. Now, can we just end this? I'm getting a damn headache. It's about a damn record contract, y'all. We're fighting for crumbs."

"When are we starting these practices?" Danielle asked.

"Let's do it now, yo," said Coco.

The words sounded more like a challenge than an arrangement for rehearsal. They all rose. The skidding of the chairs signaled their fate like the bell that begins a boxing round. Suddenly Coco remembered her calculus test.

"No. I think we better wait 'til tomorrow. I've really got to study and tighten up on da calculus thing, yo. We could do this tomorrow, yo. I still wanna go to a good college for free, know what I mean, yo?"

"Yeah, cool," said Danielle. "This kid's beeping me, anyway." She checked the incoming message on the pager, worn next to her navel. Her blue jeans were a little tighter than the other girls wore. She had a slender body that connected in a voluptuous form. She made no attempt to hide it. In fact, she accentuated it by continually showing up in outrageous combinations. She hurried to the pay phone. Her manicured fingers dialed the digits from the pager.

"Hi Cory," she said.

Coco shouldered her knapsack, lit another cigarette, and headed to the door. She threw a peace sign to Danielle, whose eyes shifted just in time to catch it. Danielle nodded.

Coco and Josephine walked to the bus stop in silence. Coco puffed, her right hand clinging to the cigarette like a drunk about to throw a dart.

"What do you think it is?" asked Josephine, finally breaking the silence. She had been thinking about the incident at lunch. Coco flipped the cigarette away. It spiraled through the air and into a puddle. The water doused the fire and soaked into the cigarette butt, turning the puddle into an ashtray.

"I don't know what you're talking 'bout," said Coco.

"The little skit at the chicken place," Josephine reminded Coco. "Or am I bugging?"

"You probably buggin', yo," said Coco.

"No, you 'n' Danielle were. I guess she wants more props."

"She gets all the props from her boyfriends," said Coco as her mischievous smile appeared.

"No, you didn't go there," Josephine rejoined. "Personally, I think she's been drinking too much."

"Well everyone takes a sip of sump'n."

"Way too much," said Josephine. "And when she does, it's not like you."

"Like me? Whatchu gettin' ready to say?"

"No, I don't mean that. I mean she can't control herself. She always be getting wild and loud. For a while at the chicken place, I thought she had a little nip of that damn Alize. 'Me 'n' my man split a bottle o' Thug Passion." Josephine mocked Danielle's way of speaking.

"She better check herself," said Coco,

"And don't wreck herself," added Josephine.

"I'm gonna take a walk over to the library next to her place. It's real quiet in there, yo."

"You could come and study at my place, my mom ..." offered Josephine.

"No, that's okay," said Coco.

The bus pulled up. Both girls showed passes and took seats. Coco reached for her headphones. Josephine watched as the huge tires of the bus splattered the puddle and the waterlogged cigarette. With a turn of the wheel, both became nothing. Coco and Josephine watched passengers board and leave the bus. As it moved uptown, fewer suits and ties got on and more got off. Then it was Coco's stop.

"Don't study too hard, girlfriend. Wednesday is

rehearsal," said Josephine.

She offered her fist, pointing to Coco. Coco touched fists and left the bus. Her bop came to life as she neared the brown glass doors of the gray library. She stopped to catch a smoke. *Danielle is just being a bitch*, she thought. *I know she ain't even close to me in dancing, and the bitch definitely can't sing. All she does is swing her long hair in your face. That's the reason I had to move up to the front. Anyway, people know I'm the lead. They know. Maybe that's the reason she hangs out with so many boys. She trying to win a popularity contest. Well, if it's a contest she wants, she's coming to the right one.*

Coco flicked the cigarette away. Now she wished she hadn't put off rehearsal until Wednesday. But the calculus test was tomorrow, and she wanted to score high.

Coco walked into the library, still dwelling on Danielle's little lunchtime outburst. *She thinks she's all that. We'll see.*

"A-h-h-h," she breathed as she sat down and pulled her calculus book out of her knapsack. *Too bad I can't study at home*, she thought. *I could study and just fall asleep. This place is mad quiet. Wish I could take it home.*

Calculus began. She let it take over her mind, and after a couple of hours it was over. She shouldered the knapsack and headed for the bus stop. On the way, she spotted Danielle and her new boyfriend.

"Hi. What are you doing around these parts?" asked Danielle, who already knew the answer.

"Trying to set up one of these nice apartments," said Coco.

"Be careful. There are plenty of cops around here. You don't want to mess around and get caught," said the boyfriend. There was lipstick all over his mouth, but he seemed ah'ight. And he was good looking.

"Oh, Coco, this is Cory. Cory, this Coco, my ace boon," said Danielle, a little giddy.

"Hi, what's poppin', Cory," said Coco. "Got to be out. Here comes my bus."

"Coco, I'll give you a ride. I mean, Cory has a car, and I'm sure--"

"Nah, that's ah'ight. You guys do what y'all were

gonna do. Nice to see ya. Peace."

The bus came, and she got on. *Now she's gonna get real nice, like nothing happened*, thought Coco. *Fuck her and her ride. That's what that nigga getting ready to do, anyway. Lipstick all over his face*

Damn! she almost said it out loud. The bus lurched forward, and Coco fell back into the seat. Her thoughts switched to home. *What kind of mood is Mom gonna be in?* she wondered as she got off the bus and moved toward the broken glass doors of the dirty brick building. The crack-heads lurched in and out. *Home, sweet home*, she thought as she pushed by them and into the building.

"Hi, Coco," they shouted.

"Peace," she said, without turning around. She headed for the elevator, but the sign on the door read "Out of Service."

"Shit." She went to the stairwell. She reached the apartment door. She thought a sign should be posted: *You're now entering hell.* The peephole looked like a bullet hole. *Let's see what the devil's gonna cook up this evening. Maybe she'll be too drunk to deal with life.* Coco's mind tried to enter before her body. This type of mind-game prepared her for whatever came next: Think it's worse, maybe it will be better.

A door squeaked open. It was Miss Katie, the widow from 3D. Her apartment, toward the entrance of the building, faced the street.

"Hi Coco. How are you doing?" asked Ms. Katie. "It's been about a month now, right Coco?"

"Yes, Miss Katie," answered Coco, politely. It was not her usual style, but Miss Katie Patterson was different from the other neighbors. She was fifty-ish and still looked young and bright. Her husband had died "back in 'Nam," she would say during times when she allowed herself to talk about him. Coco knew him only as Sgt. Patterson. But Miss Katie didn't sit around and mope; she went back to college and earned her degree. That really impressed Coco. Of course, she accomplished this while raising and sending her children, Roxy and Robert, to none other than Princeton. Coco smiled at Miss Katie, who deserved a lot of respect and love.

"Well, I'm pleased to report that she didn't go down to the dens today," said Miss Katie, as if reciting orders.

"That's good news," said Coco. She'd been getting that report since her mother came out of drug rehab a month ago and was continuing drug counseling on an out-patient basis.

"How's she on the inside?" asked Miss Katie. Coco flipped her right hand up and down, wrist loose.

"How's school and your tests coming along?"

"Fair to fine," replied Coco, enthusiasm in her voice.

"Good, good. Keep it up, Coco."

"Coco, is that you?" Her mother stood in their doorway.

"Yes, yes. I'll see you later, Miss Katie."

"Bye, Coco."

Coco entered an apartment that was well worn. It appeared every stitch of the family's clothing was laid out in the tiny hallway.

"I was gonna do laundry," her mother said, "but I just couldn't make it down them goddamn steps. Elevator still out?"

"Yeah, Ma," said Coco. "I'll get them in a few. Just sort 'em out." It would be a chance to go downstairs and use the pay phone. "Any mail?" she asked.

"Girl, you constantly asking the same question. What you hoping for? Publisher's Clearinghouse told you that you gonna be their next first prize winner? Huh?"

"No, Mom. Just checking, just checking," said Coco, reaching for a bag of chips. She slipped out a couple and crunched.

"The mail's over by the kitchen window."

Coco sauntered to the window.

"Why don't you walk properly? Ladylike? You're getting older, and you've got to learn to conduct yourself like a lady."

"Mom, please save the sermon," sighed Coco. She leafed through the mail. Bills, junk mail. No college acceptances, no record contracts. She looked down through the window. People were milling around. From above, they looked like robots, moving a few steps at a time, pausing as if trying to reach something, but never succeeding. She saw beggars with turned up palms, making the working people move faster, walking away with noses turned up in disgust. Just across the side of building, a torch was sparked--a fiend had made a score.

Coco turned her back to the window. Her mother plopped herself down on the soiled sofa. Everything was worn out like the sofa. A mouse scuttled from underneath the sofa and disappeared through a hole in the wall. *Well, maybe not everything.*

"I guess I better start the laundry." Coco grabbed the keys, along with the cart. She started out the door. Her mother approached.

"Get me a pint of Hen," she said. She handed Coco a ten-dollar bill while looking the other way. "Bring it up after you put the clothes in the washer, okay?"

Coco noted that her mother's demeanor was like that of a little girl asking for candy.

"Okay?" Her mother asked a second time. Coco wished her mother was more like Miss Katie. "No," she wanted to answer. "No more candies for you." But instead she replied with an enthusiastic, "Yeah, yeah. Ah'ight,"

"Don't be giving me that, 'yeah, ah'ight' street lingo. Just be careful with your mouth," said Mrs. Harvey.

"To the dungeon," said Coco as the door slammed shut. She stopped in the hallway outside the door.

"Nah, nah. Not yet. I need my smokes." Coco started banging on the door. Mrs. Harvey came to the door. From the outside, Coco could see her clearly through the damaged peephole. She opened the door and threw the pack of cigarettes. Coco caught them in her left hand easily.

"We've got to get them to fix this hole, yo," said Coco.

"Yeah, when you get back. Hurry. And I'm not gonna tell you again to stop da street talkin'. I'm not your yo. I'm your mother."

Calm down, little girl. You'll have your candy soon, thought Coco.

"Okay," she blurted out as she started for the stairwell, dragging the cart with the dirty laundry.

****

"Damn girl, where you going? That's a lotta shit." It was Deja. He had been visiting his son and his son's mother who lived in the building.

"Yeah, what's up Deja? What ya doing around these parts, yo?" asked Coco.

"Ya know," said Deja. He grabbed the front of the cart and guided the wheels down the steps. Finally they reached the bottom.

"Good looking out, Deja," said Coco, genuinely grateful. "It would have been hell."

"That's ah'ight. Wanna burn some weed, Coco?" She thought about the high and was tempted.

"Nah, I'ma pass." She almost astonished herself.

"Sure, now?" asked Deja, a little surprised at Coco's answer. She had always smoked with him. "Coco, I'm telling you, this some good shit you turning down." He held the blunt to her face. Its brown paper wrap was still moist from the licking it had taken.

Coco smiled. "Nah, yo. I got shit to do," she said. But her mind wandered. *Why don't I just hit it a couple of times? One or two drags an' chill. Oh, no. I don't know what's wrapped in it. It might not be weed.* Coco made good her escape.

"Well that's never stopped you before," Deja yelled. He went up the stairs, leaving out of the building. *That bitch was acting nervous, he reflected. Edgy fucking bitches. One day they on one side of da edge, next they on da other muthafuckin' side.* "That's why man has da herb's blessing," he said aloud. Then he placed the brown homemade cigar between his lips.

"Peace, God," he said and squeezed a blue-tinted lighter. Its silver tip sparked and Deja inhaled deeply, pulling the flame up to the tip of the blunt. He held the smoke in his lungs, then exhaled, extinguishing the flame's dance on the cigar tip. Another smoker, Rightchus, moved over toward Deja.

"What's up, Rightchus," Deja said. He clasped Rightchus' hand with his right hand. They bumped shoulders and held each other's hand in a tight-fisted embrace. They released each other's hands, fists clashing.

"Good to see ya, Rightchus," Deja laughed. He

choked on the smoke of the weed. "So whazzup? Want some?" He passed the blunt to Rightchus. Rightchus had never been known to turn down weed or anything else he could smoke. Rightchus never passed on a free high. They smoked and talked.

"Wow, man, this shit got some power to it," announced Rightchus. "Yo, you know about the cosmic," he continued.

"Cos-what?" asked Deja.

"Cosmic, kid," said Rightchus.

"Cosmic? I hope that don't mean Cos on da mike," laughed Deja, lightheaded from the deep draws on the weed.

"Now I see. I can't kick shit, because you ain't ready," said Rightchus just as two Rastafarians emerged. They shouted to the smokers.

"Jah Rastafari!"

"Peace, Jahman," answered Rightchus. He turned to Deja. Deja sucked on the blunt and passed it to Rightchus.

"I'm gonna go through some degrees though--know wha' I'm sayin'? Based on da science, mathematics states that all men are created equal. Know wha' I'm sayin'?"

"Word is bond," said Deja. But the grin on his face said he was less than serious. It was important to Rightchus, so he continued.

"Word is bond, indeed. Manifest in da cipher, da truth is da wisdom. Da wisdom is da wise. Take you to the sixth degree of science. Word is bond. I'm going through some degrees though, know wha' I'm mean? The degrees of mathematics is wisdom, cipher, means: That all men are born in wisdom, know wha' I'm sayin' and that's showin' and provin' that truth is in da square when you manifest da cipher, know wha' I'm sayin'? When you manifest da truth, da truth is wisdom, which is da wise word manifested by da wise and intelligent black man, with supreme knowledge of himself. Know wha' I'm sayin'? Wisdom is the wise where no more wise would be dumb and the ignorant. Wisdom is also that black women secondary, but most positively necessary to God, know wha' I'm sayin'? Wisdom is also H20, you know wha' I'm sayin'? Water. He wisdom cipher, when he wisdom cipher, he only manifest light, 'cause water is the substance of light. Therefore, wisdom is bearing the seed of light or seed of the true and living god, the black man. The Black man have to build God. Know wha' I'm sayin'?

Coco heard this sermon on the way to and from the liquor store. Rightchus had drawn a crowd. Others rolled and lit blunts. Soon they were passed around until the crowd became a big puff of smoke. A patrol car casually drove by. The officers observed the smoking crowd.

Then came an interruption. "Disperse now," announced the shotgun cop. "Get off the street corner."

"I'ma go to the store and get a brew. Peace," said Deja. The others headed into other buildings. The crowd dispersed as quickly as they had formed, but not peacefully.

"Fuck da police," yelled Deja.

The police heard him. Emergency lights flashed.

"That's why we had Tyson in jail. Don't move. You in the red jacket, walk toward the car."

Evening had begun to fall. The sun emitted a yellow-and-red hue against a gray blue sky on its way down.

"Build black man," yelled Rightchus as the cops frisked Deja. They both were out of the car. The engine was still running the doors were left open. Deja submitted to the search. He knew he was clean. Coco watched. She shook her head and kept going. Then the police spoke to Deja. No cuffs were unlocked. He was going to be arrested.

"Tin shields always showing out," Coco said. She threw the cigarette down and walked in the front entrance, now deserted. Quickly a man reached down, picked it up and puffed desperately. His clothes were tattered and dirty: street living. *I'm sorry, I didn't see you.* Coco almost articulated, but decided not to interrupt the loud conversation he was having with himself.

She entered the building. There were no visible numbers, a front door that used to be a red door, with lock-and-key security. Seven years earlier, she and her mother had moved into this building after a series of welfare motels. It seemed then to be a nice living space, but not for long. *Things are always broken; never fixed*, she thought, as she walked past the broken elevator. Its brown doors spread invitingly.

Coco returned to her apartment and left the Hennessy on the table. Her mother shouted from the bathroom, "Coco, Coco. Is that you?"

"Yeah, Mom. I gotta check on the laundry." She hurried down concrete stairs to the basement that harbored four washing machines that worked when they wanted to, and dryers that invited quarters for very little heat. She had left her laundry in the dryer. A friend, Bebop, from the sixth floor, was keeping an eye on it.

"Thanks, yo," Coco said, bursting through the door and startling Bebop, who had just settled into a comfortable position.

"Shit, Coco, slow down," said Bebop. The twenty-three year old daughter of Jamaican immigrants was someone Coco knew she could trust.

"You scared da living shit outta me, gal," screamed Bebop. The fright brought out her native dialect.

"Chill, Bebop." said Coco. "How's my laundry?"

"They should be finished. But check them. The machines are still going," said Bebop. "I heard you were at the club dancing up a storm when they jacked that girl and raped her," she added.

Coco went to the three functioning dryers. She watched briefly as the machines emitted squeaky sounds in rhythm with their rotations. She beat out the rhythm on the long, shaky table that separated washers from dryers.

"Yeah, we were at da club but we weren't involved with that, or anything like that, yo." Coco turned to face an inquisitive stare. Suddenly, she realized Bebop knew something. Bebop had a way of knowing things.

"Well, we met her on our way to the club and shit. But I don't know. I don't really know. Maybe someone she had a beef with, someone waiting outside you know, yo. All I know is I got clocked cold."

"I don't know," Bebop threw her hands up and dropped them on the table. She thumped the last note to the beat. The washers churned, then stopped. Coco moved the huge black laundry bag and cart into their receiving positions. She reached into the dryer and dumped the clothes into the bag.

"Are you gonna fold?" asked Bebop.

"Are you gonna help, yo?"

"That's a lot of folding," said Bebop.

"Well, you don't really have to, yo. I'll catch ya--"

"No, no, Coco. I'll help."

"No, ya don't have to, child. I'll be good to ya next time. I'll see you, yo," Coco joked.

"You know you want me to help," smiled Bebop.

"Ah'ight, yo, let's do this and stop whining so hard," said Coco, a smirk pasted to the corners of her lips.

Coco took the clothes out and the folding process began. Bebop waited. Coco knew there was nothing to be said. Then, on impulse, she started something.

"Yo, Bebop. Peep this, yo. What if someone called you out, to--like a performance duel, you know? Singing? Dancing?"

"C'mon, Coco. Nobody wants to do that. You're already in videos, MTV, BET and all that shit."

"Nah, but this person is good and they supposed to be down with your crew."

"You mean Josephine? Nah she wouldn't play herself like that. It's that bitch that thinks she's a Rican. Wanna be fly girl?" Bebop phrased the question as if she was on 'Jeopardy'.

Coco smiled, giving away the answer.

"I know, I know," said Bebop, humming in her patois. "I neva liked that dut-ty bitch. I told you she was a 'ore," continued Bebop. She looked over at Coco, who held the stare momentarily.

"It's not that big a deal, yo. I'm just sayin'..." Her voice trailed off. Coco knew she could count on certain people, Bebop for one.

"Watch your back, Coco" said Bebop, "'cause people like that can't be trusted. Ya know?" Bebop was staring firmly at Coco.

The long folding table between them was obviously unstable; it shook with Bebop's words, and from Coco leaning ever so slightly against it.

"It's cool," said Coco, almost automatically. "I won't sleep, sis." They continued folding clothes. They heard shuffling noises. Bebop grew angry.

"Fucking rats," she said. She lit a cigarette.

"Save me some, yo," said Coco. "I ran out."

They continued folding. When everything was done, Coco saw that Bebop had beads of perspiration on her forehead. She went to the dryer and dumped the contents into her laundry bag.

"Let me drop these off and I'll be back to help you," she said to Coco, "'cause you could stand some help."

"Ah'ight. That'll be peace, Bebop," said Coco. She accepted without so much as a second thought. "Hurry! I wanna catch *Jeopardy*, yo," she yelled after Bebop.

Bebop was out the door. The rats shuffled. Coco waited. *Everybody knows about that incident at the club*, she thought. Then Bebop was back. They struggled up the stairs with the heavy cart, full of clothing. When they reached the third floor, the long haul was over.

"Where's the elevator when you need it?" asked Bebop, trying to catch her breath.

"Yeah, right," said Coco.

"And why did you carry the cart?" asked Bebop.

"Well, this is the way Mom gave me da shit. I was gonna drag it up and down, you know.

"Yeah, you should have. Next time bring the laundry bag only. I know it was a struggle for you bringing it down alone."

"I didn't do it alone. Deja helped. Thanks. Next time, sis," said Coco with a wink and a thumbs-up signal. "Ah'ight yo?"

"Coco, I'm telling you this once and for all. Watch your back around those so-called friends."

"Okay. I heard you already, yo."

"An' try not to get thumped in your nose anymore, okay?" Bebop smiled.

"Goodnight!" said Coco.

"Coco, you should come to church with us Sunday. Try."

"See ya."

"Say okay," said Bebop.

"Okay. See ya." Coco was through the apartment door. She pushed the cart in front of her. It was dark. She stumbled as she searched for the light switch, and woke her mother.

"Coco, is that you? What took you so long?" She spoke with that telltale slur.

Coco studied her mother. She must have been prettier in her youth. Right now she looked awful.

"It was a lot of clothes, Mom," said Coco.

Mrs. Harvey arose from the sofa, which retained her form long after she stood. She turned, searched, and suddenly seemed to panic. Then she felt the bottle. It was still there.

Coco left for the kitchen. She sat on the right side of the window and looked down. *It's calculus tomorrow*, she thought. Coco pulled her black boots off and rested both feet on the lead-lined radiator. It was cold to her touch. She flexed her toes and watched as night fell.

The pipe-fiends, rats, and other night creatures now moved against their prey. They roamed the tiny park. Its benches provided space for the weary, as well as those on the prowl. Those benches were the rest stop for the ones who overdosed or had made their last score.

Coco gazed out the window at a view which bore the statistics on shoot-outs, drug overdoses and suicides. But those were regular re-runs. Calculus was important now. *Thank God for libraries*, she thought, and drifted off to sleep.

****

Her mother's raging voice awoke Coco.

"Git up and go to bed, child. Who are you s'pose to be anyway, the night watchman? 'Cause if you is, you're sleeping on the job. So you might as well take your sleepy ass to its rest. Hear me, Coco?"

"Yeah, yeah. I'm hearing you. So does everyone else on the street."

"Just go to your bed. Always wit' the smart mouth, like your dirty, singin', travelin' wreck of a father."

"Okay, I'm gone."

Coco stood up and the window displayed its scenery. It had not changed too much. The crack-heads were still stalking. The fiends were crawling, picking up anything that reflected light from the ground. The dogs were barking loudly, and the rats scampered to their holes for concealment while the night sky covered it all.

"Coco, get away from the window. Your duties for the night are over. You're dismissed," said Mrs. Harvey.

"Ma, I'll go, but promise me you won't go downstairs. You don't need anything else. I mean--"

"Coco, go to bed," said her mother sternly. "An' stop worrying 'bout me so much."

Coco had been looking at her mother's shadow, formed by the light from the window. Crack and alcohol had cooked the meat off her bones. Her appearance was disheveled from the abuse her body had taken. Hardly any liquor was left in the bottle her mother was clutching under her arm as if her life depended on it. Coco walked past the shell of her mother and headed for the bathroom.

CHAPTER 5

Deedee lay awake, staring at the bright sunshine streaming through the window. She was turned to the side, her hands clasped beneath her knees, drawn up to her chest. She watched as the sun's rays brought a flight of birds into focus. Their wings flickered as they lit on the windowsill to feed on breadcrumbs that she had put there. She observed that the large birds pounced on the food and devoured it before the smaller birds had a chance. The smaller birds hovered above the feeding flock, afraid to participate. Deedee was tempted to scare the large birds off, throw some crumbs to the smaller ones. She would have done it on any other day.

Today she rested her head against the soft pillows, and pulled the cover up so she wouldn't see the birds. Yet the rays still shone through.

Finally she got up and went to the kitchen. Deedee poured a glass of juice, spilling some on the white tabletop. Then she saw the two coffee cups and noticed Sophia sitting there.

"Sophia, I didn't see you. I'm sorry. Is Uncle E. here too?"

"Yes. He's upstairs, I think. He was about to make breakfast, but I guess I'll have to do it."

"You're not a bad cook," Deedee teased. "But I'm not really hungry."

"Well, how about some shopping, you know?" asked Sophia with a wink.

"Aren't you working today?" Deedee was a little excited at the new suggestion.

"No, I'm off, honey. I have time, " said Sophia with a smile.

"Y'all need money for shopping?" Eric announced his presence. He had been standing, unnoticed. Deedee looked rested, he thought. "How much?" He asked, barging into the conversation at exactly the right time.

"Well, ten thousand dollars would be nice, wouldn't

you say, Dee?" Deedee turned and looked at both of them. They looked as if they were waiting for the punch line. *Oh what the hell, I'll play along*, she decided. Deedee shook her head from side to side and snapped her fingers.

"You know, I could handle that very well." The words tumbled out. They were meant to be spontaneous, but the pause lasted longer than she intended. It was like a bad joke. She felt her timing was off. "So, who's gonna do breakfast between y'all?" asked Deedee, seizing the moment to patch things up.

"Well, Eric had promised to earlier," said Sophia, smiling.

"Nah, nah. It ain't goin' down like that." He smiled and his eyes widened as he turned to look at Sophia. "Sophia," he said with a big grin, "you owe me."

"Alright" sighed Sophia. "But this will be all the cooking I do today." She returned his smile.

"Okay," said Deedee. "Why don't we all eat out?"

"Sounds good to me," said Eric.

"Sophia?" asked niece and uncle together.

"Sure, sure," said Sophia.

"You guys go ahead. I'll meet y'all outside," said Deedee.

"Unh-uh, we're not going for that," her uncle said, smiling. "We know you're gonna lock yourself in the room. Oh, no. You're coming right now."

"No, I won't be long. I'm just gonna get a coat. I promise."

"Its pretty warm outside, honey," said Eric. He reached out to hold her, but she resisted, twisting her arms free of his hands.

"Get your coat, Dee," said Sophia. "Maybe I should get one while we're downtown. Yeah! And I saw this nice Versace the other day. Hmm, hmm," she said. Deedee smiled and ran upstairs.

Sophia and Eric went outside. It was quite warm. The humidity was working its way slowly up the scale. The sun's brightness made the morning glow with life. Eric, with the press of a switch, disarmed the car alarm and unlocked the doors to the Range Rover. They got in and waited for Deedee, listening to the radio.

"How much are we getting?" asked Sophia.

"We?" asked Eric.

"Stop being such a cheapo."

"Cheapo?"

"Yes. Stop being a cheapo. Tell me how much are we getting."

"Alright, alright. I'll tell you after breakfast," he said.

They waited in the car, listening to the radio, teasing and laughing at each other. Deedee emerged from the front door. She locked it and turned on the alarm. As she walked toward the car, they both noticed that instead of her usual fitted jeans and ribbed blouse, she was wearing a pink, baggy, cotton warm-up suit and a maroon spring coat. They looked at each other.

"Let her be," said Sophia, then yelled out the window, "C'mon girl, hurry. I'm starved."

Deedee quickened her step. Her plain white tennis shoes, moving with matching socks, emphasized her pace. She slid through the open door and the vehicle seemed cramped and crowded to her. She lowered the window.

"I'm ready," she announced with a sigh of relief.

"For food? Where?" asked Eric.

"Let's go to the pancake house on Lex," suggested Deedee.

"That sounds delicious," Sophia said.

The vehicle rolled toward Main Street. Eric made a right and in fifteen minutes they were on Lexington Avenue, pulling easily into a parking spot. Deedee was the first out.

Deedee put her hands in her coat pockets. She had completed her disguise with a white Colorado Rockies baseball cap. Deedee and Sophia were seated in the cozy diner. Eric remained outside, conversing on his cellular.

"Good morning. You ladies ready to order?" asked a smiling waiter. "Something to drink, maybe?"

"Well--"

"I'll have hot chocolate with whipped cream," buzzed Deedee.

"And two regular coffees. Thanks," added Sophia. "Let me go get that guy. 'Cause if we let him, we'll eat right through his conversation. Music business," said Sophia as she left the table. She returned a few lonely minutes later with Eric.

"Hey, don't you like the hot chocolate? You're looking sad, girl." Eric had been standing next to her for a while. Deedee had been unaware of this, too deep in thought to notice.

"No, it's alright. I was just thinking." She felt compelled to explain her mood.

"Well, think of how you're gonna be spending five thousand dollars, baby." Sophia winked.

"Five thousand dollars?" repeated Eric, incredulous. "Where you gonna get that from?"

"Well, how much then?" asked Sophia in mock annoyance. "I thought you said..."

"Okay," said Eric.

"We settled on..." Sophia pouted. Deedee stared. Eric fumbled for a number. Then, finally, he turned to Deedee.

"What do you think? Five G's, or not?"

It made Deedee smile, knowing she would have five thousand dollars to spend. *Wow,* she thought, *I could shop for days, non-stop.*

"Well, five sounds all right, but I was looking forward to the ten grand," she joked. Her joke made her uncle smile. He was happy that Sophia had concocted this little scheme, and that it had brought a smile to his niece's face.

Deedee reflected. The humor was sick, but a five-thousand-dollar shopping spree sounded good. It probably would bring a smile to anyone's face. But she knew not even ten thousand dollars would erase the bitter and ugly experience, and her memories of the cruelest people she'd ever met.

"What are you having, Dee?" asked Eric, attentively. The waiter and Sophia also looked concerned. *What are they staring at,* she wondered?

"Oh, I'll have two German pancakes, and eggs. Sunny side up."

"Anything to drink?" asked the well-mannered waiter.

"Yeah. We'll all have apple juice," said Eric. His cellular phone rang, and he sprang out of his chair. He left the table and headed outside, away from the other patrons.

"Yeah, Eric, this is Busta. How 're you?" asked the caller.

"I'm fine. I need a major hit. We gotta talk."

"Well, let's meet at Geez at about seven. Eric, I've got these crazy nice girls you gotta hear. And as a matter of fact, they're all dimes."

"That's fine," said Eric. "See you then." He folded the black instrument and shoved it into a front pocket of his jeans.

"Alright," he announced, back at the table.

"What did she want?" teased Sophia.

"It wasn't her," said Eric. "It was Busta. Got to meet with him later. But first we're gonna eat, and then spend some money."

The meal arrived and they all settled into breakfast. Deedee was afraid she wouldn't be able to stomach the food, but German pancakes were her favorite. After one bite, she succumbed to the pleasures of the meal.

After a hearty breakfast, Deedee and Sophia took Eric on a shopping extravaganza that really cost him ten thousand dollars, and he carried most of the shopping bags. When the clothes became too much to carry, they returned to the parking lot and stowed the bags in the Range Rover.

"Thank you, uncle," said Deedee, planting a kiss on Eric's sweating cheeks.

"You are more than welcome," he said, returning the kiss.

"And thanks, Sophia. I love your style."

"You're welcome, sweetheart." She opened her arms. Deedee lunged forward for the hug. "Movie, anyone?" asked Sophia as Eric started the car.

"How about dinner and a movie?" suggested Deedee.

"Well..." Eric looked at his watch. "Why don't the both of you go ahead and I'll catch up to you later?"

"You tired of us already?" asked Sophia. A smug expression belied her feelings.

"No, no," said Eric, taking the bait. "I've got to meet

with Busta."

"Uncle Eric, you know we're not gonna make it to the movies if we wait around for you and your business." Deedee sounded disappointed.

"Alright. Here's my phone." Eric gave Sophia the cellular. "Let's synchronize our watches. It's six-forty p.m. At exactly eight-thirty p.m., I'll call you, and we'll catch the nine p.m. movie."

"Okay. Sounds good," said Deedee.

"Yeah, because if you get in a meeting and you get on this phone," Sophia said, pointing to the black instrument, "it's all over." They all laughed.

Eric eased the car out of the parking lot and headed uptown to Cozy Geez, a nighttime hangout for the famous and infamous.

"Be careful, Babe," said Sophia. Eric kissed her soft, moist lips.

"See you later, over dinner. You guys decide what movie y'all wanna see."

"Don't forget to call us, Uncle E.," said Deedee as he gently clasped her hand in his.

"I will, Sugar. Eight-thirty, right?"

"That's right," called Deedee. She watched Eric cross the street, dodging traffic. He walked by the dark-suited bouncers and through the brown wooden doors. There was no need for a search. Eric Ascot was one of the city's hottest music producers.

Things had been difficult after his brother's death, but Dennis had left him with good connections. Eric had produced one of the year's best rhythm-and-blues albums. This raised him from ordinary to a contender for Music Producer of the Year.

Eric strolled to a table for two in the rear. The waiter brought him his usual, straight Hennessy with a twist of lemon.

"Good evening, sir," said the waiter.

"Yeah, yeah." Eric faced the door. A sudden commotion arose. It was Busta's usual fanfare.

Busta blustered his way to the table. "Why they always feeling on me? Who they should be searching, they don't. Mutherfuckin' faggots," growled Busta. His huge grin eclipsed his anger. "What up, E?" He threw his arms around Eric in a hearty hug. "Damn, you better start working out before you get like me, man." Busta landed soft punches in Eric's mid-section.

"I can never get as large as you, Busta," said Eric. His own mock-punch landed softly on Busta's protruding stomach. "This town ain't big enough."

The waiter returned.

"Two Heinekens and another shot of..." Eric paused, seemingly lost in thought. He and Busta were both distracted by a beautiful brown-skinned girl who swayed by.

"Hennessy, Sir," the waiter volunteered. He went off to get the drinks.

"Hot damn!" said Busta, turning back on Eric as she glided past. She gave Eric 'the eye.'

"Leave that alone, E. That spells trouble. Leave that to me, man."

"Yeah alright, if you say so."

"Yeah. How's Sophia?"

"Doing well. She's heaven-sent."

"No, she was Busta's blessing," Busta corrected. "Things good with da biz?" Busta tossed back his shot of cognac. He slammed the heavy shot-glass down on the table with a bang. Eric followed suit, then sipped his beer.

He had known Busta since high school. Busta had always been into hustling everything from drugs to numbers to girls. Eric wasn't sure how Busta met Sophia. He was always into a little bit of this and a little bit of that. Eric motioned to the waiter to bring more drinks.

"The biz is great. You *know* no one can touch my sound," he said, smiling as he bragged. The waiter placed two shots on the table and removed the empty glasses.

"What is it then, man? You don't look right," Busta said.

"It's my niece, Deedee. She was raped by some muthafuckas," Eric tried to restrain his emotion.

"Who? What da fuck are you sayin', E.?" Busta stared incredulously. "When did that shit happen?"

Eric picked up the slender shot glass and sighed heavily. He raised his eyebrows and his nostrils flared in anger.

"When?" asked Busta louder now.

"Over this past weekend," said Eric. The words left his mouth dry. He raised the glass and flung the liquor to the back of his throat. His lips came together in a smacking sound.

"She knows who did it?"

"She said some guy called Deja. Well, she didn't *say* anything. What happened ... Well, she woke up screaming, and when I got to her room, she said she was dreaming that Deja was tryin' to rape her again."

"So that's your man," said Busta.

"Well, that's the reason I wanted to see you. What's the word on him?"

Busta sipped his beer and pondered.

"He's small time. Crack dealer. Hang with da West Side peeps. That's who supply him. Let's bag that muthafucka," he continued. "Bum ass nigga! His boys who be hanging wit' him may all be packing, and he's probably holding nine or sump'n, too. Da muthafucka is a rapist, E. He's got to go. Let's hit..."

"I can't be involved, see. Sophia got me legal, and I can't just be doing anything to blow that," said Eric, sitting back.

"He's down with those West Side people. It's gonna be difficult. It's gonna cost. Put up a price and I'll hook it up."

Eric picked up his beer and gulped. He motioned to the waiter for more. He picked up the fresh beer and watched as Busta did the same.

"Ten grand," he said.

The bottles clinked as Eric and Busta toasted their new deal, and Eric sipped his beer with a renewed sense of calm. He knew the problem would be taken care of. Busta was deeply connected in the street. Both men burped and laughed, releasing the tension.

"A-h-h" said Eric. "This spot still gets crowded. Haven't been up in here in a while."

"Yep, it's the same. Ain't too much changed," agreed

Busta.

"But you need to come down to the talent show, E."

"Oh, you still involved with that?"

"Fridays it's open-mike night at the club. Do something for the kids, you know?"

"Alright, I'll pass through, check things out."

"Any Friday. As a matter of fact, in two weeks we're having the finals of the talent competition I've got these girls, ah, Coco an' Da Crew. Eric, you've got to see them. They are all the way live. I'm sayin', they're dimes too."

"Sounds good," said Eric. He checked his watch. Eight-fifteen. A good time to call and see what the girls were doing.

"I gotta make a call." Eric began to rise.

"Yeah, lemme go use the bathroom." Busta pushed the table away. They walked toward the men's room. New arrivals made the small place feel smaller. Eric descended the steps to the public phone and dialed the number of his cellular. Deedee answered.

"Hi uncle. Are you ready?"

"I'm ready."

"We're on our way."

"Okay." He hung up, stepped into the bathroom then went back upstairs. Busta was shaking hands. Eric went back to his table and dropped a fifty-dollar bill. He gestured to Busta, *I'll be outside,* and pointed to the exit. Busta, still shaking hands, acknowledged Eric and engaged the smooth chick with the sexy walk.

A lazy evening breeze greeted Eric when he stepped outside. It dragged the humidity down, made the air a little cooler. The moon glowed orange, its ascent caught in the setting sun. Busta came out and gave Eric another hug and a firm handshake.

"Need a ride somewhere?"

"No. Sophia is on her way with Deedee. We're gonna check out a flick."

"Ah'ight. Good seeing you, E.," Busta punched Eric's stomach. A bit hard, Eric thought.

"Yeah, take it easy." Eric countered a straight, hard, right to Busta's exposed gut. They flinched, and took a fighter's stance, then laughed and parted like men who have been friends since childhood. They were familiar with each other's weaknesses.

The valet brought Busta's black Lexus around and Busta handed him a tip.

"Stay cool," he called to Eric and jumped into the car. Eric waved and with a blast of his horn, Busta was gone. In traffic, he picked up the car phone and made his call.

"I need a hit record. Crack dealer on back. The A side with the West Side syndicate. Deja, as in deja vu." Busta clicked the phone off and placed it on the seat next to him.

"Muthafucka," he hissed under his breath, "you're as good as dead." He steered through light downtown traffic. *Dennis and I were like brothers*, he mused. *He loaned me money when no one else would. No bank, bad credit, and being a young, black man-- that equals no loans, no legal funds. But Dennis took a chance. He financed twenty thousand dollars, the money to start the club. Now he's dead. The club's doing good, but I never really got a chance to pay him back all that money. I would have done this one my damn self, for free. That crack-slinging muthafucka raped Deedee. She's like my own daughter. If Dennis hadn't moved fast, I could have been her father. Dennis had too many women to keep count.*

****

Sophia stopped at the curb where Eric stood.

"Come around and drive, Baby," she said, and moved over as Eric hopped into the driver's seat.

"How was your meeting, Uncle E.?" Deedee asked. Eric saw she was decked out in a black Versace dress.

"All good. It went well, thanks," he said. "You look wonderful in that dress."

"Thanks," answered Deedee. "But didn't you like the multi-colored one like this one?" You didn't like it earlier." By now Eric had headed the car into traffic and she was speaking to the back of his head. "Oh well. I'm glad you think this one is nice."

Eric peeked at her in the rear-view mirror. Her face showed no change in expression. He looked at Sophia for support, but she avoided his plea for help.

"What movie are we gonna see?" asked Eric.

"Well, we narrowed it down to two," said Sophia. "Which one do you vote for, Deedee?"

"The first one." She was flippant. Sophia frowned.

"I'm sorry," Deedee quickly said. "I mean the one we discussed first."

"Okay, cool," said Sophia. "I haven't seen that one yet, and I'm sure Eric hasn't either."

"I'm down. I'll enjoy any movie. It's just hanging with you guys that's cool," he said with a quick glance at Deedee.

In the theater, Eric's nose tingled at the overpowering smell of hot buttered popcorn. "Get the tickets," he said. "I'm gonna get on the food line."

He nearly jogged to the concession stand. On the ticket line with Sophia, Deedee heard two guys behind her comparing notes. She assumed they were discussing her.

"But da bitch up front is all that," said loudmouth Number One.

Number Two agreed sternly. "Yeah, she right. She got that shit going on."

Sophia heard this, but she had a clearer idea who the guys were discussing.

"Look!" She rolled her eyes in the indicated direction. She recognized Danielle, from Da Crew. "She must think she's all that," said Sophia, inspecting Danielle. She drew every eye, and every man's approval. The women were less enthusiastic, but they feasted their eyes on Cory Miller, her escort. He was a student athlete at a New Jersey college.

The beautiful couple was on their way to the concession stand. As they drew close, Cory's eyes flashed. He paused in front of Deedee.

"What's up?" he asked. Danielle sniffled and walked on. Cory shrugged his shoulders and followed her.

When Sophia saw his shoulders, she said to herself, *Wow*. Then, irrepressibly, she blurted, "Oh, he's all that." She looked for a reaction, but Deedee only raised her brows.

I won't say anything, Deedee thought when Danielle walked by her. She and Sophia reached the head of the line and she concerned herself with the tickets. Then a minor commotion broke out. Danielle hurried toward her.

"I knew it was you," she said. A lobby full of people watched the encounter.

"Yep, nice dress," added Danielle. "You seem to be all healed." She eyed Deedee incredulously.

"Well, thanks. Just a good makeup job, thanks to my good buddy," Deedee answered. "Danielle, right?" she asked. Danielle nodded.

"Yes, I'm Danielle," she said, testily. She extended her arm. Sophia shook her hand.

"Nice to meet you, Danielle," Sophia said. Her smile did not betray the yearning not to shake Danielle's hand, but to grip it tightly, squeezing her rings between her fingers. Sophia resisted. *She's only a kid,* she thought. "You're very beautiful. You guys know each from school?" asked Sophia.

"No, not really. We met over the weekend," said Danielle.

Sophia's smile changed to a frown. She perked up her legal ears.

"She gave me and my two girlfriends a ride to the club," said Danielle. She looked to Deedee for any hint to stop, or elaborate. Deedee was weary. She turned to Sophia.

"Yeah, I picked them up and drove them to the club," she said.

"I was so mad when I heard that shit they did when you and Coco left the club," said Danielle. "I'm sorry," she said as an afterthought.

Deedee stared at her. She nodded and grimaced.

Then Danielle told Sophia, "Yeah, but I know Coco should have done something, you know. Everyone knows us. I mean, Coco at least had to have seen or done sump'n, ya know? She just let that shit happen to this innocent girl."

Deedee turned away. She couldn't believe what Danielle was saying. She sounded as if she was blaming Coco for the rape.

"I mean, Coco...Coco is, like, very well known. I mean, we've performed at that club several times. I don't know," she said touching her black tights with newly manicured, multi-colored fingernails.

"Well, maybe she saw who was there," said Sophia.

"Coco probably couldn't do anything," said Deedee, exasperated.

"C'mon. Coco was dead drunk," said Danielle. "That's why she couldn't do anything. She was drinking the whole night."

"Even if she wasn't, it really wouldn't have made any difference," said Deedee, looking away. "They had guns. I really don't wanna talk about this right now. So let's just drop it." Her voiced showed her anger.

"Okay. Sorry for bringing it up."

"That's okay," said Deedee. She looked up to find two pairs of eyes examining her.

"Well, here comes the popcorn," said Sophia as Eric rejoined them.

"Let me help you, dear," said Sophia. She helped herself to some popcorn and noticed Eric's eyes wandering over Danielle's figure. "Have you checked her out enough?" Sophia whispered as she elbowed him in the ribs. Eric lowered his eyes to the floor.

"Danielle, this is Deedee's Uncle Eric," said Sophia, turning to face the others. She positioned herself to block Eric's view of Danielle's tight frame. Danielle became perky. She rushed toward Eric, extending her right hand.

"You're Eric Ascot. Pleased to meet you. I'm Daniela. I think you're the best."

Eric smiled. Sophia compressed her lips and raised an eyebrow. She sure this young girl had changed her name for Eric's benefit.

"Pleased to meet you, Daniela," said Eric, reaching out to shake her hand.

Deedee looked away. She saw a small video arcade off to her left. Two small kids challenged each other. The machine soon turned their game into a battle. Now Cory joined the group, also bringing popcorn. After introductions, they headed off to separate movies. Sophia detected Eric admiring Danielle's rear end a second time.

"You need to start going to the gym, baby," she said, and gave him a harder jab to his gut.

CHAPTER 6

Coco and Josephine sat on a wooden bench next to the school auditorium. It was three thirty-five in the afternoon. Coco had been resisting the urge to light up a cigarette. She gave in, put the cigarette to her lips and shoved both hands in the front pockets of her oversized jeans.

"Let's walk down to the store. I'm taking a smoke break, yo," said Coco. She walked away. Josephine scurried and caught up to Coco.

"Where's the señorita?" asked Josephine.

"She's making us wait, that little..." Coco caught herself, lit up and then inhaled.

Josephine spotted Danielle driving up in Cory's car.

"On her way in a new carriage." She directed Coco's attention with her body language. Danielle and her escort had arrived.

"I'm sorry y'all, but we had to stop to do something on the way here," Danielle announced. Cory got out of the car with a video camera slung on his chest.

"Remember Cory? He's gonna be the cameraman so we can videotape this rehearsal. To be used as a reference." Danielle aimed the words at Coco, who continued smoking, not showing any interest. Then Coco addressed Josephine.

"If it's cool with everyone, then yeah, I'm wit' it, yo."

Cory approached, camera at the ready.

"I'm in," said Josephine. "Hi, Cory," she cooed.

"How you doin', Josephine?" They touched cheeks.

"Hi Coco," said Cory. He looked at Coco as if he was waiting on her table.

"Whazzup, Cory?" she puffed. "Let's do this then, yo."

The group headed for the auditorium. This was no ordinary rehearsal. A showdown had been shaping up ever since Danielle had confronted the girls. Threatened or not,

Coco had been put on her guard. Josephine played peacemaker. She was happy that the rehearsal would be recorded and critiqued. Da Crew knew they were ready. They exchanged wary smiles, except for Coco, who didn't smile.

On stage, Danielle moved enticingly. The camera rolled. Coco moved back and forth, heels and toes tapping street-sounds to the beat. Josephine circled, moving faster and faster, as if on ice. They balanced one another.

It was like the first day, when they met at the audition for the video shoot. All three danced with different groups and each girl was chosen from these groups. It had been that easy for them. They completed the dance video, and when Coco learned that the other two girls were recent transfers at her school, they started hanging out. The girls became a trio. But now a little competition didn't hurt.

The dance movements were complex, but the girls made them look easy. Coco, at the lead, performed a combination of hip-hop jazz steps, moving out against the girls. A simple tap and a few rolls to the floor brought Danielle's kicks to the changes in the beat. It was high-tempo. The girls were getting warm. The pace was furious. Coco flopped to the background with a two-knee slide. Now it was Danielle's turn. She seductively jumped and pranced for the camera and the man. She ended on beat with a split, a la James Brown. The place was wildly funky. Josephine perpetuated the beat by skipping, taking flight and vaulting over Danielle's cat-like, crouched figure. Josephine bounded with acrobatic skill and landed in a graceful ballerina's pose. She rolled up into hip-hop contortions. Coco prowled and leaped, flipping her body into the middle of the hoopla. The three danced easily together, moving in time to rehearsed steps. Cory recorded it all, and the camera intensified the mood.

It was Coco's turn again, or was it? She relinquished the lead. Josephine moved to the forefront with a split and quickly put down the break moves. She slid easily into a snail's crawl, freezing herself en vogue. Coco came through like a butterfly, landing softly on petals, wings beating a seductive rhythm. For one moment, time froze as the camera caught Coco in flight. Her gestures, her steps, said she was a dancer. When she was sure that they had enough, she quickly tumbled and rolled up on her stomach. She showed complete mastery of her muscles and limbs. It shook the other girls. The cameraman turned his head and held the camera in place. He watched Coco dance an unbelievable groove to up-tempo sounds. Josephine refused to follow.

"Yo, hold up, hold up. I think we've all flexed enough. Let's not lose focus, ah'ight? The winner is Coco," Josephine shouted and clapped. "Let's take a break."

Cory stopped filming and applauded. The girls had danced for nearly an hour.

"That was no rehearsal. That shit was for-real dance warfare," Josephine said between sips of water. Coco turned and looked at her. She lit a cigarette without answering. Danielle walked over to Cory, a few feet away. They huddled for a minute.

"I'm saying you were the best out there, baby. But Coco is bad."

"What do you mean?" Danielle was annoyed. "Did you get it all?"

"Think so," said Cory.

"We're gonna do voices next, and that'll be it. So take five." She kissed him on the cheek, twitched her hips, and rejoined Coco and Josephine.

"Did he get us?" asked Josephine. Her emphasis on 'he' made Coco look up from her smoke break.

"Yep, he did," answered Danielle. "Okay, instead of singing one or two numbers as a group, how about each of us solo on a song of our own choice?"

Coco and Josephine looked at each other.

"Oh, the contest is still on?" asked Josephine.

"Who says it's a *contest*?" retorted Danielle.

"Ah'ight, stop bitchin' at each other. Let's do it, yo," said Coco, putting out her cigarette.

"Josephine, you go first. Or do you want me to?"

asked Danielle. She was eager to show her vocal range. She had taken voice lessons with a trainer and she claimed the trainer had coached a couple of famous singers. She felt that put her in another class.

The equipment and the cameraman were ready. Danielle took the microphone and belted out "Neither One of Us," Gladys Knight-style. Even without the Pips, Danielle did an excellent job. She received applause from a new member of the audience.

"Don't worry. I'm not the heat. I'm just gonna sit here and check y'all nice, talented people out," he shouted, still clapping.

Josephine was next. She chose a difficult number by Whitney Houston. Her enthusiasm kept her going and when she was done, it was Coco's turn. Sitting at the edge of the auditorium stage, Coco lit another cigarette. *My turn came quickly*, she thought, inhaling. *Well, I could try "Diana the Boss," but there are no Supremes.* She dragged on the cigarette and the microphone amplified its hiss. Coco held cigarette and mike in her right hand. With her left hand, she removed her sweat-laden baseball cap and tousled her hair. She was searching her mind for something. Then she found it: her mother's favorite. Coco raised the microphone and the cigarette, and sang Billie Holiday's "My Man."

The newcomer was clapping from the beginning of the first stanza. He shouted, "Yeah" each time Coco paused. She held the other girls captive with her nonchalance. She was good. They thought of Diana and the Supremes, but when the Supremes sat down, Coco became Ms. Holiday. Then it was over. The newcomer raced down the aisle to the front of the stage. He got down on his knees, begging Coco to continue.

"Do some more for me. I'm your new Number One fan," he shouted. Coco beamed and jumped off the stage.

"Y'all are some *talented* people," said Rightchus. "I watched and listened to you, and you--" he pointed to each of the girls in turn. Then, he turned to Cory. "And you look like you have talent too, being the bodyguard and the cameraman." He was amused with his joke.

"Thanks," the girls said. They walked toward the exit. Cory joined them, as did Rightchus.

"You *did* that song, girl," said Josephine. "I didn't know you dug Billie Holiday like that."

"Well, she's my mom's favorite," said Coco. She was visibly overcome by the admission.

Danielle locked the door as they left and ran off to return the key to the maintenance staff. She had chosen that role ever since the girls got permission to use the small auditorium when it was idle.

"So, we'll be seeing you, yo," said Coco to the newcomer.

"Oh, yo. My name is Rightchus. When I do my thing, folks call me da Shorty-Wop-it Man. Hey, y'all can call me Shorty-Wop, cuz I seen y'all's performance an' y'all are there. Bad! Know wha' I'm sayin'?" He raised his arm. He was only four-feet, ten-inches tall. Coco, five-ten in her boots, towered over him. He was decked out in an inside-out *Free Mike Tyson* T-shirt, rolled-up blue jeans, and sandals.

"Yeah, I could sing too. I could do my thing. Can I get a cigarette?" asked Rightchus. They gathered around the car. The girls were relaxed most of the pre-rehearsal tension gone. Coco gave Rightchus a cigarette and a light. Josephine and Danielle shared a joint.

"Anyone want a Bud"? asked Rightchus. He produced a brown paper sack. "But y'all probably don't want this light stuff. Y'all probably want da gasoline stuff, da crooked-eye stuff." He winked. A big smile appeared on his face. Cory moved closer and took two cans from the package. He gave Danielle a can. Rightchus moved over to Coco, offering her a can. She hesitated, then took one. He looked at Josephine, she looked at Danielle.

"I'm not sharing. Take a beer," said Coco, sipping on the now-open can.

"Yeah, I can tell you're good peoples. See, I know. When you've spent your whole day talkin' to people who are constantly tryin' to beat you outta shit, then you know good peoples," said Rightchus. The group nodded and guzzled their beers.

"You from around here?" asked Josephine.

"What do you care?" Coco asked.

"Nah, nah," answered Rightchus. "This guy I met at a job interview told me whenever I was in da hood, jus' stop by. He's large in da hood. I stopped by and da muthafucka had nothing." He grinned. Cory laughed, encouraging Rightchus. "He was begging me. I had to give him a dollar bill," continued Rightchus. "Is she your girl?" He pointed to Josephine, spoke to Cory.

"No," said Cory. He pointed to Danielle. "That's my girl."

"No disrespect. I know you love her, but I'm telling you, don't get married. When you marry, you stop growing. Two people can't grow together. One has to stop growing and let the other, or they will wind up butting heads. I'm telling you."

"People make it," said Josephine. "I mean there are a lot of successful married people out there."

"Yeah," agreed Rightchus. "But they have the minds of eight-year-olds. They'll be forty years old, acting like eight-year-olds. They've got the minds of children." The group broke out laughing. Cory clapped his hands.

"See, I knew y'all were nice people. So far, nobody tried to beat me outta shit. That's what it's all about. You have to enjoy life. Like me, I got crazy, Bobby Brown style. Whenever y'all ready. My name's Rightchus, but you can call me Shorty-Wop. An' when I do ma thing, I'll be blowing up da spot. Peace. I've got to be out before da police escorts me into da cell. Y'all know how they love to fuck wit' da black man cuz he's da true an' living god." Rightchus hobbled down the street, tugging at the brim of his cap. He vanished as quickly as he had appeared, leaving the group with beer on their lips and smiles on their faces.

"I'm out, yo." Coco tossed her empty at the trashcan.

"We'll give you a lift. Let's do something, hang out for a minute," said Danielle.

"I'm down," said Josephine.

"Ah'ight, yo. Sounds ah'ight to me, too," said Coco. She was feeling the beer. Coco and Josephine got in the backseat, Cory and Danielle sat up front. As Cory started the car, he looked back. Coco gazed out the window, and Josephine smiled at him, approvingly.

"Where to?" asked Cory.

"Downtown," said Josephine. Soon they were on the way downtown. They passed Deja on Tenth avenue, doing his hustle; drugs, whatever.

"Down for some smokes?" asked Danielle.

"Sure. Here's two dollar," said Josephine, "and a dollar from y'all."

"Hold this, yo." Coco gave a dollar to Danielle.

"Get it from Deja, yo. His shit is always best," Coco whispered.

****

"Wha' nigga, I'ma take the bank. Yeah, that's right, muthafucka. Jus' watch," said a player, kissing the dice before he threw.

"Head crack," burst a chorus as the dice landed, showing a loss. They all laughed, picking up dollar bills.

"Next game, try again," said the winner of a lot of singles. It was Deja, wearing a red Pelle Pelle jacket zipped to his neck, and baggy blue Guess jeans. He went bopping over to the car. The dragging of his unlaced Timberlands made the bop seem difficult.

" 'Zup?"

"Nickel," said Cory, offering Deja a handshake with five one-dollar bills folded in his palm. Deja slipped him the small bag of weed with the handshake. The exchange went smoothly, no fumbles.

"Yo, Coco. Whazzup?" asked Deja, peering into the car.

"Chillin'," replied Coco with her index and middle fingers extended in the street sign.

"Peace," said Deja. He walked away from the car,

back to the game.

"Those da honeys that be dancing and shit. Word, they kinda got it going on," said a dice-player.

"Roll da dice, you pimpin' mo'fucka. Git ready to lose your money," Deja taunted.

"Uh," grunted the roller as he let the dice fly. "Mama need a bigger TV." The dice landed and the car occupants watched a scuffle over the exchange of dollar bills.

"Yo, there goes that preaching ass nigga," said Coco.

"Yep," said Danielle as she pulled on the joint. "I heard his raps. We are nice people, an' all that, but I bet if he were smoking an' getting' high, he'd be the first to jump off wit' shit about what women shouldn't be doing," said Danielle.

"Uh-huh," agreed Coco, pulling hard on the joint. "He be kicking shit 'bout da true and living righteous black woman and black man, yo." Coco knew the origin of Rightchus' street name. They watched as he approached Deja urgently. He pulled at one arm of the red jacket.

"Yo, whazzup Rightchus?" asked Deja. "Can't you see I'm busting these niggas' asses?" He saw the serious eyes of Rightchus. "You buggin' off sump'n, nigga?"

"Yo, man, my brother, word from the snake's mouth is you've been fingered to die. Your life has been jeopardized, black man." Rightchus was emphatic.

"What da fuck?" asked Deja. "Fuckin' talk straight to me before I have my niggas do *you*. What's this word-from-the-snake shit?"

"Deja, you're my brother. There are snakes, devils, plotting to kill you."

Deja was doubtful. He knew Rightchus had a history at Bellevue, smoked a lot of weed and crack.

"Yo, everyone strapped?" Deja spoke to the three lanky teens he had been shooting dice with.

"What you think, nigga? We turned our toasts in for food and toys?" asked a dice player, laughing and clutching his waist. "Muthafucka, hell, yeah, we strapped." The laughter ceased, stalling the game.

"Whazzup?" they demanded.

"Ah, just checking y'all muthafuckas, makin' sure shit is tight," said Deja. He smirked, and gave Rightchus a small plastic vial with an orange top. Rightchus walked away at a furious pace.

"Don't worry 'bout who's strapped, nigga. Just watch this strappin' your ass will receive, right here. Ugh," he grunted as the dice bounced off the wall.

"Crack head," shouted the girls in the car.

"Whose dice is it?" shouted Deja.

"Put your money down an' find out about this C-low, nigga," said a player.

****

"Let's go check Open-Mike. See how our competition is doing," said Danielle.

"Yeah, cool," said Josephine.

"I'm wit' it, yo," said Coco. The beer and weed had relaxed her. She gave Danielle a high-five. Josephine welcomed the return of camaraderie.

"Let's do this, Cory," she slapped his outstretched palm. Cory drove off, a smile on his face. When they arrived at the club, the girls and Cory were escorted to the head of clubhoppers' queue. They were announced over the club speakers, and the crowd cheered. *This is annoying,* thought Coco, before she entered the trance of the groove. All thoughts aside, the music insisted. She gave in and glided in step to the beat. The girls came alive as the rhythm took their souls. They danced around, laughing. All the air had been let out, and now they were running on beer and weed. They exploded, pretending to be one another, mimicking each other's favorite moves.

They applauded as each act took the stage, and jeered or encouraged attempts to sink or swim. Josephine kept a tally on the good acts, the ones the crowd liked. At their table, it was non-stop chatter.

"They nice," said Josephine.

"Nah, nah. I like da other ones who wore those funky outfits. That shit was dope," yelled Danielle.

"I like them and the other ones, too. That lead kid was wicked, yo," said Coco.

Cory brought sodas to the table. As the evening advanced, jokes spilled from the girls' lips, replacing anxious frowns with smiles. They were happy.

"Of course, the people who are favorites so far are here tonight. They are Coco and Da Crew. Let's hear from them," said the master of ceremonies. A beam of bright light struck the table. The girls stood, acknowledging the applause.

"Would you like to give us a taste of y'all good stuff?"

The emcee could not be denied. The girls walked down a short corridor and onto the stage. Coco, last to get there, hugged the other girls.

"Yo, before we do this," she said to the audience, "I just want y'all to know that we're sistas. It's me, Coco, Josephine to my right, Danielle to my left, and we started this and we're gonna finish it. It's no more Coco and Da Crew. We're just Da Crew, yo."

"All three of us are Crew," yelled Danielle.

"That's right. C-R-E-W. *Crew*," yelled Josephine.

"C-R-E-W. *Crew*." Coco clapped her hands. The girls picked up the rhythm and the club hoppers clapped, stomped and chanted. They needed something to lift them and they were caught in Da Crew's hysteria.

"Yeah, yeah, Mr. Deejay. Drop the beat, yo," yelled Coco. The stage exploded with the fire of Da Crew. They began setting lightening-quick moves to the hard beat. Their first love, dancing, came as natural as the electricity in the wave of moves crashing against the audience, who continued to chant "C-R-E-W. *Crew*," long after the girls had shared high-fives, bowed and left the stage.

"What can I say?" asked the emcee when the audience subsided. "We asked for it, right? Another round of applause." It came with ease. The girls were ushered back to their table. They raised their glasses of soda to acknowledge the audience's generosity.

"Wow! What a night. I'm worn out. Let me sit," said Danielle.

"It felt great up there tonight," said Josephine.

"Now nobody else wants to follow y'all," said Cory. "Here comes the emcee."

"Yeah, he's coming over here," said Danielle.

"Y'all were so bad. The people in the open-mike section don't even want to perform behind y'all," said the emcee. He motioned to a waiter.

"Whatsup, Busta?" Coco asked the portly, neatly denim Nehru-clad man.

"You is up. Y'all are what's up. Keep it up." The waiter came. "Give them as many rounds of sodas as they can handle. Don't give their bodyguard too much though, we don't want him to OD." He slapped the waiter's back too hard and walked away. The waiter stared at Busta as if he wanted to return the favor.

"Okay," said the waiter.

"That Busta is tough on you, yo?" blurted Coco.

"Nah, it's his jokes. He has to slap you with the punch lines. Anyway, what kind of sodas y'all having?" He had fully recovered from the joke now.

The group partied and the feeling of camaraderie intensified a while longer. They lent their celebration to a couple more acts. Then with more hugs and kisses, the girls got up and followed Cory Williams.

"Yo, Coco. That shit was real cool, with the intro and all," said Cory. Danielle beamed. "What you said on stage, about the name change and all that held the crowd. They were behind y'all. Y'all almost wrecked that whole set."

"Word, they were open from that point on, yo," said Coco. She stepped into the car and took her place in the backseat, next to Josephine who gave her a smile.

"What are you smiling 'bout, yo?" asked Coco, smiling herself.

"That was really cool, yo," answered Josephine. She assumed a smirk when the 'yo' left her mouth.

"That's Coco, I swear, yo," said Danielle.

"Well, that shit's better than y'all wit' da 'oh, hi, I'm cool, y'know.' 'Cause that shit be making y'all look foul. Little Ms. fucking Muffet," Coco laughed loud.

"Oh no, you not calling niggas Miss fucking Muffet. That's what your whole shit is about," said Danielle. She and Josephine clapped a high five and they stared at Coco.

"Well, bein' that I am a little fuckin' Muffet, at least I ain't out there chasing after niggas like chicken heads. An' y'all know who I'm talkin' 'bout." Coco eyed Josephine.

"Unh-uh, you ain't gotta go there. You know that's right," said Josephine, play-punching Coco's left arm.

"See, now you're gonna make me dust your shit off," Coco cautioned Josephine.

"I got your back. Go ahead," Danielle taunted Josephine. The girls laughed. Danielle sipped the soda she had sneaked out of the club.

"Alright, everyone out," yelled Cory. All three girls looked at him in surprise.

"Just kidding," said Cory. He sounded unsure. The girls burst into laughter. Cory headed the car uptown.

The girls continued laughing and high-fiving one another. No team could come back to defeat them after the tremendous step they had taken tonight. They enjoyed the small victory, hugging and touching checks at each stop and departure. Cory dropped off Josephine first, then Coco. Cory and Danielle were now alone, riding further uptown.

"Where do you think you're going, Mister?" asked Danielle, sly now.

"I'm...Baby, you wanna go home?'

"That's not what I asked. I want to know where you're headed."

"Well, it's still early. It's only eleven fifteen."

"Damn! I was havin' so much fun an' all, I forgot to tell them I saw that bitch Deedee."

"Let's go chill for awhile, close to da park," said Cory.

"Uh, excuse me," said Danielle with mock scorn.

"I'm sayin', d'ya want to go to my place or to da

park?"

"It's a cool night. Let's chill by the park. Your dad is too fuckin' nosy."

"C'mon. You know he's a cop, right?"

"Well, does he have to stay on duty when he's home? We ain't fuckin' criminals."

"That nigga stays on duty twenty-four-seven. That's why my moms left his ass. We'll chill at the park."

"See, your pops don't give me a chance to do this," she said, rubbing the ripple of his stomach with her right palm. The bulge in his blue jeans grew larger. She kissed hard on his chest, then blew in his ear.

"Let's do it while you're driving real fast," Danielle whispered. She blew a wet kiss in his ear. Cory shivered. His palms became sweaty and he gripped the steering wheel tight.

"You're buggin'," he breathed.

"Think so?" She kissed his stomach. The car raced. His heartbeat kept pace with the engine. She toyed with his zipper, sliding the nail of her index finger up and down the ridges of his zipper, then his stomach. His muscles tightened at her touch. Cory breathed deeply, trying to control himself behind the fast moving car. Danielle slowly unzipped his fly and greeted his hard member, protruding proudly from its perch. She leaned over and gripped his left leg with her right hand. The penis disappeared between her lips as the car moved faster. Her tongue lapped at his exposed genitals.

"Yeah, ahhh, yeah, yeah," murmured Cory as excitement took his mind for a ride.

Danielle sucked hard. Cory gripped the wheel of the fast moving car, holding on for dear life. Danielle's lips slid up and down his rock-hard member. Then she parted her legs and straddled his hardness. She leaned her hand on the top of the dashboard and rocked her exposed ass back and forth in Cory's lap. Cory squirmed in his seat. She moved gently, riding him skillfully and watching the highway disappear beneath the car. Cory stabbed, jerking his muscular torso, and Danielle grunted. The car hopped over potholes Cory was unable to locate. The potholes forced her up and down, and then she was swinging back and forth, up and down, back and forth, until he felt the explosion. It was the front end of the car.

"Damn!" he yelled.

"Oh, keep moving, baby, keep moving," shouted Danielle.

"Baby," he said stroking up, "I think we're stuck."

"Wha', what are you talkin' about?" asked Danielle.

"We must have hit a big hole, 'cause we can't move," he said. Danielle continued to ride his shaft. Cory caressed and squeezed her breasts, shoving harder into the moistness of her flesh.

"Baby, we gotta stop and get out of the car before we get hit," he said, still shoving his erection deep inside her. He switched the hazard lights on.

"Oh...oh...oh," she screamed and moved faster and faster. She yelled again, "Oh, ohhhhhhh." Then there was complete quiet. Cory gunned the engine and pulled on the steering wheel, trying to direct the car out of the pothole, but to no avail. They were stuck, indeed. The ticking of the hazard lights was like a time bomb. Danielle sat back in the passenger seat. She noticed cars going by, the drivers honking their horns.

"Damn," she said, "that shit was good."

"I'm glad you enjoyed yourself," said Cory. "You got yours." He sounded a little annoyed. He zipped up his jeans and stepped out of the car.

****

"Yo, your ass is stuck, kid?"

Danielle heard the voice and knew that it belonged to Lil' Long. Vulcha was driving. They pulled up alongside Cory.

"Damn," said Lil' Long. "How did you miss this big hole, kid?"

"My girl was driving. She didn't see it coming. Sorta snuck up on us." Cory covered his tracks. Lil' Long peered into the car. Immediately he recognized her.

"Yeah, yeah. That bitch is da funky dancer from da club. Yeah, you're gonna miss some potholes. Shit, the way I'd be all over that bitch, I would falling in holes too, kid. Up under that dress an' all that, you know wha' I mean?"

Danielle watched as Lil' Long spoke, not able to clearly hear the words. She saw how the light of the street reflected from his gold-capped teeth whenever his lips parted. *Tacky nigga*, she thought, as she stepped out of the car. A speeding car barely missed her.

"Oh my freaking God! Shit!" screamed Danielle.

"Get back in," yelled Cory. "Danielle, start it and try to move it slowly when me and my man lift."

"Lil' Long," he introduced himself. Cory, busy with the task at hand, ignored him.

"On three," yelled Cory. "One, two, three. Oomph," he grunted. The wheel remained captive in the deep pothole.

"Gimme another count," said Lil' Long.

"Let's change positions," said Cory.

"Cool," said Lil' Long.

Cory moved directly above the stuck wheel. He heaved without saying anything. The wheel made it over the edge, and Cory eased the front of the car down.

"You is a cock-diesel muthfucka, kid," said Lil' Long, noticeably impressed. "Do you lift? I used to, back in da days in da penal, but I ain't done that shit in a while."

"Thanks, man." said Cory with a handshake.

"I'm Lil' Long, kid," he said, pounding his fist against Cory's outstretched palm. "Yo, a cock-strong nigga like you, I know you be fuckin' da dog shit outta that bitch, kid."

Cory flinched. "Ah'ight, man. I'm out, and that bitch is my girl Danielle," said Cory, getting in the car.

"Stroke her twice for da brother, kid. See ya." Lil' Long swung into the Jeep and Vulcha, still behind the wheel, screeched away.

"Yo, that bitch is bad, Vulcha."

"Oh yeah?"

"Real bad, son."

"Why didn't you bag it, then?" Vulcha watched Lil' Long clutch his crotch.

"Bidness before pleasure." Lil' Long smiled and removed the Glock-17 from inside his shorts. "That muthafucka was showin' out. I should've bagged dat bitch. What time is it, kid?" asked Lil' Long.

"Eleven-fifty."

"Yeah, that fucka should be home fuckin', or sump'n."

"Let's make a check," said Vulcha.

"Yeah, yeah, let's go check that nigga." Lil' Long nodded.

CHAPTER 7

Deja stepped out of the red Maxima and checked his waist. The gun was there. He unlocked the door and walked to his second-floor apartment.

The phone rang. He picked it up on the second ring.

"Who dis?" he yelled.

"It's Bebop. What's up?"

"Just walked through the door, girl."

"What are you gettin' into tonight?"

"You, girl. Bring that ass on over here."

"Nigga, you wuz just wit' your baby's mother. Her ass is enough. You don't need no more ass."

"I had to drop some loot off for my seed. Shorty is growin'. But I need some o' that sweet, ragamuffin-style punani. You saw me when I was up in da building?"

"No, Coco said you helped her wit' her laundry cart. You probably tried to push-up on her, too."

"Bring that ass on over here, girl."

"Alright. I really don't feel like it, but I'll be there in about thirty minutes to keep you company. And I'm not staying the whole night, either."

"That's all good, sweetheart. I'll see you in a half hour." He hung up. *Cool. I'll chill, watch a flick and get my swerve on wit' Bebop*, he thought.

Deja showered and changed into a red silk robe and matching boxers. He sipped on a glass of Hennessey while flicking through the channels on his big-screen television. He rolled a blunt and lit it. Easing into the pleasure, his mind reflected on his two-year-old son. *Yeah, he's growing. I've got to make sure he gets his*, he thought.

Deja puffed on the cigar, thinking about things like school for his child. Deja never completed school, but he vowed his son would. He puffed on the blunt, licked his lips and reached for the Hennessey. He had the money to do something for his kid. He had survived foster care and group homes. He had hated everyone, but enjoyed learning. The formal education abruptly came to an end the day his friend, Mark, was shot to death in front of the school. Deja, who had run back into the school for what he thought would be a quick second, returned to find Mark's dead body. His life came to an untimely end. The bullet-hole was so deep that he saw all of Mark's insides. Deja ran away from the group home and never returned to school.

The street offered a different education, and Deja was a fast learner. He learned to deal drugs. He was good at it and it rewarded him. When he displayed the fruits of his labor, girls flocked around him, lusting for cash.

Deja had chosen Kimberly. She was good looking, wifey material and had a nice ass. *She's Number One. She is the mother of my seed*, he thought.

There were always girls. Bad guys attracted them like flies. Bebop was one of his. She had been living in the same building as Kimberly for six years and had been sharing Deja's bed for three. She knew about the situation with Kimberly, but had never made a fuss. *And Bebop has that ghetto butt, too.*

The doorbell rang. *And boy, doesn't she have some sweet trimmings to go with that ass?* The reflection turned to lust. He got up to buzz his expected company into the building. He checked his gun on the table and dimmed the light. Then came the knock. He moved quietly and checked the peephole. It was Bebop. He unlocked three bolts and opened the door wide to greet her. She flung herself at him. But then he saw the other faces. *Oh shit! It's a hit.* He jumped back, but it was too late. Lil' Long and Vulcha were on him. He stumbled backwards, falling onto the carpet. He realized that he had been shot. The bullet had come through Bebop's back. Deja felt the burning and saw his blood. He had not heard the gun go off. He grabbed at his chest. The blood spurted out of him at a rapid rate.

"Why da fuck are you doing this to me?" Deja gasped. He glanced at Bebop. Her body, with that nice ass, lay still.

He wished he had his gun. The phone began to ring. Even if they didn't mean to kill him, he may still bleed to death. Lil' Long walked past him and picked up the receiver. Vulcha closed the door with a backward kick of his right leg. *Maybe they just wanted money*, thought Deja. He looked at Vulcha's nine millimeter. The place was quiet. He could hear the caller.

"Deja, Deja, Deja, I know you're there, fucking that Jamaican slut. Deja, fuck you. I'm coming over to kick your ass." It was Kimberly. He wanted to scream out to her *Call da cops. Call my niggas.* He couldn't move his lips. He lay helpless, blood gushing from his chest. Lil' Long put the phone down.

"I know you're there with that fuckin' ho. Don't bring any disease she gives your ass to me."

There was a click. Deja saw Lil' Long pick up the gun on the table, next to the blunt he'd been smoking. *My seed.* As much as he tried to squeeze the words out, they remained stuck in his throat. It was too late.

Lil' Long walked over to Deja. He put Deja's gun to his head.

"In my quest to become immortal, a whole lot of weak muthfuckas must die." He fired twice. The bullets smashed Deja's frontal lobe and destroyed his thoughts. Blood rushed from Deja's ears, mouth and eyes. His body collapsed on the soft blue carpet, now stained with bright red blood.

"Da bitch is alive?" asked Lil' Long.

"Not anymore," said Vulcha. He sent two more slugs through Bebop's back. Lil' Long wiped the guns clean. He walked over to the phone and wiped it, also.

"Take that nigga's Rolly. He won't need da shit," he ordered.

Vulcha searched Deja's pockets.

"Muthfucka had a lil' loot." Vulcha was pleased at the discovery.

Lil' Long, using a towel, placed his gun in Deja's fingers. He folded Bebop's fingers around Deja's gun. Then he stepped back and admired his handiwork.

"This shit will confuse da fuck out of da police. This nigga is dead. Let's bounce." They left by the fire escape.

"I neva liked him. Fuckin' crack dealer," said Lil' Long. He jumped in the black Jeep and settled down comfortably as Vulcha drove away. They both puffed on a blunt; Deja's last smoke.

"Yo, man. Let's go to the topless bar," said Lil' Long. "Let's go fuck around wit' da bitches."

"Yeah, yeah. Git a bottle of Dom P. and fuck wit' dem bitches wit' da big titties," said Vulcha. The idea excited Vulcha. He screeched the Jeep's tires as he swerved in a new direction.

****

In the strippers' bar, where topless waitresses served drinks and Buffalo wings, the two got VIP treatment. They were known as heavy spenders and the prospect of big tips licensed them to rub, touch and finger the waitresses. Lil' Long took full advantage of the privilege. Usually, Vulcha just stared at every pair of huge breasts that passed by. Occasionally he would explore them like a blind man reading Braille, using nipples as reference points.

They ordered two bottles of Dom Perignon in rapid succession. Lil' Long visited the men's room, pausing to kiss a few exposed belly buttons on the way. Men sat at small tables, watching the dancers take turns peeling off clothes, each in their own style. The beat was constant hip-hop. Lil' Long danced back to the table, where Vulcha now drank champagne from the bottle.

"Aw shit," said Lil' Long. He plopped down on the soft seat.

"Whaddya doing?" asked Vulcha. He put the bottle down. "Nigga, did'ja piss on yourself?"

"Nah, nah, da muthfucka left blood on my Bill Blass. Had to wipe it off. Ya know, it's bad manners to be drinking from da bottle, kid."

Vulcha resumed chugging. "That's why I ordered one for your ugly ass," he said.

The waitress, Kamilla, arrived with more champagne. She was pretty, with an ass to Lil' Long's taste and breasts just right for Vulcha. Lil' Long tipped her generously. She snuggled up to Vulcha and he buried his face in her huge chest.

"Down," said Lil' Long, laughing and clapping his hands. He stroked her buttocks as she walked away. "That bitch is ours, kid," he added.

He sucked at the champagne bottle and the bubbly ran all over his black suede jacket. They drank steadily and watched the girls stripping into the wee hours. Finally, Vulcha ordered a spliff to go. Kamilla brought it nicely rolled. Her breasts gleamed with heavy oil.

"I wanna fuck that bitch, kid," said Lil' Long, clenching his fist to signal his enthusiasm.

"Yeah. Me first, nigga."

"Yo, I never seen her here before. She must be new."

"Fuck that. New or not, that bitch is bagged, kid." They laughed and pounded their right fists together.

"Yo, we made ten G's tonight, nig," said Vulcha. The realization seemed like a pleasant surprise to him.

"Yeah, lil' loot. Yo, man, I want a hun'ed grand for the next one, kid," said Lil' Long.

"I hear you, muthafucka, cuz them mo'fuckin' cock-suckin' bosses be makin' five, six, seven times da amount we be makin'," said Vulcha. He grasped the bottle at the bottom, thrusting it at Lil' Long, who did the same with his. The bottles clanked in a toast and they guzzled. Vulcha put down his bottle and lit the spliff.

"I'm tellin' you, kid, I'ma be famous like muthafuckin' Tyson. Mug gonna be on T-shirts. Like, whaaaat! I'ma be like muthafuckin' O.J. Peoples gonna be like 'how da fuck he do it,' an' all." Lil' Long guffawed. Vulcha joined him.

"Yeah, yeah, they gonna be like, 'I know he couldn't have done all that shit by himself,'" said Vulcha. He laughed so hard his weapon fell. The sexy waitress stooped, displaying all her assets, and picked up the weapon. She handed it to Vulcha, who continued laughing as he rubbed his face in her breasts.

In this club, the only ones who stripped were the women. The patrons, a hundred percent male, entered with all their clothes on and kept them on. Even their hats and coats stayed on, because there was no place to hang them. And displaying a gun was as normal as having your hat and coat. So no one but the waitress even seemed to notice Vulcha's weapon when he dropped it.

Vulcha staggered off to the men's room. On his way back, he picked up a couple of hits of cocaine. He shoved the small porcelain receptacle in front of Lil' Long, spilling some in the process. Lil' Long lifted the stem and made two sucking sounds with each nostril. He handed the dish to Vulcha.

"Yeah, yeah, that's what a nigga needed. Now all we got to do is..."

"Is what, muthafucka? Ah, oh yeah, for Lil' Long. I'm there wit' you," said Vulcha, following Lil' Long's gaze toward the strippers. Vulcha sniffed cocaine until the white powder was all gone and he set the dish down. He clasped both hands to his nose and sucked in his breath until his face looked purple.

"Ah, ah, that shit was ah'ight. Yo, let's bag honey an' take her back to da crib."

"That's wha' I'm talkin' 'bout." Lil' Long motioned to Kamilla.

"Yo, this my man, Vulcha, and my name is Lil' Long, and since you're da one we chose, yo, you've got to come back to da crib wit' us."

"Huh?" she said, straining to hear.

Vulcha stuck a hundred-dollar bill between her mountainous breasts. The bill stayed wedged until she removed it.

"I'll go get my coat," she said. He stared at how her ass cheeks rubbed each other with each step.

Lil' Long and Vulcha laughed and slapped five. They rose from their seats and headed for the bar, where they ordered more hits of cocaine. They shook hands all around. They fondled the buttocks of nude dancers on their way out.

Kamilla, now dressed, waited at the door. They headed for Vulcha's place in the Jeep. But as they drove by the park, Lil' Long impatiently asked Vulcha to make a pit stop.

"Yo man pull over anywhere."

"Whazzup nigga?" asked Vulcha. He stopped next to a tree.

"Yo, Vulcha, I gotta piss. Here is fine." Lil' Long jumped from the Jeep. He stood next to the tree and broke the silence with a shower on the grass. He returned to see Vulcha attempting to suck both nipples at once. The girl was on her back, showing her taut stomach, curving to wide hips, decorated by red bikinis. Lil' Long moved close and tugged at the bikinis.

"I'll get them." She eased the panties off.

"Let's take this shit outside," said Lil' Long. He saw no reason to restrain himself.

With that, she stepped out of the Jeep. Vulcha sat on the hood. While she ran her tongue up and down his huge dick, Lil' Long unwrapped a condom, rolled it on, and mounted her like a horse. She grunted, but kept on alternately sucking Vulcha's dick and rubbing it between her breasts. Lil' Long stabbed, grinding his body into her flesh, all the while groping her fleshy buttocks.

"Uh, uh," he grunted.

"Come on, Daddy," Kamilla massaged Vulcha's shaft.

Lil' Long and Vulcha traded places. Lil' Long now received the slurping and rubbing. Vulcha grunted and Kamilla squealed as he pushed his member all the way in. They fucked her long and hard; both of them alternating until she thought there were two dicks attached to a single body, splitting her in half.

"Yo, this bitch is doin' shit, kid," said Lil' Long, thrusting.

"I wuz tryin' to tell ya, nig," yelled Vulcha, his penis snug between sweaty breasts.

"Ah, yessss, bitch do ya thang," screamed Lil' Long. He slapped her ass, thrusting faster and faster. He slowed down, then began hissing.

"Yssst yssst ... Ahh, yes-s-s." He withdrew and leaned against the Jeep, panting.

Vulcha, who used an extra-large condom to sheath his member, thrust into the girl immediately. They rocked back and forth, each body movement in support of the other, Vulcha holding on to her mountainous breasts to balance himself.

Lil' Long rested against the Jeep, smoking and enjoying the show. As he puffed on his cigarette, he noticed through the smoke cloud other eyes watching the scene. The eyes belonged to the people who were stuck on the highway earlier.

Lil' Long smiled then he yelled out, "Hey, yo big man. You wanna come get some o' this shit?" He chuckled. "Bring ya bitch too, kid."

This was the park where Danielle and Cory came to escape his father. Now they were discovered, caught in the act. Cory started the car and hit the accelerator. They raced into the street. Then Cory switched on the lights and considered a new side of Danielle. She had definitely been turned on watching the orgy. Her hand had drifted over and grasped his swelling member. She seemed to be in a trance-like state; her gaze fixed on the dance in the park. She jerked hungrily to the rhythm of the movements. *Damn she had some big breasts.* Cory's thoughts were rattled.

"What're you so busy thinking 'bout?" asked Danielle, nudging Cory with her elbow. He reached over and drew her closer.

"Just busy thinking 'bout doin' ya, baby."

"Yeah, sure." She hugged him.

"They were really fucking da shit outta her," said Danielle. The words broke Cory's concentration, causing the car to swerve out of control.

"Hey, hey, chill," Cory said, regaining control of himself and the vehicle. But he imagined again the woman's breasts and buttocks and he felt lust.

****

At the park, Vulcha rested on his hands on the grass. His body seemed suspended by the huge appendage to the dark inner crevice between her thighs. She rocked back and forth, kneading her own breasts. Vulcha sprung from the grass. His force thrust her forward. She toppled in front of him, but recovered immediately, spinning around like a cat. Kamilla arched her back. She was on all fours. Vulcha rammed her from behind.

"Ugh, ugh, ugh," she grunted.

"Yesss bitch, gimme that shit," he exalted, riding his charge. She wiggled and screamed. Vulcha held on as long as he could, then he exploded into the condom.

"Agh, agh, Aaahhhh."

Lil' Long applauded. "I thought you were gonna kill da bitch, kid. Yo, you better ease up off that coke shit, ha!" He continued to laugh at Vulcha, sprawled, out of breath, on the grass. Kamilla got to her feet. She put her long coat on over her bikinis, buttoned it, then walked over to Lil' Long and grabbed his crotch.

"No, no. Just suck me off." He thrust a hundred-dollar bill in her coat pocket. Quickly, she was on her knees and his hard dick disappeared in her mouth. He lay back against the Jeep and watched her head bob. Vulcha was still on the ground. Lil' Long's eyes rolled upward as his head tilted back, seduced by the pleasures her mouth gave him.

He saw the dark clouds of night mesh with the bright-tinted clouds of dawn. The sun's rays welcomed the early morning. Lil' Long's dick slid easily in and out of Kamilla's rounded lips. *I gotta get mines, kid*, he thought as he drifted into the depths of pleasure.

****

Loud bangs awoke them. Vulcha ran toward the Jeep, gun at the ready. Instinctively, he paused to check the source of the noise. Sanitation workers were throwing the park's empty trash containers back in position. Patches of smoky clouds overtook the sunlight. These heavy clouds brought an overcast morning, which shielded the two in its shadow. Vulcha stuck the weapon in his belt.

"Da bitch left?" asked Vulcha.

"She hit me off lovely, kid, an' stepped. Son, let's go eat and then drop me at my rest," said Lil' Long.

"Yeah, yeah, some food sounds lovely. Let's do that."

"Now you awake, huh?"

"Yo, I wuz lying there like, 'what da fuck,'" said Vulcha, getting in the Jeep and cranking the engine. The vehicle hurtled forward at breakneck speed, flinging both driver and passenger forward. Lil' Long braced his arms against the dashboard.

"That bitch really fucked da dogshit outta you, son. Let me buckle up for safety." Lil' Long checked to see if Vulcha was all right. Vulcha gripped the steering wheel tightly.

"It's da fuckin' gas pedal. I'm tellin' you."

"Yeah, muthafucka. It's always this or that. It's never your muthafuckin' non-driving ass."

"Nah, Nah."

"Nah, nah what, muthafucka? Just admit it."

"Admit what?"

"That your ass is a no-driving son of a bitch, that's all." Lil' Long thought of softening this with a smile, but decided not. Instead, he sniffed the cocaine he had lifted from Kamilla. He handed the foil to Vulcha.

"Hit some more of this shit. It might wake your sleepy ass up. Help you navigate, get you right. Know wha' I mean?"

"Yeah, yeah," said Vulcha. He vacuumed the foil with two quick sniffs.

"Damn, kid, I would've bought your ass some mo'

shit from da club if I knew you were fiending," said Lil' Long as Vulcha licked the inside of the foil.

"Yo, that bitch wuz bad for a muthafuck," Vulcha reflected. He pulled up in front of an all night cafe and they got out. Lil' Long reached up with both arms, as if trying to touch the darkening sky. There were no more rays peeking to make things bright. The two struggled to the entrance of the cafe, dragging along like the dark sky of the night seeking to cover the earth. The fading moon had lost the battle.

CHAPTER 8

They walked into the dimly lit place and sat at the table with a shaded lamp above it.

"I gots to see what I'm eating, kid." Lil' Long plopped against the wall. "Ya ah'ight man? You look kinda drunk," said Vulcha.

"Chill, I ain't drunk, kid. Fucking seat is too low."

"Now you wanna blame it on da chair?" asked Vulcha.

"Whatcha tryin to say, nigga?" Lil' Long did not enjoy the way the joke was working. The tension broke when the waitress came for their orders.

"Pancakes, cheese omelet with toast twice. Sausage for me. Bacon for my kid," said Lil' Long.

"Anything else?"

"Yeah, juice," said Vulcha, greedily.

"Yeah, yeah but I want a hot chocolate wit' whipped cream," added Lil' Long, hungrily eyeing a passing tray heaped with food.

"Is that it?" asked the waitress, already on her way.

"Oh yeah. That's all," said Vulcha. "For now," he called to her back.

"Oh shit!" exclaimed Lil' Long.

"Whazzup, nig?" asked Vulcha.

"Yeow," Lil' Long chuckled. "I'm either seeing things, or that's da bitch from back at da park standing over there." He pointed to a waitress six tables away.

"Nah, that couldn't possibly be her, man. We fucked da dog-shit outta da bitch. That bitch is at her rest, sleeping. Recovering from that train ordeal, nigga." Vulcha was trying to convince himself, as well.

"I'm telling you, it's that same bitch. Look at her ass, kid. That's da bitch!"

"Nah, nah. Lemme see her tits when she turns

around. I'm telling..." Vulcha's voice trailed off as the waitress faced them, then turned away.

"I should've bet your ass," said Lil' Long. "Yo, I never forget a good ass."

"I'm saying, dog. I fucked da hell outta that bitch. I'm sitting here, tired like a mutha and da bitch is walking around, taking orders. I'm telling you, Star, I need a women like that, word is bond," said Vulcha. Lil' Long stared at him, half amazed. He didn't know what to think.

"You whipped, kid?" asked Lil' Long. "Must have been. I ain't never heard your ass say shit like that. It's always, 'fuck a bitch. Dog a bitch, cuz a bitch ain't shit'... aahhh."

The hot chocolate arrived.

"Hey, yo, waitress. You know da name of da big ass...I mean nice looking black lady over by that table?" Lil' Long pointed.

"Oh, that's Kamilla." The waitress briskly walked away.

"Ah'ight, bust a rap on her, kid."

"I don't wanna rap to her. I wanna bitch like her," said Vulcha.

"Son, how are you gonna git da bitch if you don't rap? Hit her over da head with a club? Capture her and drag her back to your rest?" Lil' Long laughed at Vulcha's dilemma.

The food arrived and they attacked it. Kamilla passed by during their feast. Lil' Long passed her a napkin on which he'd written Vulcha's beeper number. She unfolded the napkin and read it. Kamilla turned and looked at Vulcha, then addressed Lil' Long.

"My man would be very upset if he knew I had your number. You know where to find me," she said, and turned to walk away. Lil' Long reached for her. She easily evaded him.

"No touchy-feely in this establishment," she said. "Are you enjoying your meals?" Kamilla refolded the napkin, slipped it into a pocket and undulated away.

"Damn," said Lil' Long. "Sure wouldn't mind some sloppy seconds of that, kid."

"Yeah right, nigga. You were about to grab da bitch when your rap was failing, huh?"

"Pay da tab so we could be out," said Lil' Long.

"Yeah, before you get charged for assault."

They paid the cashier and trudged to the Jeep. Vulcha lit a cigarette and started the engine. Lil' Long sat back, relaxed and slightly exhausted.

"Yo, we caught two bodies, kid. One was for free," said Lil' Long.

"Smoked that bitch, hmmm? She was in da wrong place at da right time," said Vulcha.

"Word," said Lil' Long. "If she hadn't come along...Know wha' I'm saying? We would've had to do shit different. Maybe it woulda been a lil' difficult."

"Fuck that. That nigga was so soft for a mo'," said Vulcha.

"No question. We woulda caught up to him, anyway. They just got a body for free, that's all." Lil' Long's outstretched hand collided with Vulcha's in a hard shake. The vehicle lurched forward. "Aw, shit. Learn to drive, muthafucka."

The Jeep settled. Lil' Long reached into the backseat for his blue-tinted, gold framed Polo shades.

"They wanted that muthafucka dead, kid. Offered ten G's straight up. It's all good, man."

"Well, they asses came to da right spot. 1-(800) YOU DEAD. Bang!" shouted Vulcha. He shot an imaginary pistol at the windshield. "You're history, drug dealer."

Lil' Long's head lay back on his seat, his mouth open, snoring loudly.

****

When they arrived at Lil' Long's destination, he got out and staggered to the front of the car. Vulcha hit the horn and the gas simultaneously. The car lurched forward, barely missing Lil' Long before the brakes took hold.

That nigga is a fucked up driver, Lil' Long repeated on the way to the elevator. He dragged himself to 8G. There he found his mother, Lerlene Lowe, getting dress.

"Ma, where you going?"

"I have a face-to-face at the welfare office," said the beautiful woman. It was hard to believe this genteel, youthful woman was the mother of a thug. Friends teased him by saying he was adopted. As a young boy, he stuttered. When the kids taunted him with, "Is tha'choo, mammy?"

"N-n-no," Lil' Long would stutter. "I'm her Lil' man." He felt badly about this. Even though he knew it was only a game, it would hurt. Lil' Long often wound up fighting because of his stutter. He could control the stutter now, except when he lost his temper.

The door slammed, shaking Lil' Long out of his recollections.

"Did ya feed da snake, Mom?" he yelled, but the only answer was the click of Ms. Lowe's heels.

Fuck it. I'll feed that bitch later. Hope that muthafucka don't crawl out and hunt my ass for food.

Lil' Long showered quickly and emerged wearing a blue robe. He lay back on the soft, plush, baby-blue sofa, remote control in hand. Channel surfing, he caught a music video. Still buzzing, the video seized what remained of his senses. *Ooh, that bitch is bad. Work it, work it.*

The television blared the latest video by the Chop Shop Crew. "*Say, Silky Black is gonna blow da spot up. I say Silky Black is gonna blow da spot up...*" The TV blared on. Lil' Long drifted in and out of sleep.

Was it that easy to make ten grand? Where was that stuttering kid? His own mother had called him Lil' Love. He evolved into Lil' Long once he hit the streets. The transformation was tough in the beginning, but in time Lil' Long earned big money by doing some of the dirt and taking out the garbage. He was a lookout at first. Then he dealt drugs and guns. Soon he was selling protection for drug turf and received rewards from the small-time pushers. For the big pushers, he kept the small-timers in specific territories.

Each territory was defined by its own graffiti markings. When a dealer crossed the border, Lil' Long sent him back. If it became a problem, Lil' Long would settle the border dispute. He thought of himself as a realtor. The nine-millimeter enforced the contract. Sometimes disputes were settled with guns, leaving mutilated bodies.

He had met Vulcha while doing his first and only bid in an Upstate jail. Lil' Long, fifteen years old, had been sentenced to a correctional facility for juveniles. His stay was supposed to be three years. The judge had wanted "to teach this young animal a lesson in humanity."

The system taught Lil' Long nothing except improving his skills in the areas of chess and video games. It gave him props and confirmed him as a criminal. When Lil' Long and Vulcha joined forces, they wreaked havoc.

In the prison, Vulcha was well-known for his violence. The other inmates left him alone. He became Lil' Long's bodyguard and brother. Outside prison, Lil' Long threw some of the street business his way, and they became partners.

Their business ventures include shaking down dealers, pimping prostitutes, car jacking and murder. But they took the greatest pride in the hit-man service. Like the street fighter in video games, Lil' Long ripped through his targets with the ease of a semi-automatic pistol-cum-joystick. The price was ten thousand dollars a body. The bosses were like deft video-players with time on their hands and bags of money. Lil' Long and Vulcha were their street fighters. The outcome was hit after hit, body after body.

The last hit made by Lil' Long and Vulcha had left two people dead. They knew nothing about the ramifications, and they didn't care. They never read newspapers or watched the news. Families whose lives were destroyed were not known. Lil' Long and Vulcha would collect ten thousand dollars for the slain Deja.

The girl's family would have to pull together and mourn. They would be completely ignorant of exactly what role Bebop was playing at the time of her death. The police would discover her bullet-ridden carcass rotting in the drug dealer's expensive apartment a few days later. Wrong place, wrong time, she had paid the ultimate price.

The television blared. The phone rang. Lil' Long snored. Then, in a pause between music videos, the ringing penetrated. Lil' Long groggily reached for the phone and brought it to his ear.

"Who dis?"

"It's me, nigga," said a girl.

"Me, who?"

"Tina. Whatcha' doing?"

"Sleepin'," replied Lil' Long. "Whatchu want?"

"I'm coming over to get some money and give you a taste of chocolate loving."

"Ah'ight. Don't wake me. Use your keys. See ya." He hung up, uninterested in the proposition. *All she wants is money, money*, he thought, and went back to sleep.

****

Tina smiled at the sight of Lil' Long, laid out and snoring loudly. She found the remote and reduced the volume. She intended to do the same with his cash.

She kissed his parted lips, his drool touching her chin. Tina wiped her face on his robe. Lil' Long remained fast asleep. She removed her silk Versace shirt, exposing her matching silk bra. Her hand slid down Lil' Long's inner thigh, seeking his penis. She ran her nails lightly along the shaft, but it didn't respond to her usual petting. She swooped down, mouth open wide. She gently sucked his penis. Lil' Long stirred. With half opened eyes he peeked down at Tina.

"Oh, so you had some already, mo'fucka?" she asked between sucks.

"What is your ass talking 'bout?" asked Lil' Long, now groggy.

"You know, cuz I know," Tina replied. She kept on sucking. "Cuz you should be hard already." Tina checked for rigidity with the tip of her tongue. Lil' Long began to rise to the teasing occasion.

"Oh yeah," cried Lil' Long. "See, see. That's what your ass shoulda been doing from jump." Lil' Long savored Tina's lip service. Now he was hard and ready.

She wiggled out of her Guess jeans and climbed out of her black, silk underwear. Mounting him easily, she slid up and down, slowly at first. Lil' Long, fully aroused, laid back with his hands clasped behind his small Afro. Her actions brought a smile to his face.

"Yeah, yeah, baby. Work it." After some minutes of continuous sliding action, Lil' Long climaxed.

"Oh, oh, oh yeah," he screamed. Tina remained perched on his dick. She laid her head on his chest. He kissed her hair and face.

"Baby-baby, I need a G for shopping, and..."

"A G?"

"Well, if you'd let me finish, you'd see why." She put her face directly in front of his. Her hazel eyes recorded the strained contortions of his facial muscles. Her vagina still gripped his erect member. She flexed her muscles around his erection and squeezed harder. She had his attention.

"See, I wanna get this dress, Sweetheart, and you *know* I just gotta get the shoes to go. And my hair, it's gotta get done." Tina kept her eyes on his facial reactions. She continued alternately flexing and relaxing her vaginal muscles. Now she rotated her rear end.

"Well, Baby? Baby," she said softly, "do you agree?" Lil' Long thrust hard. "Well, Baby?" Tina realized the decision was going her way. "Well?"

"Aahhh. Yeah, yeah."

"You agree? You're not gonna change your mind, are you?"

"Yeah. Yeah. Yeah." He writhed. His body shook violently. "Oohhh. Ah."

"Do you have the G, or not?" Tina stood up and

looked down at the helpless street-fighter.

"Yeah. Check over by the video collection, in da Mack video case. Just take da Hamiltons and da Jacksons. Just a G."

He knew exactly how much cash was in each video cassette case. He had chosen them carefully. Tina went to his bedroom where he stored sixteen of his favorite old movies. The movies' colorful jackets bespoke fame. Pam Grier, "Sheba," shown in her glory, had in its jacket twenty-five thousand dollars in five-hundred-dollar bills. "The Mack," Julian Bond, displayed the elegance of fur and a fedora. Within was three thousand tax-free dollars. It once held five thousand five hundred. He had spent the rest partying and shopping. "Enter the Dragon," on which Bruce Lee's ripped skin dripped blood, held an extra nine-millimeter and a thousand. Tina emerged, smiling.

"What's da time?" asked Lil' Long.

"It's four, Babe." She kissed him and retrieved her clothes from the floor. Tina began dressing and checked her reflection in the huge mirror on the wall. "I'm out, Babe."

"Oh, yeah. Do one more thing for me before your ass be out."

"What, nigga?"

"Page Vulcha." Lil' Long sat back. He retrieved the remote and began flipping the channels.

Tina dialed the number. "I'll beep you later. Be good." She blew him a kiss and left.

The phone rang. Lil' Long grabbed the receiver.

"Who dis?" he asked, shouting into the receiver.

"Someone beeped my ass, muthafucka," said Vulcha.

"It's me, muthafucka. Who else gonna beep your ugly ass?"

"Well muthafucka, how am I gonna know it's you? I ain't seen your code. It could be your girl or sump'n, beeping my ass."

"Whatever, nigga. Yo, don't get too technical on da shit. Jest come git my ass. We need to collect this dough."

"Ah'ight son, I'll be there in a flash. Chill."

Lil' Long put the receiver down. He went into the bathroom, smoking a cigarette. Soon after, he emerged in oversized blue FUBU jeans and blue denim shirt. He shoved a Glock nine-millimeter in his waistband, using the shirt to cover it, and adding a black, denim Guess jacket for complete concealment. He partially laced his black Timberland boots and strode out.

In front of the building, a bus stopped. Some kids from the apartment building hopped onto the back of the bus. Vulcha parked behind the bus. Lil' Long swung into the Jeep. They brandished fists in greeting. Lil' Long hit Vulcha's fist hard--definitely not a regular handshake. As the bus drove off, Lil'Long's attention was diverted.

"Yo, yo, pull up next to that bus," commanded Lil' Long, very serious.

"Whazzup?" asked Vulcha. He gained on the bus. "You want me to go around it? You saw some big-ass honey on it? Whazzup? Tell me, nig." Vulcha saw Lil' Long's expression change. He guided the Jeep closer.

"Yo, shorties, all y'all git da fuck off da back of dat bus! An' don't be trying to jump back on when I'm gone, cuz I'm coming back and sneak up on y'all."

The kids jumped off the bus, momentum propelling them forward. The Jeep swerved as Vulcha tried desperately to avoid them.

"Son, be careful," said Lil' Long.

"Them fucking kids need to git outta da street," said Vulcha.

"Pull over and stop blaming da kids for your non-driving ass, mo'fucka." The smile returned to Lil' Long's face. He hopped out of the vehicle and stood with the kids, who edged away from him.

"Y'all should be careful. Know wha' I'm sayin'? Life is precious. It giveth and it taketh...Here." He pulled out some money and handed each kid a five. Skulking kids quickly came out of their hiding places for their share.

"Each o' y'all got some money, so now y'all gotta wise up and spend it right. And don't spend it all on video games." The eight kids gazed in awe at Lil' Long, as if hypnotized by the huge platinum cross swinging from his neck like a pendulum.

"Thanks Lil' Long," they chorused. "You're cool. We down wit' you, 'nuff- 'nuff respect." They ran off to the neighborhood video hang-out.

"Remember, don't spend it all in da same place," yelled Lil' Long. He strutted back to the Jeep. Vulcha had waited impatiently, tapping both thumbs on the wheel to the beat of the street.

"Yo, muthafucka, you on some community service type shit, man?"

"Nah, nah. Them kids are our future. Somebody gotta look out. Know wha' I'm saying? When I wuz that age, no one really looked out for me. I had to look out for self, know wha' I mean?"

"Yeah, yeah. I hear you, boo. I got your back, mo'fucka," said Vulcha.

"No question."

Vulcha started the Jeep, then struggled with its bucking motion.

"Plus, your non-driving ass might've ran into the back of the bus and killed em, anyway," said Lil' Long. "I need those shorties around. Them lil' mo'fuckas are da ones who'll be wearing T-shirts with my face on da shits."

"You'll be like a mo'fucking role model and shit," said Vulcha.

"Know wha' I'm saying, kid?" said Lil' Long, slapping a five. "Let's get paid, kid." He turned up the volume on the Chop Shop Crew. *Blow up, blow up,* yelled the chorus.

They pulled up to the waterfront meeting site. A beautiful woman in a white pants suit walked casually up to the Jeep. Vulcha got out. Lil' Long fingered his Glock and watched from the passenger side. The woman tossed a brown envelope to Vulcha, then walked away, as casual as she had come. No words were exchanged. Vulcha moved to the vehicle and threw the envelope in Lil' Long's lap.

"Yo, you count da shit, kid?"

"I glanced, muthafucka. You count da shit. I'm busy driving," said Vulcha. He took the vehicle through the bucking routine, and finally got it moving.

"Yo, here's your half. You should get less, mo'fucka," Lil' Long joked. "It was only da bitch's body *you* took. *I* took da bitch-ass, drug-dealing nigga. A service to da community."

Vulcha drove the Jeep uptown. Lil' Long negotiated on the phone.

"Yeah, it's all here ... No, that bitch's body was fo' free man ... Yeah, we always deliver ... No bullshit ... Yeah later." He clicked the 'off' button and turned to Vulcha.

"Another hit, another job well done, son. They'll be in touch wit' da details Friday."

A smile suffused Vulcha's face. He stayed focused on driving, eyes staring intently ahead, nodding his head in agreement with the offer.

"They didn't say why? Drugs? A birdie?" asked Vulcha.

"Since when you wanna know shit, nigga? You just hit da muthafucka. Some husband wants his bitch on da side done up." Lil' Long grinned.

"Right up your alley, mo'fucka."

Lil' Long's laughter ricocheted off the windshield and drowned the blare of the CD. Then Vulcha joined in and the Jeep swerved out of control. He braked so hard that the vehicle jerked wildly to a stop, barely avoiding another car.

"You better invest some of dat loot in driving lessons, mo'fucka. You gonna kill our ass." Lil' Long clutched the dashboard.

"Chill, chill. I got things under control, nig. Let's get some lobster."

"Yeah, yeah, kid. Let's go by da fish spot. Lobster! Yeah, I could feel it," said Lil' Long.

"Oh. They said that nigga had five G's in his place," said Lil' Long.

"Which nigga?" said Vulcha.

"That drug-dealing mo'fucka from last night." Lil' Long was annoyed. "You be sleeping, mo'fucka?"

"Nah. That nigga had about five hundred and change on him, an' all them drugs. Crack and coke. That's it? Five Gs?" Vulcha concluded in disbelief.

"Yeah, mo'fucka. Could have an extra five G's."

"Well, fuck it. We would've had to stay around and search. Fuck that. We did what we were in there for, an' got da other shits in a flash," said Vulcha.

"But five G's is five G's," persisted Lil' Long.

"Ah'ight. Five G's is five G's. Don't beat me in da head wit' it."

They arrived at the fish place and grabbed trays. They headed for the lobster section. The hunger for seafood had taken hold. They craved satisfaction.

CHAPTER 9

Deedee returned to school after a week. Da Crew saw her head for the building that housed the actors' workshop. They watched the green van drive off.

"Isn't that Eric Ascot?" asked Josephine. Danielle nodded.

"Si, Señoritas," said Danielle. "That's Eric Ascot and Sophia."

The girls separated, heading for their classes.

"Rehearsal later," they shouted in unison. It was like a battle cry echoing through the empty halls.

Coco wondered how Deedee felt, but she had other things to worry over. Bebop was missing, and her parents had dogged Coco constantly for the past five days.

"Have you seen or heard from my daughter?" they would ask.

How am I gonna be seeing Bebop? I have to be looking out for my mom. They wouldn't understand, thought Coco. She sat in class, replaying memories of the street. She realized the problems of the world made calculus seem like child's play. Eventually calculus claimed Coco's attention. She was all ears.

****

For Deedee, however, school slowed to a crawl. Classes were made up of students with inquisitive stares. After a few classes and hours of stares, Deedee wanted to do nothing but leave. She sought refuge in the girls' room with a lit cigarette, but still felt the whispers of classmates through their looks of scrutiny. It was unbearable at times. Deedee overheard bits and pieces of conversations when she removed her headphones from the Sony CD player. What she heard made her body cringe. *This shit's awful,* she thought. Her fingers shook so much that her rings rattled. Deedee wanted to cry. *Be strong*, she told herself. At times, she felt guilty for being the victim.

"Shit stinks," she repeated as she left a classroom, hearing her name being called.

"Ms. D. Ascot, please report to the guidance counselor's office immediately."

A few minutes later, Deedee knocked on Mrs. Martinez's door.

"Come in, please," said Mrs. Martinez. Deedee walked in and closed the door. She stood facing the chubby, friendly woman.

"Have a seat please." Mrs. Martinez waved her to a row of chairs against a wall. Deedee sat, staring uncomfortably at the guidance counselor. Mrs. Martinez rushed over and sat next to Deedee.

"Our deepest sympathy goes out to you, my dear. We know what happened and we know this is not a fair world. Bad things happen to good people sometimes, but good always triumphs in the end."

It was a nice gesture, Deedee supposed. She tried to return the woman's smile.

"Thank you," said Deedee, not exactly sure why she was saying it. She wanted to get up and escape the interrogation. Deedee felt that there would be more questioning, more probing. Paranoia awakened her body and gnawed at her thoughts.

"How are you feeling?" asked Mrs. Martinez. Deedee forced something she hoped was pleasantry.

"Ah, I'm okay. I'll be ah'ight." She struggled to find the correct response.

Mrs. Martinez saw the struggle. She went to her desk and picked up an envelope with a card inside. She returned and handed Deedee the card. Deedee accepted it, fighting back the tears. She stood up. Mrs. Martinez reached forward and held Deedee by the forearm.

"If you need any kind of assistance, please feel free to call," she said.

Deedee nodded and turned to leave. Then she looked at Mrs. Martinez's face; it displayed a smirk, which did not seem reassuring. Mrs. Martinez was also trying to hold back her tears. The expression didn't completely hide the pity she felt. Deedee smiled at the realization. She waved and slammed the door, heading toward the exit. This day had to end, she thought, reaching for her cigarettes.

The world is such a fucking wicked place, she almost said aloud as the tears sprung, filling her eyes with water and making her vision blurry. As she took out a cigarette, she bumped into Coco. Deedee's head rose. She wiped her eyes and turned to apologize.

"I'm sorry, I..."

"Need a light, yo?" Coco eyed the cigarette Deedee was trying to hide. "Can't smoke in da hall, so we gotta take it to da toilet or da streets, yo."

"Cool. I was heading to the streets," said Deedee. She was noticeably shaken.

Coco noticed the uneasiness immediately. *Maybe this is the way all victims react*, Coco thought as they walked to the exit together. As the two girls left the building, they paused. Coco gave Deedee a light. The smoke rushed to her lungs and Deedee immediately started to cough. Her eyes filled with tears.

Coco patted Deedee's back. "Let's get something to drink, yo."

"Yeah, sounds good." The girls walked into the corner store. Deedee chose apple juice and Coco brought a soda. They moved to a bench in front of the school. Deedee felt better after a few sips. Coco lit a cigarette.

"So, how ya feeling?"

"Oh, I'm better. That juice really hit the spot. Thanks," said Deedee. She inhaled easily now.

Damn, did she forget already? The rape was only last week, she thought, watching Deedee from the corner of her eye.

"Yeah, true. Da soda is on time. But I'm saying, how are you *really* feeling, y'know?" Coco gestured with her cigarette.

Deedee smiled. She had actually misunderstood Coco's question. It made her cheerful, even if she had to recall a bad ordeal. Coco marveled at Deedee's smile.

"You're funny," said Deedee, through a chuckle. "I didn't mean to laugh, but I'm doing better. It's the first day back. It's kinda rough, y'know. Y'know?" She surprised herself with this burst of energy.

Coco nodded. They smoked and sipped and gazed lazily at passing pedestrians. Then they spotted Danielle and Josephine hurrying their way.

"Figured we'd find you here," said Josephine. Danielle and Deedee exchanged greetings.

"Hi, what's up? How you feeling?" asked Danielle. She passed Coco to kiss Deedee's cheek.

Coco stood aside as Josephine did the same. Being with these girls again renewed the feeling of innocent camaraderie for her and brought a flood of emotions. Deedee cried as the girls hugged her. She motioned to Coco, who joined the group hug. Josephine and Danielle sniffled. Coco's eyes seemed damp. They huddled for a few more minutes, then released one another.

Coco reached for a cigarette. Danielle and Josephine sat on the bench. Coco handed the lit cigarette to Deedee. She puffed smoothly and passed it back to Coco, who took a drag and passed it to Josephine. Josephine inhaled and it was Danielle's turn, then Deedee's. The cycle continued until the cigarette was finished. They all stood when the green Range Rover stopped across the street. Eric waved.

"Oh, that's my uncle," said Deedee. "Y'all wanna meet him? Maybe get a ride to somewhere?"

"We're gonna rehearse in da school auditorium," said Coco.

"But thanks, anyway," said Danielle, waving at Eric Ascot.

"Yeah, thanks. You're always looking out," said Josephine. She gave Coco a challenging look. Coco shook her head. Eric Ascot spun the vehicle around in front of the girls.

"Hello, young ladies." He greeted the girls from the driver's seat.

"Oh, Uncle. I want you to meet Coco, Danielle and Josephine. They have a group called Coco and Da Crew."

"No, not anymore. We just Da Crew, yo," said Coco.

"Yep, Eric," Danielle stepped forward. "It's Coco, the crowd motivator, yo, Ms. Flamboyant Jo, and myself."

"Love-lay Ms. Dani," said Josephine, completing the melody. The girls laughed. Deedee opened the door and got in the van.

"Come check us this weekend. We gonna wreck shit at Busta's Open- Mike contest." Coco launched her verbal assault at Eric Ascot.

"I will, I will," he said. The van pulled away and Deedee waved.

The girls raised their hands. "Peace," they called in unison. "Let's go rehearse," they chimed, taking the energy of the battle cry to another level.

They walked determinedly toward the auditorium, ready to engage their talents in their high energy dance steps.

****

Eric Ascot tapped his thumbs to the beat of the music from the stereo.

"How'd it go?" he asked. He searched Deedee's face, waiting for an answer.

"Okay, I guess." She reached for the volume button. "Who are these guys? They sound kinda nice."

"Oh, yeah. They're nice. They're called Chop Shop Crew. They have some good stuff," said Eric, a little excited. Deedee leaned back into the soft leather seat of the van, ready to learn all about this new rap group. She relaxed as her uncle continued. Enthusiasm shone in his voice.

"Yeah, it turns out they're all barbers. Four of 'em have been working in the same barber shop all this time."

Deedee listened to her uncle rattle off the history of the barber shop rap quartet. His voice communicated confidence that the group would do well. He talked for the rest of the journey. She had become his connection to her father, his silent partner. Deedee nodded as he unfolded the story. It hadn't been such a bad day, after all.

CHAPTER 10

"Ah'ight, ah'ight, yo, I think we ready to take this," said Coco. She fumbled to find a cigarette and lit it. She luxuriantly inhaled, well pleased with the rehearsal. The girls had bonded closer since the minor squabble between Coco and Danielle. Things had been patched up through some hard hours of rehearsal, made more intense by the scepter of rivalry. Josephine welcomed the energy, which was the by-product of the small feud, but she felt uneasy with the settlement. She was hoping there wouldn't be any other fallout. Cory was there from the time he videotaped the act, and remained for the entire rehearsal.

"Well how'd you like it?" Danielle asked Cory after a light kiss.

"Oh, don't even bother showing up. They could watch the videos of y'all's rehearsals. Butter." He kissed her again. Danielle held him.

He really likes the group, she thought, holding his gaze. *His admiration couldn't be directed to Coco. She's not the attraction. It's about me!*

"Um, let's go, lovers. Out, Out, Out." Josephine gently shoved the embracing couple. Coco jumped off the stage and walked out. She wiped sweat off her brow as the others approached.

"Got to go, yo," she said. "See ya."

"Coco. You wanna ride? We'll all ride." Cory opened the car door and looked expectantly at Coco. Coco paused for a beat, returning the gaze.

"Ah'ight, since you insist on being nice, yo."

"Save me some shorts," said Josephine. Coco still had her cigarette. She handed it to Josephine. They got in the back seat.

"Let's get some weed," said Danielle.

"Yeah. Let's go by da spot an' see Deja. His shit is

always on time, yo," said Coco.

"Last time, da shit had us pumping," Josephine said. "We had mad fun at da club after smoking that shit."

"Remember where the spot is, honey?" Danielle asked Cory.

"Yeah." Cory headed for the Tenth Ave weed spot. They stopped where Deja had earned his living. They didn't have any idea of his ending.

Deja's decomposing body had been discovered earlier that day, after neighbors had complained about the stench coming from his apartment. When the police entered the apartment, they discovered two bodies. The police first thought what Lil' Long had intended, that Bebop had killed her boyfriend. The drugs and cash the police found, together with scales and other drug paraphernalia, was proof enough that the man with his face ripped open was a drug dealer. Kimberly Jones identified his body and verified that Deja was a drug dealer. However, she did not know where or with whom he had plied his trade.

Bebop's parents went to the city morgue and confirmed her identification. The parents and friends cried immediately on seeing the body. They left completely distraught.

"Bebop is dead," the family members cried as they went through the building. Their sadness spread through the apartment complex. Their phone rang non-stop as neighbors called to offer condolences.

"Yes, yes. She's dead," a family member would say and the weeping for Bebop would begin anew.

The family gave permission for an autopsy. Coroners found that the bullet that killed Bebop was not from the weapon in Deja's hand. The police now knew that there had been at least one other person, and one other gun, in the apartment at the time of the killing.

Coco and the girls didn't know any of this as they approached Deja's spot on Tenth Avenue, where they witnessed Rightchus painting the colorful memorial mural.

"Oh shit," said Danielle.

"Looks like someone's been killed," said Josephine.

"Yeah," said Coco, straining for a better view. "Deja done fucked around an' caught a bad one, yo."

"Oh shit! It's the weed dealer. That's fucked up. Where are we gonna get good weed from now?" said Cory.

They sat in the car and watched as the mural took shape on the wall. The large artwork was a testament of Deja's standing in the hood. *In memory of Déjà vu, now macking on another level* read the graffiti inscription Rightchus painted. The art style was concluded with the traditional R.I.P.

Cory and the girls watched the mural as Lil' Long and Vulcha cruised by. The music from the Jeep brought the sad serenade of a drive-by. Lil' Long rode shotgun again. Head tilted, gun in hand, he chugged from a forty-ounce bottle. The Jeep stopped and he ceremoniously poured half the beer on the asphalt. Then the Jeep jerked away. The music blared, surrounding the scene with noise.

"Yo, that nigga had mad props," said Vulcha.

"Yeah, yeah, I saw how big that shit was, kid," said Lil' Long. "Vulch, wasn't that them bitches wit' that cockdeez nigga from da club?"

"I ain't seen them. Know wha' I'm saying, nig? I wuz looking at his boys, standing around like what an' shit," said Vulcha.

"Fuck 'em. They ain't trying to do shit, kid. They muthafuckin' bitch-ass drug dealers." Lil' Long grabbed the black Glock. "They don't really wanna fuck around or they asses will be laying around like bitches."

Vulcha laughed and bobbed to the beat. His action caused an erratic shaking of the vehicle.

"Chill, kid, before you make my ass puke," said Lil' Long. Vulcha laughed harder and the Jeep rocked harder.

"Hey, look what da fuck you're doing," yelled a passing male driver. His female companion stuck her middle finger up. Lil' Long pointed the nine-millimeter at them. They screeched away and quickly changed lanes.

"So what about this job, kid? Wanna do that shit tonight? Shoot a fat lady?" asked Lil' Long.

"Da bitch is blackmailing this rich married muthafucka, huh?" asked Vulcha. "We should be hitting that muthafucking married mutha. He wuz da one cheating on his family. Word up."

"Son, we getting paid to kill da muthafucking bitch. When we paid, we could discuss who should've been hit and all that other shit. Right now, tell me if we gonna hit da bitch tonight or not."

"Ah'ight. Let's check da strip joint. See that bitch do her thing, get a nigga's dick hard." Vulcha grinned.

"Ah'ight, cool. But I ain't tryin'a sit up in that piece all night while you stare at bitches' ass an' all that bullshit, kid. We got work to do," said Lil' Long.

"A hour or so," said Vulcha.

"Ah'ight. That sounds cool. One hour, muthafucka. Don't be tryin'a slip away wit' some bitch, saying shit like, 'yo, I need another hour, man,'" Lil' Long laughed. Vulcha parked near the *Live Girlz* neon-lit billboard and entered the club.

CHAPTER 11

"Let's be out, y'all," Cory said, moving to the car. The girls piled in, seated as before. Their faces were solemn. They had just witnessed the completion of the mural dedicated to Deja.

"Yeah, drop me at my block, yo," said Coco.

"Take me home. I don't feel like hanging out, y'all." Josephine was clearly shaken by her experience at the weed spot.

"Death just seems to be waiting, huh?" said Cory.

"Cory, your father is a cop, right? I know he be seeing a lot of this shit," Coco said.

"Aw, c'mon. Why do you need to discuss that shit, man?" asked Danielle.

"No, no, it's cool," said Cory.

Coco stared off into the distance. Lights flickered like fireflies. She lit another cigarette. She saw the candles at the end of the block. *Deja is on this block too*, she thought.

"Right here is ah'ight, yo," said Coco. The vehicle stopped. She shook hands all around, and with a slam of the door she was off with a bop. Coco stopped at the corner and looked at the picture behind the candle.

"Bebop." The name slipped from her lips. The cigarette fell to the ground. Coco turned and walked away quickly into the building, straight to the stairwell, eyes stinging. Tears flowing, she bounded to the roof, pushed the door open and let out a scream in the evening air.

More tears flowed as Coco released the burden of her latest discovery. She cried for Bebop, who sometimes had been that big sister to her. She became more and more confused as she pondered Bebop's death. She heard someone approaching as she left. Going down the stairs, she felt something close to fear.

Coco knocked on Miss Katie's door. She heard

movement from within. After a metallic click, Miss Katie opened the door. Coco walked in. She was taken aback by the neatness of the apartment.

"Hi, Coco. I guess you heard, huh?" said Miss Katie in a hushed, gentle tone. She motioned Coco toward the kitchen.

"Oh, Miss Katie," Coco began. "I really don't know what happened. May I use your bathroom?"

"Sure. Go ahead, Sweetheart. Then join me in the kitchen. I'm almost through with supper." Coco hardly heard her in her rush to the toilet. She joined Miss Katie at the kitchen table.

"Here, have some Kool-Aid," said Ms. Katie.

Coco accepted the glass and sipped. It was too sweet, but she drank it anyway. It left a cloying sweetness. Coco was sure Miss Katie knew the facts of Bebop's death.

"What happened? I mean Bebop..."

Miss Katie looked past Coco and glanced up at the ceiling before she spoke. "May the Lord have mercy upon our souls," she said.

Then, registering Coco's anxious expression, she said, "There has got to be a better way for us all." Coco was patient. She knew the story would eventually emerge from the piety.

"You know, during the war and all the other times my husband was fighting for this country, even after he met his death, God bless his soul, never ever have I gone looking at another man. I mean, never," said Miss Katie. There was such finality in her voice that Coco began paying closer attention.

"But these new jack women, they just can't leave other women's men alone. She wouldn't leave that drug dealer alone. It cost her," said Miss Katie. She got up and walked away from the table.

Coco watched her go to the oven and remove fresh-baked bread. She cut it in two and wrapped one half neatly in foil.

"For you and your family, Coco." Miss Katie pointed to the wrapped half.

"Thanks," said Coco. But she wanted to learn more. "Where did they find her?"

"Oh, I thought you had heard the full story," Miss Katie searched Coco's expression. "They found them dead together, Bebop and Deja, in his apartment. She had a gun in her hand. Lover's quarrel. Coco, is you mixed up in anything like..." Miss Katie's voice trailed as her eyes locked with Coco's. Coco gazed stonily at Miss Katie. "Coco, I know you are a sweet child. I know you will take care and continue to do so with God's help." Miss Katie tendered a caring smile. Coco rose and hugged her.

"Thanks a lot, Ms. Katie. I better head over and see what's going on," said Coco, parts of a smile making its way across lips bitter with emotion. She tried to hold back her tears by pursing her lips.

She took the wrapped bread. It felt warm to her touch. They embraced again at the front door. Coco was face to face with the elderly lady. She planted a kiss on Miss Katie's cheek and the tears began to flow. Miss Katie held her as Coco's body heaved with the burden of her emotional state.

"She was like a sister to me, Miss Katie," said Coco. Her voice broke.

"Yeah, I know child. Sometimes there's a price that we must pay for our sins. Coco, you have to continue with your education. Don't worry about your mother. She will be alright, and she's been doing a whole lot better," said Miss Katie.

As Coco neared her own door, her mother flung it open. "Get inside, girl. I heard you bawling your lungs out. Must be for that Miss Hottie, Bebop," she said. Her motherly face, an expression of seriousness shattered by too much alcohol. She was drunk. There would be no sympathy for Bebop.

"Ma," said Coco, "you don't even know what went down. You're just running off at da mouth."

"Well she was fucking around wit' some other girl's man from da building. It ain't as if she didn't know. I would've shot them both dead, too. They probably deserved it."

"Ma," Coco lashed out, "save your theories. I'm gonna go take a shower. Miss Katie sent this over." She placed the halfloaf of bread in her mother's hands and walked away.

"Why d'ya have to jump in da shower right after you walk in here? If it's sex, you better be using rubbers. Don't be coming up in here wit' any pregnancy or HIV bullshit. You little ho."

Coco vanished into the bathroom, closing the door, seeking solitude and trying to make sense of what had happened. *Bebop and Deja were killed together. Did Bebop have a gun?* The thought ran counter to the sweetness of the Kool-Aid she had drunk. Here, alone in the bathroom, her mother's voice rambling loudly in the background, Coco's thoughts were filled with the way the ugly end of a friend released a bitter taste and left her nauseated.

She turned the shower on and cried again. She did not understand. It just didn't make sense, any of it. Bebop was alive just a week ago, going to school and taking care of her biz. Now she's dead in a drug dealer's apartment.

The shower continued to run. Water sprayed hard on Coco's head. She stepped out of the shower and shook off the water. Sad thoughts of Bebop's death clung to the inner parts of her mind, displayed like an upside down flag, clinging to its post in a storm. She couldn't shake the thoughts.

She didn't even hear the knocking. "You've been in there long enough. What da fuck 're ya trying to do, drown yourself? Listen, she deserved what she got. You're from a different set. Them West Indian gals, drug dealers is what they all about. I know shit. I should know," said Mrs. Harvey, barging into the bathroom, drink in hand and smoke puffing out of her mouth with the words.

Coco screamed back at her. "Okay, so she wuz wit' someone's man. That's no reason to kill a person. C'mon, Ma. That's no reason to put bullets in her." Coco wept again.

"Well, that's your generation, yo!" said Mrs. Harvey. She raised the glass, sloshed the drink and smacked her lips. "What is it y'all do?" She said and poured some of her drink into the sink. It left a brown stain. "Peace to those who ain't wit' us," she mocked. Then closing the door, she walked away.

That night, sleep did not come easy for Coco, and in the morning she left the apartment building way too early for school. She could hear the mourner's chant. Coco strolled away, her bop coming in a hurry. With sadness close at her heels, she sought to escape.

CHAPTER 12

"Check, muthafucka. I got your ass now. Yeah, nigga, you thought you were gonna avoid this one. Make that move so I can take care of that ass. It's da only move your non-chess-playing-ass got," Lil' Long taunted.

Vulcha stared at the chess pieces. He knew Lil' Long was right. He made his only move.

"Checkmate, nigga," yelled Lil' Long. He got up from the table. "Can't fuck wit' da muthafucking Whiz. Four games to zip, kid. Can't fuck wit' me."

"Ah, lucky streak, nigga," said Vulcha. "You know that sometimes I be whipping that ass dead, muthafucka."

"Now when wuz da last time you whip my ass, nigga?"

"You know when. I ain't got to..."

"Damn. That's da time, man?" Lil' Long exclaimed as he looked at the clock.

"Aw, shit. I guess we can't kill that blackmailing bitch," said Vulcha. "Nah, nah, kid, we could hit da bitch on her way to work. Like we wuz gon' rob her or sump'n," said Lil' Long.

"Yo, da bitch is all that," said Vulcha.

"Yo, I don't give a fuck about that shit. We's got business to take care of, kid," said Lil' Long.

"Yeah, I'm just saying da bitch is bad," said Vulcha.

"Which bitch are you fucking dealing wit', kid?" asked Lil' Long.

"Yo, I wuz talking 'bout da bitch from da strip joint. Fuck that other bitch. She's dead and stinking."

"You talking 'bout da big - ass bitch? Da one you spent da whole night wit', muthafucka?" asked Lil' Long. "After two nights, you're pussy-whipped now?"

"All I'm saying is da bitch is all that," said Vulcha.

"She must've dropped some shit on your ass last night, got your head all fucked up. She ain't nothin' but a ho. You need money to pay that ho."

"What if she becomes my personal ho? Yeah, I'm gonna make her my personal ho."

"You buggin', kid," laughed Lil' Long. "Let's go bag this blackmailer," he said, checking his waistband. The nine millimeter was there.

"She goes to the office about now."

They walked out of Vulcha's tiny apartment. They had taken two women there from the strip club and spent the night. Both were satisfied now. Lil' Long held the elevator as Vulcha locked the apartment door.

As the car neared the selected station, they saw their target. She was a beautiful woman who stopped to buy the morning paper like so many other commuters, only she was marked for violent death. She was guilty of blackmailing her ex-lover, who happened to be a rich, respectable family man.

Lil' Long jumped from the slowing Jeep. The target was leisurely crossing the street. He ran up behind her, grabbed her handbag, and passed her. Instinctively, she ran after him.

"Stop! What are you doing? Thief! Thief," she called, in pursuit. Vulcha blocked her with the Jeep. Lil' Long hopped in.

"In my quest to become immortal, whole lot a bitches and weak muthafuckas must die," yelled Lil' Long. They both opened fire on the surprised woman. The shooting pair riddled her body with holes. Their weapons sprayed even after she fell into a pool of her own blood. Vulcha stepped on the accelerator and the vehicle was gone with a screeching of tires as commuters emptied the train station and watched.

"Da bitch wuz like, coming after you, nigga," laughed Vulcha.

"Yeah, yeah. 'Stop thief.' It's like, bitch, you're da thief, bitch. Put my mug on muthafucking T-shirts. I'll be back. Let's get some food," said Lil' Long. Vulcha drove uptown. They laughed all the way, and Lil' Long continued his tirade.

"You know da deal. Many weak muthafuckas will have to die in my quest. Shit is real, kid."

"But I'm saying," said Vulcha as he parked in the diner lot. "I think we should've hit da fucking cheating husband, man."

"Nah, we got the right one. She ain't paying us, kid. It's all about them Benjamins," said Lil' Long.

"What she had in her purse?"

"Sixty dollars, credit cards, condoms. I threw that shit away already." Lil' Long peeled the black gloves off.

"Muthafucka, you just love to come to this spot. Bitch got'cha open, kid."

"Nah, nah, da food's good," said Vulcha.

"So why we sitting on da side where that bitch be serving?"

"Cuz we gonna get served right. Know wha' I'm saying?" Vulcha winked.

"You might as well take over for her pimp. Da muthafucka probably a old-ass nigga and can't handle it anyway," said Lil' Long, a big grin completely polishing his mug.

As the two settled down to their breakfast, the police asked questions at the train station. The latest victim still lay outside in a pool of blood, the bullet-riddled body contorted on the pavement.

The commuters had not seen much, but had heard her yelling "Stop, thief!" They also heard the sound of gunshots. It could have been one, two or three men, they said. It could have been a robbery. The crime-scene unit moved in. The police were unsure, but leaned toward a robbery motive. Whoever had done it definitely wanted to make sure that the victim identified no one. She herself remained unidentified. Her body had been converted to a bloody pulp by a shower of bullets. She had paid the price. Shortly after the medical examiner arrived, she was pronounced dead.

****

Vulcha studied the waitress's plump backside. He puffed slowly at his cigarette. The rings on his fingers clanked as he raised the cigarette to his lips. Lil' Long got up from the table.

"Yo, you keep dreaming. I'm gonna drain my tank." He headed for the men's room. Vulcha watched Kamilla's body as she moved from table to table. She sensed his gaze and flashed a smiled at him.

Lil' Long returned. "Nigga, you in a daze or bugging out?"

Vulcha came alive. "Yo, she likes me. I'ma get her," he said.

"Nigga, I told your ass. Girls like that, they always got a man -- a Mack on da side, kid."

"I'ma be her Mack. She need a nigga like me. Know-wha'-I-mean?"

"You're gonna have to get rid of da other Mack-daddy", said Lil' Long as he stood and watched Vulcha peel a hundred dollars from a wad of bills. He left it as a tip. Lil'Long smiled and shook his head.

"She got'cha open, kid," said Lil' Long as they headed for the exit. Vulcha stumbled, looking back. Kamilla picked up the hundred, her smile stopped Vulcha in his tracks.

"Will you look where da fuck your ass is going? Think you're Superman or sump'n, muthafucka? That bitch is like a drug, kid. Damn nig," complained Lil' Long. Vulcha was almost smooth driving the Jeep away.

"Let's go shopping," said Vulcha.

"No, let's go get our money, kid," countered Lil' Long. Vulcha drove to the pre-arranged pick-up spot.

CHAPTER 13

Uncharacteristically, Coco walked the six miles to school. Even so, she was early. Sitting on the bench just outside the school, she searched for cigarettes and found none. She stood and started the walk to the shop at the end of the block. Coco paused when the green Range Rover circled and stopped in front of her. Deedee hopped out. Both Eric Ascot and Sophia waved at Coco as Deedee approached.

"Whaz-zup?" shouted Deedee. Her yell shattered the morning air. Birds took refuge in nearby trees. Eric honked, and Deedee waved goodbye.

She must be feeling a lot better, thought Coco.

"What's popping? I'm going to da corner store, yo," said Coco.

"I'll walk with you, if you don't mind," chirped Deedee.

"Ah'ight, yo." Coco eased into a leisurely stroll.

"This seems like such a nice morning. I mean, the sunlight, the water on the grass. Damn, how could it be such a nice day?" Deedee lit a cigarette, puffed and passed it to Coco.

"Yeah, yeah. Know what'cha mean, yo," said Coco. They walked on to the store. Coco bought cigarettes and a Coke. Deedee, apple juice and chewing gum.

The girls stood outside the store, sipping and smoking. They left as other students descended on the shop. Coco and Deedee walked back toward the school and sat down on a bench.

"Still early," said Deedee.

Coco nodded. "Yeah." Her voice trailed off in sadness.

Was Coco's behavior just early morning blues? Deedee wondered. Maybe she was tired. She knew Coco and the girls had been rehearsing for the talent show finals.

"So, how's rehearsal?" asked Deedee. Coco nodded

again and reached for her cigarettes. She lit one and stared upward, blowing the smoke out slowly. Deedee watched her, and Coco started.

"Life's some fucked-up shit, yo," she said.

It occurred to Deedee that her own situation fitted the phrase better than Coco's.

"Yeah, I know just what 'cha mean, Coco."

"But it could always be worse. No matter what, there's always gonna be worse," continued Coco, looking away. "I mean, yo...d'ya wanna take a walk?" asked Coco. She paused thoughtfully. "We best chill," she said. "Cuz I'll wind up not fucking bothering wit' this shit. I need da education, yo."

They remained on the bench. She lit another cigarette and Deedee joined her.

"You're ah'ight, yo. Know wha' I mean?" asked Coco.

Deedee thought about that. "Yeah," she finally said, not fully understanding. It didn't seem to matter.

Coco slumped back. "You're looking better, anyway. But I'm saying the feeling stays with you, yo," continued Coco. Deedee stared at her, still unsure of exactly what was going on. Then Coco came up with the clarification. "Da feeling of being vick. That shit never leaves, yo. It becomes your fucking shadow, pops up in different situations. You be seeing faces, like it wuz that muthafucka, or this one."

Deedee listened, dangling her cigarette. She watched Coco's expression change from sad to anger.

"I know wha' da shit feels like, yo," said Coco. "See, I wuz fucking raped. Muthafucka got drunk wit' my mom and when he wuz finished wit' her, he came for me. My mutha, yo, she tried to fight him, and I did too. That muthafucka was big, yo. He kicked my mutha's drunken ass and then took mine. I be staring at muthafuckas now, having flashbacks. Yo, I'm telling you, if I had a gun, that muthafucka would be spitting up lead. I'm telling you, I be staring in muthafuckas' eyes, they be looking at me, yo. If I ever see his ass... Whaaat! He's dead, yo."

Students began entering the school. First they had to pass through the metal detectors. Some waved to Coco.

She managed to ignore them and stared off, over the trees.

"I'll kill a muthafucka like *what*!" Coco summed up a feeling that had haunted her for a long time. Deedee was surprised. She had no idea the morning would bring this revelation. She had planned on going to school, enduring as much of the stares as possible, and leaving early if they got her down. Now, she too would stare back at 'muthafuckas,' possibly locating the one who had caused her pain. It was a scary thought. Coco's grim expression made her realize that things really could be worse.

"Do they know about this, too?" asked Deedee when she saw Danielle and Josephine heading toward the bench.

"Nah," said Coco. "They wouldn't understand da half. You had to be there like a vick to fully get it, yo." She got up and greeted the girls.

"Whaz-zup," said Danielle and Josephine.

"Hi," said Deedee.

"Whaz-zup? Y'all late, as usual, yo," said Coco.

"This crazy girl made me late," said Danielle.

"I'm telling you, I couldn't get into da station. They robbed this lady and shot her like twenty times. So da police had the shit blocked off. You should've seen all the blood! Yuck! Ugh," said Josephine.

"Let's not go inside, y'all. Well, not until later. I mean, fuck it, let's cut," said Deedee.

The three girls looked at her, surprise in their stares. Josephine swallowed hard. She and Danielle directed their attention to Coco. She was looking with interest at Deedee.

"Why not?" asked Coco. Deedee noticed a slight smile.

"Yeah, why not?" Danielle and Josephine chorused.

The girls walked hastily to the corner store. Danielle and Josephine bought snacks and cigarettes.

"Just a little juice. My throat is dried out," said Danielle, leaving the store. She held the straw up to her lips and spoke between sips.

"It's all that sucking," laughed Josephine. The comment caught Danielle off-guard and some of the juice spilled on her chest. She attempted a smile.

"Ah, you just jealous cuz you ain't got a man like Cory, bitch," she said.

"No," said Josephine with mock vexation. "If I had done all that sucking, my tongue would've been tired and I would definitely be thirsty."

"What're they talking 'bout?" asked Deedee.

"Get yourself looking this good and you won't have to wish about anything, and," Danielle licked her lips, "you won't have to suck." She patted her hip and arched her chest.

Josephine kept on laughing. Coco and Deedee stared at the other two. Then all four girls began laughing, not really knowing the whole reason.

"Let's go check out that new movie wit' Tyrese. I heard it's all that," said Josephine, still giggling.

"Oh yeah, it's called 'Baby Boy'," said Deedee.

"No, let's check out some breakfast. Now that will hit da spot," said Danielle.

"That sounds good to me," said Deedee.

"Ah'ight, yo. Where?" asked Coco.

"Mickey's," came the chorus They continued chattering as they headed to the breakfast place. Josephine continued teasing Danielle.

"I can't believe you be telling people your name is Daniella, wit' accent and everything, like you're Spanish," she giggled.

"Well, you be walking up to people saying, 'yo, my name's Jo,' like your ass is somebody an' shit," said Danielle.

"Well I *am* somebody," said Josephine.

"And I get the men sweating me because I'm exotic," said Danielle. She batted her eyes like Betty Boop.

Coco and Deedee walked ahead, within ear-shot, glancing over their shoulders and laughing along with Danielle and Josephine. Deedee was caught up in the moment. She laughed freely, completely enjoying the exchanges. Memories of the rape faded. The energy of the moment seemed to burn away all bad memories. For a while Deedee lived free.

Coco stopped, lit a cigarette and kept on walking. She had enjoyed Danielle and Josephine's performance, but what was important was sharing the ordeal she had gone through with someone she knew could truly understand. She slowed into her bop.

For breakfast the girls had only fruit juices and sodas. This 'hooky day' was nourishment enough for them.

"Yo, that nigga was walking like he had shit up da ass, yo," said Coco.

"He wuz dead into Daniela", said Josephine.

"Who's Daniella? You mean Danielle, right?" asked Deedee.

"Daniela. You know, that fake-ass, wannabe-Spanish girl sitting right next to my black ass," said Josephine. She laughed loudly. The other patrons, seated and standing, looked their way.

"Oh, no. Don't even try it. That little nigga knows a fine sister, no doubt," said Daniele. "You're just jealous that he ain't all up on you."

"Si, lo que se. Si, si. Mira, mira," said Josephine. The jovial mood infected the entire restaurant. They heard the rest of the patrons snickering from all directions.

An old lady hobbled over. "What did y'all mothers give y'all today?" she asked.

"Vitamins."

"Well, aren't y'all s'pose to be using all that energy in school?" The old lady waited for another answer. She didn't get one.

"Let's go check out that flick, yo."

The girls rose and walked away from the table. The old lady's stare followed them out the door. They strode past rushing pedestrians and homeless people waiting for a break.

****

They walked side by side as they entered the movie theater, laughing and throwing verbal pellets at each other.

Like bored kids throwing spit-balls, it was done just for simple fun. The jocularity extended until they left.

"Yo, yo, let's go window shopping," suggested Danielle.

"Deedee can show us where she gets that phat stuff she be wearing," said Josephine. She winked at Deedee, who grinned at Coco.

"Yo, that's cool. You wear some funky stuff, too," said Deedee.

"Ah'ight, yo, let's go already. Damn clothes addicts," said Coco.

"That's because you're always wearing them baggy jeans. Try something else, something that'll show your figure, girl," said Danielle. "That shit that be making you look like a nigga sometimes," laughed Danielle.

Coco didn't laugh. She lit a cigarette and hung it between her lips. She tilted her collar upward and slid her hat down to the top of her nose. She mimicked a boy's body language.

"Well, at least my jeans ain't wedged up into da crack of my ass causing me major discomfort, yo," said Coco. She lit the cigarette, a smirk on her face. Josephine laughed and applauded as Coco pulled her baggy jeans tight and imitated Danielle's walk. Deedee laughed, too, and pointed at Coco. Even Danielle, with the proverbial egg on the face, managed a smile.

"Hey, yo, let's go by the rink and rent some skates," said Josephine.

"Sounds good," said Deedee, still laughing.

"Okay, yeah, let's," said Danielle. Coco, who had moved further up the block doing the imitation of Danielle, rejoined them.

"Wanna hang at the rink?" asked Danielle.

"Yeah, yo," said Coco with sudden urgency. "There some cops giving out summonses to some other kids. We better be out, yo." The four girls ran for the skating rink.

Two hours later, they emerged, still laughing. Deedee phoned Uncle E. She asked him to pick her up a few hours later than usual. She was going to watch Da

Crew rehearse. Sunlight strained against heavy dark clouds as the girls slowly made their way back to the school. The mood was light as they shared cigarettes and a joint.

"This shit taste kinda nice, yo," said Coco. "Where'd ya cop it?"

"Oh, yo, from Cory. I don't know where he copped it." It gave Danielle a greater high when Coco was impressed. It was as if she had gone one-up on the not-so-easily moved and streetwise Coco.

They passed a group of guys on a corner and ignored their advances.

"And pleased to meet ya and suck my Johnson. Bee-itches."

The girls kept moving in silence. They heard chuckles from the guys.

Josephine broke the silence. "What if we ran back there and be like, yeah, nice to meet you Mr. Johnson, but you rather short. Too short to be sucked. Now, all the little Mr. Johnson need is someone to whip that ass for him. A nigga try to pull some shit like that, 'bout 'bitch, suck my dick,' we fighting, cuz that's big disrespect."

"What if they got guns?" asked Deedee. "That makes a huge difference." She wanted to share her experience. "It's really no joke when it happens. You just start wishing it's a bad dream and it will all be over real soon."

Danielle passed the joint to Deedee. The smell stung her nostrils, but she took a drag on the rolled cigarette with the brown tar on the tip. She passed it to Coco, who took it with a smile. Josephine and Danielle continued yakking.

"I'm telling ya," said Josephine "I be beatin' up my cousins, and they're guys. Puh-leese. Some guy try that shit on me..."

"You be so scared, your ass probably faint right there," said Danielle.

"Well, your ass probably would start loving da shit," said Josephine.

"Listen up, Sista Josephine. I'd probably bite Mr. Johnson's head off, so there wouldn't be too much to enjoy," said Danielle. "They know who to pick on."

"We be rollin'. I would scratch them niggas' eyes out," said Josephine, fingernails at the ready, scratching the air.

"This some good weed, yo," said Coco. She pulled on the joint so hard, the tip glowed. "Where he got this shit?" Coco managed to ask between tokes.

"Prob'ly uptown. That's where they got good shit. Cory said they call it cookies 'n' cream," said Danielle. She grabbed the center of attention once occupied by the burning weed.

"Yeah, this shit does smell like cookies `n' cream, yo."

"I'm serious," said Josephine. "Baskin Robbins, special flava."

"You need to take your serious ass to rehearsal," said Danielle. She toked on the last bit of the joint and flicked the tiny roach away.

"Yeah, yeah, it's that time again, yo," said Coco, heading for the small auditorium. Deedee and the girls followed. The auditorium was like a boxing ring before a fight. It had been the main hall of the old school, and was nearly abandoned after the new building went up. Now it was about to be transformed by the winds of human energy.

Deedee watched Da Crew calmly shift to their ready position. The whole place became energized with their emotions. She saw the raw expressions on the girls' faces as they moved--sharpening each turn, weaving, pivoting and stepping on cue.

They're good, thought Deedee. *They are incredible.* She felt the excitement as the girls' liveliness burst through, causing momentary delirium. Above the noise of rehearsal she heard the blast of a car horn. She went to the window and peered out. It was her Uncle E. She went out and invited him inside. They sat and watched Da Crew fine-tune their act. At the break, Eric Ascot applauded and approached the stage.

"Hey, what y'all have is really good," he called up to them. "Y'all looking sharp and ready."

"Thanks," came the reply.

This, they knew, was a compliment from a producer,

and not just any producer. It came from Eric Ascot. It surprised them. And the compliments got better.

"You are Jo, with some smooth flow, Danielle and Coco," said Eric, pointing as he named each girl.

"Oh, oh, you got us down to the point," said Josephine.

"Yeah, yeah. We feel big time already," said Danielle.

They all laughed. Coco drank bottled water and watched. Then she saw Deedee's smile and she smiled back.

It was time to go. Deedee waited as her uncle offered compliments and promises, then they said good-bye. Deedee reviewed the day as the car moved into traffic.

"I had a very good day," she announced, without any prompting. They both smiled, relieved.

"Think we should sign Da Crew? Get them into the studio?" asked Eric.

"Oh, yeah. That'll be really good," said Deedee. She looked directly at him.

"Yeah, I think so, too. We better make a move before someone else signs 'em up."

"Uh-huh, 'cause y'know they're gonna win that talent show. They're so good, I mean onstage and off. They're really not the same." Deedee elaborated on the girls' versatility.

Eric drove on with a smile. Deedee sounded excited, and it felt like old times. He listened to her opinion on the girls' strengths and weaknesses. He thought about signing the girls after the talent show, win or lose. Da Crew might be the antidote Deedee needed for a full recovery.

CHAPTER 14

"I'm telling ya, that shit's foul."

Coco continued walking up the block toward the apartment building that was now home to another wake. She heard the hushed tone of the street's voices, and Coco was staring at Deja's son along with his mother. Tears were in Kimberly's eyes.

"Coco, you knew? Cuz if you did, then that's real foul, girl."

Coco reacted quickly. "Knew what, yo?"

"Knew that your girl wuz sleeping wit' Kimberly's child's father." The words came from behind her. She realized there were two girls back there who weren't just mourners. *Oh shit*, she thought, eyes on the angry Kimberly and the fatherless boy at her side, eating candy.

"Yo, you think I knew about any of this shit? That's why you brought these bitches to jump my ass, yo?" Coco lashed out. She was angry, but she tried to control her temper. She felt a hefty shove from behind. She fell against the wall.

"Ain't no bitches here but your silly ass, bitch. You best chill, 'fore you get your video-mug ripped wit' fucking tribal markings."

"Leave her alone. Leave that girl alone, you big cowards," yelled Miss Katie from her window. She threw pots and utensils at the girls who threatened Coco. Coco jumped away from the wall, ready to fight. She hugged the little boy when her attackers ran away, shouting insults at Miss Katie.

"Fuck that ol' ass witch."

"Let go of my child," yelled Kimberly.

"Come on, take him. I had no beef wit' you or his father. And I didn't know what the fuck was up wit' him and Bebop." She softened her voice for the boy. "Go to your mother, sweetheart. She needs you." For a while, the little boy held Coco's hand tight. Then he let go and ran to Kimberly's outstretched arms.

"Coco, are you alright?" asked Miss Katie from her third-floor vantage point.

"Yeah, I'm ah'ight. Thanks Miss Katie, for looking out. I don't need no ass-whipping." Coco dropped her voice on the last phrase, walking into the building. Miss Katie met her at the top of the stairs.

"You better get right inside and see about your mother," she said. "She slipped out earlier today." Miss Katie didn't need to finish. Coco darted into her apartment. She was still trying to unlock the door when Miss Katie called out, "She's in there with someone."

Coco caught the horrible stench of burnt plastic when she opened the door. She headed straight for her mother, who stood in the hallway.

"Why couldn't you wait?" Coco shouted. She wasn't fully conscious of the presence of the stranger.

Mrs. Harvey was disheveled. Her hair looked as if it had not been combed for days. She stared at Coco with eyes that seemed red and fiery. Through parched, gray lips, she croaked something unintelligible. Coco looked where her mother's shaky finger pointed. A man came out of the bathroom, zipping up his pants.

"Hi. I'm--"

"Can you excuse us, please?" asked Coco. He walked into the kitchen and pulled out a chair.

"Excuse me means go. Your time's up, yo," Coco pointed to the door.

"Listen, you lil' bitch, me an' your mom got some unsettled shit to deal wit'," said Mrs. Harvey's crack-smoking partner, his voice urgent with anger.

Coco turned and stared at him. *Nice homecoming,* she thought. She gritted her teeth, ready to lash out.

"Now, you better listen da fuck up--" Coco's retort was cut off by her mother, who emerged suddenly from her crack-blurred mindset.

"We have nothing to settle," she said. "Just do like

my daughter says an' git da fuck outta here." Mrs. Harvey threw the round glass vial, with the crack still cooking, to the floor at the man's feet. He dropped to the floor and scavenged through the residue, burning his fingers. He shouted as he shuffled out the door and his voice carried from the stairwell to the apartment.

"Bitches! They fucked up my shit. Must be fucking each other up in here. Bee-itch!"

Miss Katie shut her door and walked into her apartment, shaking her head. Coco did the same and turned around to confront her mother. *Why? Why?* she wondered. Her mother was half-lying on the sofa. She seemed to be asleep.

Coco shook her head at the thought. The incident brought back memories of Bebop's death. Coco headed for the bathroom. *Was her mother, too, cracking with Deja?* Coco wondered as she turned on the shower. *I'll recommend a cold shower to my mother.* After showering, she walked past Mrs. Harvey, who remained motionless.

"That shit must've been sump'n else, or you're outta practice, Ma. Ma, get up and take a shower. Ma, c'mon now. Stop laying around, mother." There was no response. A look of disgust spread across Coco's face. "I can't believe you went out an' did this shit to yourself. I don't believe it. Now get up." Coco shook her mother's unresponsive body. The older women fell to the floor, with the thud of a tree hitting the ground. Coco gasped in fear.

"Mom! Ma!" She bolted banging on Miss Katie's door.

"Miss Katie, please open up. It's my mother." Coco, in a T-shirt and boxers, clutched at her throat in panic.

"Coming, child. What is it?" she opened her door.

"It's my mother," said Coco. "She's not moving."

Miss Katie grabbed two jars from a black bag as she told Coco to phone for an ambulance. She went across the hallway into the stench of burnt plastic. Miss Katie quietly said a prayer.

"Thy soul unto God you must give and you'll feel peace within." She soaked a towel with two solutions and wiped Mrs. Harvey's face.

CHAPTER 15

"Yeah, yeah. You know the scoop. Uh-huh, yes, it was cool. Everything was love-lee. Played the hooky all day. Deedee could be fun. I got another call. Hold on a sec. Yo, it's Cory."

"Ms. Busybody herself! Wish Coco had a phone. Need to talk, you know? Party line, us girls," said Josephine.

"My girl's mom be sniffing, drinking and smoking the line up. She got a problem."

"You need to check yourself before..."

"Save it. I got to go. My man's on my line. See ya."

"Bitch!"

"Just don't be late for the train, Jo. Call your man, girlfriend," said Danielle. She clicked over to Cory's call. "Hi, baby, I'm sorry I kept you waiting. Running my mouth with girl talk. What're ya doing?"

The transition was smooth. Cory hugged the receiver in delight. He fumbled for the answer.

"Nothing, really. Kicking back, thinking 'bout some special boots."

"Don't tell me. Let me guess. It's only ten p.m. and I'm getting a booty call?"

"Babe, the last time was a week, week and half ago. C'mon."

"Maybe after the dance finals. I've been rehearsing. Well, you know how that is. You play football."

"Yeah, but can't we sneak a little snack prior to the big one?"

"Snack? Cory, you don't snack. You wanna have everything on the menu. So no snacking. Baby, chill. After the finals, I'm gonna need you to do me right. You know, hit a home-girl off proper-like." Danielle smooched into the phone and the blood rushed to Cory's crotch.

"Ah'ight, I'll chill. So how's rehearsal? Still battling Coco?"

"Oh yeah, it's a daily struggle, let me tell you..."

Cory interrupted. "Babe, hold on a sec while I terminate this other call... Danielle, why don't you get some rest and I'll call you back, okay?"

"Okay. Cool. I'll talk to you later, honey. Maybe we can get together tomorrow in the evening or--no! I've got rehearsal."

"Don't sweat it. Chill. We'll catch up with each other at some point, ah'ight? Get some rest, babe."

"Love ya," said Danielle as she cradled the phone in its charger. *Why did Cory hang up so quickly and who was he speaking with on the end of the other line?* she wondered. Danielle wanted to call back, but the urge left as quickly as she found the comfort of her mirror.

She stared at her reflection and contemplated the girls on the frenzied day. *Coco, why doesn't she get a phone?* Coco was always telling her and Josephine things about guys. *Coco always say, "Don't sweat 'em. Let 'em sweat you".* Why doesn't Coco ever have a boyfriend?

Danielle walked back to the phone and dialed Cory's number. No answer. Next she paged him. She set the receiver down. Danielle returned to the comfort of her mirror.

"Ah-h, it still was a great day," she whispered.

CHAPTER 16

"That's it, nigga, I'm serious. Honey wuz looking kinda fly. Tits 'n' ass in place, nothing really jiggling. You know wha' I mean?"

"Yeah, true. No question, son, but she had mad trophies, son!"

"Them kids. She only had those two, one in da carriage and one beside her."

"Nah, you bugging. Them three walking behind her were there for real too, son."

"Se-e-rious nigga!"

"I'm trying to tell you, muthafucka. Open your eyes and look."

"Ah'ight, listen. Why you gonna try 'n dis me on da low?"

Lil' Long and Vulcha passed the stores as shutters came down at the end of the day. They had spent much of the day shopping for clothes. Both of them had two big bags in each hand. Lil' Long shifted through the restless evening crowd. They took turns pinching and fondling women as they walked and shared a "coolie," a marijuana joint laced with cocaine.

"Where are we fucking parked, kid?" asked Lil' Long. He sat the bags on a parked vehicle, setting the alarm off. "Damn, this shit is loud," he commented. He kicked a dent in the car door.

"We parked over there, Lil' Long," said Vulcha. He led the way to the parked Jeep.

"Yo that meter maid got da mad big, apple-shaped ass," said Lil' Long.

"Don't mind her ass, she's fucking giving us a ticket." said Vulcha, walking faster. "Hey, baby doll. Yoo hoo."

They arrived as the traffic summons was placed on the windshield.

"We in da car. Why you still ticketing us?" asked Vulcha, feigning disbelief. The meter maid looked as if she was about to explain.

"I'm telling you, baby-baby. Baby-baby got the nicest ass I've seen all day," said Lil' Long. The meter maid walked away with a smile. "Ain't that the nicest ass you've seen all this day?" asked Lil' Long, raising his voice so she could hear.

Vulcha was disgruntled. "We be seeing all flat, ironing-board ass, so no question that's some ass. But that ass left us a fifty-dollar ticket." Vulcha picked up the summons and examined it, skeptically.

"Fuck her big ass," he said and started the vehicle.

"Yeah, yeah. I sure would like to. Pull up close to her, Vulch. Let me kick some shit, right here."

"Man, that bitch is getting in a car. Whatcha want me to do? Follow her around?"

"No, no. Ah'ight, I could see this ticket here is causing some problems. Lemme handle it. Give it here, kid." Lil' Long grabbed the ticket and ripped it to bits. "See how easy that was? Let's go by the video store and re-up."

"Yeah, let's go check out Carlos," said Vulcha.

A few minutes later they alighted from the Jeep and hustled through the crowd in a busy video store. They walked to the back of the store.

"Carlos, Carlos. Where are ya, you Colombian muthafucka? Yo, Carlos," shouted Lil' Long, searching the back of the store. Then they saw a chubby-faced, light-skinned man, wearing a blue T-shirt, a size too small.

"Hey, my friends," he exclaimed, displaying a big toothless grin.

"Carlos, aren't you afraid of eating yourself to death?"

"No, it's how do ya eat so much?"

"Ah, si. Have mucho, lotsa space," said Carlos, tapping his stomach gently with the palm of his right hand.

"No, I mean, how?" said Vulcha, pointing to his teeth.

"Oh, oh. Ha, ha," chuckled Carlos. He slipped the set

of false teeth in his mouth and came closer.

"Business, mi amigos?"

"Got any new joints, Carlos?"

"Always have new gifts for mi amigos."

He led them to a corner of the store for special customers. He lowered a shelf of videos and a row of new artillery emerged.

"This joint come wit' silencer? It's some space age shit. Sigma Lasermax, hmm."

For the next half-hour, Lil' Long and Vulcha marveled at the display of arms. They decided on four black Kalakos, four magazines and four hundred rounds of ammunition.

"Mix in some silicone tip and Teflon shit, ah'ight? Yo, Carlos you got any of those Rhino rounds, penetrate anything, huh Carlos?" asked Lil' Long.

"No fuss, no problem." Carlos always gave his customers complete satisfaction. He brought out two magazines filled with blue-colored bullets. He set the magazines apart from the other goods. "I have veinte black rhino rounds, straight from Texas. I give you both one magazine a piece for free."

"Ah'ight, Carlos, my man. You all this an' that," said Lil' Long.

"Yeah, we'll tell you how these joints work," added Vulcha.

After paying, Lil' Long and Vulcha strolled to the front of the store.

"Enjoy the viewing, mi amigos," said Carlos with a toothed smile. They left with what appeared to be a case of videos and set it gently in the back seat.

"Let's drop the shits at my rest, son," said Vulcha.

"Sounds good, nigga. Then we can get some food. Seafood, you know wha' I'm sayin'?" With that, the vehicle jerked away and rolled forward into the traffic. In the back seat were a couple of Donna Karan leather jackets and accessories, as well as four new Kalako nine-millimeter weapons, with all the trimmings.

At Vulcha's apartment, they changed. The weapons fit perfectly. Lil' Long snorted through a small straw and rubbed his nose reflectively. Vulcha, completely dressed down in a leather outfit, toyed with the guns.

"Yo let's go to da spot, son," said Vulcha, closely examining the trigger mechanism.

"Don't tell me. Your ass is pussy-whipped for a..."

"Nah, bust it. It ain't even like that. Just wanna cool out wit' peeps like us," said Vulcha.

"Ain't no one like us--at least, like me. I'm da one, da two and da three. That's me. L-i-i-l' Long," announced Lil' Long, compounding his stutter as he beat his chest.

"I'm just saying..." Vulcha began.

"Listen up. I un'erstan' 'bout that shit."

"What shit are you referring to, son?"

"Being pussy-whipped, nigga," laughed Lil' Long.

"How you figure that?"

"Every time we got sump'n to do, your ass wanna go to da spot. When we don't have shit to do, your ass still wanna be in da spot. Now you tell me, uh?"

"I like that spot. Everyone know who's who, know wha' I'm saying? No fronting allowed," Vulcha countered.

"Ah'ight. You're gonna tell me that da bitch don't have your ass open?"

"Nah, I'm saying I ain't open yet. Bitch still got a man," said Vulcha.

"Ah'ight. Why da fuck don't ya get rid of his ass?" Lil' Long asked. "C'mon, let's go pay that muthafucka a visit. Shit we already know where he at."

"Yeah. Let's go make that nigga an offer he can't refuse."

"I'm wit' that," Lil' Long smiled as they packed away the new guns and walked out. The smell of new leather camouflaged the atmosphere of death as the traveling companions set off to do business with Kamilla's pimp.

CHAPTER 17

Hank Boller was a proud man. He dressed well and indulged in the best money could buy. He received regular payments from six girls. His favorite was Vulcha's latest interest. Lil' Long and Vulcha strode into the dimly lit bar and spotted Big Hank immediately. He was dressed in gray pinstripes, with a white collar and a golden tie-pin. He wore a yellow rose in his lapel.

The pimp rose as Lil' Long and Vulcha approached. He knew who they were. Since he didn't know the nature of their business with him, three burly men stepped up to block the visitors. They quickly disarmed the pair. Lil' Long and Vulcha realized their mistake; they had misjudged Big Hank Boller's size and status.

"Hank! How are you doing?" asked Lil' Long.

"What's your business wit' me, kid?" Boller had an eagle glare.

"Ah, Mr. Big Hank, see me an' ma man here ... well, ma man, Vulcha, he sorta dig your-- know wha' I'm saying-- one of your girlies. So we figure we'll make an offer."

"An offer?" asked Big Hank, in disgust. He chuckled a bit. The men around him joined in. Then he burst out in a roar of laughter. Hank Boller stood six feet four and carried good body weight. The outburst began in his stomach and came splattering out in a deep-throated roar.

"What kind of offer?"

"We were thinking monetary measures. See, we got this Mercedes 600, fully equipped." Lil' Long was taken aback by the heaviness of Hank's laughter. Both he and Vulcha seemed to shrink into their leather garments. Big Hank merely stared. The tension heightened as the hit-men realized how vulnerable they were without guns. Suddenly, their situation was grave.

"I'll tell you what. We're gonna forget about this entertaining session an' y'all are just gonna slide your little, new-jack asses outta here," said Big Hank.

"We don't get our guns back?" asked Lil' Long.

"Unh-uh. Y'all may start acting wild. Shoot up da place, new-jack style. No way. Y'all look good together. Try comedy, rapping, whatever. Y'all got it going on like that." Big Hank's cronies erupted in laughter.

Lil' Long and Vulcha walked out, their expressions stinging with wounded pride. The night air smacked them with the reality of live and learn. They had been taught a lesson in street living: *Never underestimate the next man.*

"Glad we could fucking entertain y'all!" yelled Lil' Long.

"Yo, they fucking enjoyed that lil' show. Them muthafuckas couldn't stop laughing," said Vulcha, a wry smile appearing on his face.

"They fucking played us. Them fat, ugly muthafuckas fucking p-l-a-y-ed us like we was their bitches an' shit," said Lil' Long. He was in Vulcha's face, breathing heavily. Vulcha's smile left in a hurry.

"We gonna make that big nigga another offer. Let's get da fuck outta this muthafucking piece," said Lil' Long.

Vulcha drove to a take-out seafood restaurant. They ate in the Jeep. "Them niggas kept our joints an' that muthafucka almost died laughing. They just straight-up dissed us and all we represent, you know wha' I'm saying?" Lil' Long tore at the fish.

"They weren't trying to hear jack-shit. Them muthafuckas just kept laughing and laughing," said Vulcha.

"We were their joke for da evening. We were getting fucked for pleasures, like bitch-ass, pussy niggas. We ain't no pussy muthafuckas, an' we ain't going out like that, neither." Lil' Long pounded Vulcha's chest. Vulcha pounded back. It was a pact, renewed now in reaction to their encounter with Big Hank's pimp world. Age and experience had brought Boller props, street fame. But he had permitted punkish tendencies to color this meeting with two up and coming killers. A line had been crossed. Now, they had been violated. Lil' Long and Vulcha sat in the vehicle staring at the clouds of smoke being made by the burning 'coolie'. They noticed the arms of the law as a patrol car drove up toward the fast food eatery.

"Let's go get da other joints, kid," said Lil' Long.

"Word up," said Vulcha.

****

They were waiting when Kamilla left the club. She got in a waiting limousine and it drove away. Lil' Long and Vulcha followed. The limousine stopped in front of the huge apartment building and Kamilla got out. The limousine waited. Kamilla took the keys from her handbag to open the ornate doors. The doorman jumped up to greet her, then turned and watched the steady swing of her backside with admiration. She got into the glass-sided elevator and went to the twenty-third floor.

Kamilla returned to the limousine a few minutes later. Now, the doorman gained proximity, holding the door for her and helping her into the limousine. Then the limousine drove off leaving the doorman whistling with pleasure.

CHAPTER 18

The sun shone through thick, dark clouds as the morning air brought the smell of a new day. The Jeep rolled into a parking spot outside the diner where Kamilla served food only. Lil' Long and Vulcha found an empty table in her section. She smiled at the big-tippers, then brought their usual breakfast order. They chowed down angrily. Vulcha kept his eyes on Kamilla as she undulated back and forth. He blew a smoke ring.

"Is that bitch worthy of a war?"

"Fuck da bitch. That big, fat muthafucka dissed first. We gonna dis him back," said Lil' Long.

"Word," said Vulcha. "He's gotta pay."

Lil' Long puffed on a cigarette while Vulcha sipped water, swirling the ice. He smelled Kamilla's perfume. She deftly took his empty glass and replaced it in his waiting hand, filled. He took a swallow and gazed into her eyes.

"How much are you worth?" he asked, gazing into soft brown eyes.

"Every bit of your gold, Mister." She rapidly dodged his pawing and moved to the next table. The hit-men arose and walked out, leaving heavy tips. They left the smell of new leather and cigarette smoke in their path to the Jeep.

"That muthafucka should be getting ready to nod off just about now," said Lil' Long. He glanced at his watch as the sun's rays reflected from its surface. Both Lil' Long and Vulcha's thoughts wandered.

Lil' Long rolled a 'coolie'. Vulcha snorted the white powder with a straw. Kamilla watched them from the restaurant. *They must not be on their way home*, she thought as she positioned the shades of the diner to block the assault of daylight.

****

Vulcha pulled into a parking space a block away and walked to Hank's apartment.

"Let's see if these joints can cause damage," said Lil' Long, screwing a silencer on the tip of his weapon.

"These joints feel so new. Let's go ketch wreck," said Vulcha.

"Let them count these muthafucking bodies, kid," said Lil' Long. He eased the weapon between his leather coat and sweatshirt.

They entered the building, carrying empty boxes. They got on the elevator and pressed the number twenty-three. When they got off, they used the boxes to cover their faces and searched for the stench of the underworld. They caught the familiar scent of breakfast. One of Hank's burly body guards buzzed twice at an apartment door. They had found their quarry. Lil' Long hit the polished floor and slid between the guard's legs, squeezing off bursts into the second bodyguard, while Vulcha shot the man carrying the food.

"It's breakfast?" Big Hank had asked through the door. But when he heard the gunfire, he ran out the back and down the fire escape, car keys in hand. He was sure no one had seen him. He had made a getaway, but he knew the shooters would be back. Big Hank began thinking of how to repay them.

Lil' Long and Vulcha lay on the floor and surveyed the interior of the huge apartment. Lil' Long pointed. He rolled up behind the third guard, who was sneaking up on Vulcha. Lil' Long took aim, then fell. A fist from nowhere caught him flush on the face. Vulcha whirled around, and the room erupted with the explosion of his Tech Nine. The blast picked up the third guard and threw him back against a wall. He lay slumped over, blood flowing like the spray from a park statue.

"Vulcha, yo, this bitch clocked me as I wuz about

to...Chill, bitch!" Lil' Long struggled to subdue his attacker, a woman.

"Ain't nobody else here 'cept for two other bitches. That muthafucka got away, son," said Vulcha to Lil' Long, who was still struggling with the woman. Vulcha slapped her with force. She fell to the bloody carpet.

"So that's it. Da muthafucka ran like a bitch. We got to find his bitch ass," yelled Lil' Long. Rage stirred within him. Vulcha was silent.

"B-b-bitch where d-d-did da m-m-mutha-f-fucka g-g-go?" Lil' Long stuttered in his towering anger. He drew his face close to hers, then held her at arm's length, staring in wide-eyed anticipation. She struggled, in vain, then she answered.

"I-I-I-I d-d-don't k-k-know." Her stutter came with fear.

Lil' Long released the girl and took a couple of steps back. He raised the gun with the silencer and pointed it at the screaming girl's face.

"D-d-don't m-mock me, bitch. In order for me to be immortal a lot of weak motherfuckas must die." Screamed Li'l Long and squeezed the trigger. Bullets flew, ripping the flesh of her face at close range. She fell, faceless, to the soiled white carpet. The action alarmed the other girls. They began to shriek. Vulcha spun the automatic weapon on them and squeezed the trigger. The gun chopped them in two and they dropped, silenced forever.

"Let's take his loot. He had to have had a stash. That muthafucka wuz being paid," said Lil' Long.

"Yeah, all this shit had to have cost him some change," Vulcha agreed. He started searching. "Probably chump change for that nigga."

"I found da stash," said Vulcha. He held up a briefcase. In it was stacks of hundred dollar bills.

"How much?"

"Too much to count right at this minute."

"Ah'ight, put that shit in a paper bag. I'ma clean off

some shit and then we bouncin'."

They slipped out of the apartment and onto the elevator, then walked down a flight to the lobby and left by the service door.

"We'll find that bitch-ass, muthafucking Hank," said Vulcha, starting the engine.

"That muthafucka ran. He ran," said Lil' Long. Then he emptied the bag and began to tally the consolations. After a few minutes he looked up.

"Da muthafucka wuz holding thirty Gs an' change," he announced. When he looked up he caught a glimpse of a slick, black Mercedes.

"Damn, that shit looks real nice..."

"I could deal wit' sump'n like that," said Vulcha.

"Muthafucka, you can't even deal wit' this, kid. C'mon, remember a couple of weeks ago when you jacked that bitch wit' da car an' crashed? You a non-driving, need-to-take-your-ass-to-remedial-class mothafucka."

"You're always complainin'. I don't see your ass trying to drive." Vulcha smiled, slyly.

"That's your job, muthafucka. Your gig, nig. You think you're all that, so I let you play yourself, see. Don't wanna embarrass your ass."

"Oh, embarrass me, huh? Go ahead. Take da wheels and try that shit."

"Yeah, be sitting with your heart broken. Like damn, mo'fucking Lil' Long got mad skills. He should be at Indy and shit. Acting up on me like you a chicken head."

They both laughed and Vulcha lit a cigarette, guiding the car through the light traffic. As they exited the highway, they spotted Kamilla alighting from a cab.

"She live up in this hood?" asked Lil' Long. "Back this shit up, Vulcha. Let's pay that bitch an afternoon visit." Lil' Long gave Vulcha a tap on his raised fist.

"That muthafucka ain't skip town so quick. He around somewhere. I can smell them bones."

****

Kamilla hurried to her building. She was weary as she got off the elevator and headed for her apartment. She arrived as quickly as possible. Hank Boller, former lover, pimp and father-figure was waiting. He had always been there for her, she reflected. Now he sought something more than money in return. As Kamilla fumbled with the keys, she heard his voice inside.

"So what do I do now?" asked Big Hank.

"Ya just have to leave da city for awhile," Hank heard the caller on the other end say. "These kids are ruthless and they work for real connected peoples. Take some time in Florida, try Texas. I hear Houston is getting real pretty. These kids, they gonna burn out like streetlights, Hank."

"And then what?" questioned Big Hank.

"Well, they just get replaced, like light bulbs. There's a lot of hungry kids out there. Right now, these two are bright stars. They'll burn out, soon enough. Take a little vacation. Call me in a couple months. Bye," said the voice, with finality.

"Bye!" shouted Hank into a dead receiver. He slammed the phone down. Kamilla walked in. Lil' Long and Vulcha busted in behind her. Hank tried to run. Lil' Long pounced like a ravenous leopard.

"Hey, hey, you did that once. Your ass is not pulling da same shit twice. No sir. How are you?" Lil' Long pointed the gun at Hank's throat.

"Sit. Please sit," he continued. "We have a little change from your stash, an' we know you would like to have it back for da bitch...I mean lady, of course." He looked meaningfully at Hank, then Kamilla, and then Vulcha, who stood motionless at the door.

Big Hank smiled. "Hey, I know we could reach some understanding, gentlemen."

"Oh yeah," said Lil' Long. His smile held a hint of goofiness.

"Well, gentlemen, y'all are welcome to Kamilla. She's yours," said Big Hank.

"Well, she's actually for da homey wit' da lovesick look standin' over there." Lil' Long pointed to Vulcha, whose frame was blocking the door.

"Since we, me an' you, got further biz to address, I suggest we do it outta sight of these love birds. Give 'em privacy, know wha' I'm saying?" Lil' Long smiled at Vulcha and Kamilla with the same goofy look. He winked as he and Big Hank headed out the door.

Alone with Vulcha, Kamilla was uneasy and fearful. Vulcha lay back on the huge, soft bed and smiled. *She's mine*, he thought. *No more pimp-daddy Hank.*

Lil' Long walked slowly behind Big Hank, who kept trying to eye him as he talked about his other girls. Now Lil' Long's smile was genuine. They walked around the corner to Big Hank's car. There, Lil' Long pulled out the brown paper bag full of money.

"Hey man, I need a ride," he said.

Big Hank was rattling like shingles on a roof in a windstorm. "Sure, sure," he said.

Lil' Long handed him the bag. Big Hank was reassured. He stepped into the car and started the engine.

"Where to?" asked Hank.

"To da left, bitch-ass," said Lil' Long. He now held his gun to Big Hank's temple.

"Ya know, I never did get my guns back from you an' them big-time niggas you wuz wit'. That shit pissed me da fuck off."

"Listen, if it's da money, then here, take the bag. I think that'll get you some more guns. Many more..."

Lil' Long was waving his weapon carelessly now, causing Hank to sweat profusely.

"Pull over," yelled Lil' Long. "I gotta take a leak. Yeah, over there."

Big Hank felt better when Lil' Long reached over and opened the door. Lil' Long began speaking to himself.

"In my quest to become immortal, a lot of weak niggas must die."

He then fired twice into Big Hank's sweating face. His head exploded with the hiss of the gun, the silencer muffling the noise. Hank's cranium was splattered all over the window and the dashboard. Lil' Long retrieved the moneybag. Then he lit some matchbooks and tossed them into the back seat. He ripped Big Hank's shirt, avoiding the blood on it as much as possible, and walked to the rear of the car. He stuffed the shirt into the muffler. He lit the shirt and walked away, the brown bag swaying gently in his hands.

The car exploded as he rounded the corner. He hailed a cab and showed a twenty-dollar bill as he got in. The cab driver took the money and instructions from Lil' Long. Then, Lil' Long closed his eyes, and with a sense of accomplishment, leaned back.

CHAPTER 19

Vulcha looked at Kamilla and felt lust. He wanted her to feel the magic again. But Kamilla was not interested in his fantasy.

"What's gonna happen to Big Hank?" she asked, cautiously.

"Well...Well, Big Hank's gonna get his loot and then he's gonna hit da blacktop." Vulcha examined Kamilla's body language. He saw she was afraid. Maybe he wasn't convincing. He reached out. She moved backwards. "We're all alone, honey. No one can bother us. You don't have to be scared anymore. Ol' Vulcha will put your fears to rest, sweetheart."

"What is da blacktop? What's that like?" Kamilla hoped for the best, but she sensed Big Hank was a dead man.

"Oh, yeah. Blacktop? That's da way outta here." Vulcha reached out for Kamilla again.

This time she let him touch her. They embraced. She wanted to trust Vulcha, even though every instinct urged her to run. Kamilla stood while Vulcha pawed her clothes off, and before long they fell onto the large bed. His shaft penetrated her warm, moist flesh as her body readily accepted him.

Kamilla's mind turned again to Hank. *I hope he's alive*, she thought. Big Hank had always helped her through ups and downs. Tears welled in her eyes. Vulcha moved his hips back and forth. She held firmly onto his piston-like hips for the ride. Kamilla suddenly became aware of a surprising feeling; She was free! She clung tightly and sobbed quietly as Vulcha's eruption calmed her. She drifted off to sleep, her juices still flowing as her mind drifted to thoughts of her former pimp.

Kamilla had met Hank sixteen years ago, after her

parents dumped her in a group home. Hank seduced her, gave her money, and took her out of the home. Finally, she moved in with him. He made her complete a high school program. Then he put her out on the street, peddling. But Hank didn't keep her on the street for long. Soon, she had a furnished apartment and handled only special clients. And in time, he supported anything she wanted to do.

She chose college. She graduated and tried several entry-level jobs. She decided they weren't for her and wound up quitting each of them. Kamilla returned to work for Hank. She managed the finances of his small empire. She was good at it and Big Hank rewarded her well.

But, Kamilla couldn't manage her coke habit, which eventually broke her down. Increasingly, she blundered; in her own life at first, then in managing Hank's money. Hank had been aware of the coke habit, but thought she was able to handle it.

When Kamilla hit bottom, Hank convinced her to check into a rehab program and supported her through five, long years of rehabilitation. When she recovered, he rehired her. Using her ample assets and her knack for the business, she quickly blossomed into his top shelf girl. He had been loyal and generous to her and she pledged her loyalty in return. She knew that Hank had created her dependency to suit himself. It was his way of always holding on to her. Now that he was gone, she knew physically he had sold her out. Mentally she would be free.

CHAPTER 20

"Everyone has to make a choice. Sometimes we already know it's the wrong choice, but we go along with it anyway, for friends, for fun, even though we know it's wrong," said Miss Katie. Coco's sleepy head rested on her lap. They had waited hours in the crowded emergency room to learn if Mrs. Harvey had any signs of life. Then a nurse approached, shaking off other anxious families waiting for news of their relatives. She smiled down at Miss Katie.

"Miss Katie, you should go home and come back to visit her tomorrow."

Coco jumped up. "She's gonna be ah'ight?"

"We're gonna keep her a few days. It's up to her. Who's signing the papers?" Miss Katie signed and the four-hour ordeal ended.

In the cab on the way home, Coco pondered about the beginning of a new stage in her mother's life. Maybe she would go to a full-time drug rehab program. Miss Katie had begun to nod off. She opened her eyes and stared at Coco.

"Just a little shut-eye," she smiled.

"I understand," said Coco. "My mom should go to a full-time rehab, don't you think, Miss Katie?"

"Well ... you mean a residential? Yes, I think it would help her a lot. She'll be away from all that temptation."

"How can we get her in one?"

"Well, it's really like what the nurse back there said. It's up to her. It's up to her."

Coco leaned back in the seat and shut her eyes. She wanted to help her mother, but it seemed that all she could do was cheer from the sidelines.

The cab pulled up to the curb and they faced the gloom of the building, where Bebop was being laid to rest.

"I guess we better be getting ourselves ready for this. Miss Katie said. "Coco, I think you should stay with me.

Okay? It would make your mother feel better."

"Thanks, Miss Katie." Coco jumped at the invitation.

"Just bring your stuff over to my place and lock your apartment."

Coco was quick to obey, and once she sat down in Miss Katie's apartment, she fell asleep. Coco closed her eyes, but her thoughts didn't fade. She was at the hospital and she saw her mother was very ill.

"Ma, ya gotta do what they tell ya. Ma, Ma, stop ignoring me."

Coco began running through subway cars in search of her mother. She had to be in this car; the conductor had seen her there. Coco walked through the doors of the car and immediately noticed a frail woman in a side seat. The woman tried to shield herself from the sun. Coco sat opposite the wispy woman, blocking the rays. The woman could see her face and Coco's stare beheld what was left of her mother's smoked-out shell. Her black jeans were dirty, and though the blouse seemed too tight, it hung as if on a hanger. The woman smiled, revealing a couple of brown teeth.

"Break a leg," she said. The woman was now smoking the butt of a cigarette and chewing on a big, shiny apple. Coco closed her eyes. She turned. The woman laughed and brandished Coco's wallet. "Ya missed yer stop. Yer stop is long gone. Ya went to sleep an' missed yer stop. You've been riding this train wit' me," the woman chanted.

Coco found herself in front of the concert hall. Lights off and people leaving, Coco opened her eyes, halting the dream. She smelled cooking. She fumbled for a cigarette and realized she had been sleeping in the same clothes she wore in the emergency room. Miss Katie called from the kitchen.

"Coco, you up? You were tired, huh? Jump in the shower, and when you're ready, there's some food here for ya."

CHAPTER 21

Danielle went through her morning ritual. She made sure to apply judicious amounts of mascara and bright red lipstick. After mirror-time, she phoned Josephine.

"Hello?"

"Josephine."

"Danielle. I knew it was you bitch. Are we through playing Ms. Hollywood?"

"Girl, mind yer own. Question is, are you ready?"

"I've been up all night."

"Doing what, bitch?"

"Couldn't sleep. But I'm ready, baby-o."

"You're bugging, girl."

"You're the one bugging. Muy bonita, thank you."

"What, bitch? Just meet me at the train, bitch. An' don't be late. I'll kick your..."

"Tramp," said Josephine. She hung up quickly. With the morning formalities completed, she finally put it together: Blue jean suit, mild makeup and a change of gear in an oversized bag.

Josephine stopped for breakfast with her parents, as always. It was the only time the family could eat together. Then they drove in silence to the train station.

"Break a leg," her parents told her. She gave them a smile and left the car, approaching Danielle.

"Five minutes after. Your ass is late," said Danielle. She waved as Josephine's parents drove off.

"Your parents, they always late, too? Is there a family trait?"

"Well, you're looking an' acting loud today, as usual. Buenas Dias, bonita mamie."

"At two o'clock we'll be on stage competing an'..." Danielle began.

"It's only eleven thirty. We got lots of time. Do I detect a moment of nervousness happening here?"

"No, I just like to be ready so I don't have to be rushing, dealing with y'all..."

"Y'all?"

"Yes, y'all. Ms. never-on-time Josephine and Ms. Cool Coco, speaking of whom..."

"Have you heard from her?" they asked one another in unison.

"No."

"Neither have I."

****

Coco sat at the table in Miss Katie's well-kept kitchen. She heard the whistle of the kettle. Miss Katie placed a cup of hot chocolate in front of her and took a seat across the table.

"Worried about your mom?" asked Miss Katie. She sipped from a ceramic blue cup. "She'll be fine. We just got to take it one day at a time." She swallowed hard, then burped. She smiled. Coco giggled.

"Hmmm, hot cocoa's good, huh? I'm gonna try an' talk her into going to a residential right after she gets out of the hospital. That would be best for her," said Coco. She slurped from her own cup.

"You're right, Baby girl, but let's not be weighed down by that. You still have things to do in your life. How's school and those tests coming?"

Coco paused. Then she spoke in a saddened tone. "It's not school an' it's not so much my mom." Tears brewed in her eyes and traced down her cheeks. "It was seeing that casket lowered into the ground, Miss Katie. That was awful. Bebop was like my sister," said Coco, wiping away her tears.

Miss Katie rushed to Coco's side. She hugged the weeping girl. They exchanged smiles when Coco saw tears on Miss Katie's face, too.

"Life goes on, Miss Katie."

"It does, child."

"Well, my friend has been laid to rest an' mom's

laying in a hospital bed from a drug overdose, and I have a talent show to win," deadpanned Coco.

"I didn't know you had a show coming this quickly. I thought it was still weeks off. Are you ready?" Coco got up and smiled at her.

"After all that, who wouldn't be ready?"

"When is it?"

"Well, the preliminaries are in a few hours. We--our group, Da Crew--are guaranteed a place in the finals. So the prelims are like warm-up for us." Anticipation lightened her mood.

"Really?" asked Miss Katie. Coco nodded. "That's good. Seems as though that singing and dancing is beginning to pay off."

"Oh yeah. We get a--I mean, the winner gets a record contract and five thousand dollars."

"Wow! That's nice," said Miss Katie. "Well, you better get set and go take first prize, baby." Miss Katie was caught up in the excitement.

"So, I'm off, then. I'll give you a call an' tell you if we won. I mean..."

"What time are the finals?"

"Supposed to start at eight, but you know these people an' how their time goes."

"Aw, but y'all gonna just knock 'em dead. Well, knock 'em out. Good luck," Miss Katie hugged and kissed Coco on the cheek. "Here's a set of my keys. Take care and be safe."

Outside, Coco lit a cigarette and headed down the block. Miss Katie watched her bop around the corner, puffing on her cigarette. Then she was gone from sight.

At first, Coco thought the other girls had not arrived at the parking lot across from the club as planned. She headed for the deli on the corner. Then she spotted them sitting, hugging each other. *I wonder what could possibly be up*, thought Coco as she approached the girls. Danielle sat on a fire hydrant, her arms around Josephine. They looked as if someone had just lost the family pet.

"What's up, yo?" said Coco. She saw tears on their

"It's man trouble. Who's zooming who?" Josephine cleared her throat and nodded toward Danielle.

"No, no, no. Don't tell me Mr. Loverman is..." began Coco.

"That fucking bastard," yelled Danielle. "I'm walking down da fucking street to find a phone to call his nasty ass and guess what? Da nigga was ridin' around with some other bitch. He wasn't even answering da beep."

"Well, what? That doesn't necessarily mean she's anything to him," said Josephine.

"C'mon Josephine, if she didn't mean anything, why did he make a U-turn as soon as he saw us? Huh? Tell me, why?"

"He didn't do that. He did, yo?" asked Coco.

"Yo, as soon as his eyes caught mine, he was out. The car made an illegal U and almost caused a couple of accidents. He was up to no good," said Danielle.

"Well, y'all know my steeze, yo. Fuck a nigga. I don't want one! Don't need one!"

"He's cut off. Off like, 'see ya, Cory.' I still have some more of the chronic."

"Da one that smelled like cookies, yo?"

"Yeah, yeah," said Danielle. "Let's break ourselves off a piece, yo."

Coco deftly rolled the spliff. The three girls took turns toking. Before long, the weed had all three mellow and calm.

"Fuck a nigga. There be plenty more," said Josephine.

"I ain't sweating that shit. That's behind me, Jo," said Danielle.

"That shit was like, pow. Don't want no more. I'm chilled, yo," said Coco.

"Let's go check out da competition," said Danielle.

"Yeah, yeah, let's start da show outside right here," said Josephine.

"You are absolutely bugging, girl. Whatcha had for breakfast?" asked Danielle.

"I'm just amp-up, know wha' I'm saying?" Josephine swung around and hopped up on the hood of a parked car. She made a couple of ballerina twirls and jumped on another unfortunate car.

"Yeah, I feel lifted too, yo" said Coco. Coco jumped forward and bounded onto the hood of a third car. She sang loudly. Noise erupted from several car alarms. Danielle joined in. She leapt from hood to hood, setting off more alarms. The noise caught the attention of the parking attendant in his booth.

"Hey," he shouted, peering out of his small window. Then he made his way toward the girls, still dancing on cars, singing a repertoire that ranged from Diana Ross through Grace Jones.

"Get your jail-bait assess outta here," yelled the attendant.

The girls jumped to the pavement. "It's show time," they announced and dashed for the club. There, they quickly sought refuge in the restroom. But the attendant anticipated that. He and two security guards waited outside the restroom. The girls were resourceful, though. They emerged at staggered intervals. Coco, in an Afro wig and make-up, greeted Josephine, also disguised in a blond wig. They watched the three men stare in lustful wonderment at Danielle.

"Yo, we should sit up front," said Josephine.

"We go on in one hour, right?" asked Danielle.

"C'mon, we could see much better over there," said Josephine.

"Unh-uh, it's much better over here," argued Danielle.

"Fuck it. Let's just sit, yo," said Coco, finally settling things.

They enjoyed the other performers and applauded each act. Then they were introduced.

Da Crew came together onstage. Coco wore an Afro and Danielle and Josephine were in blond wigs. The ensemble was complete with bright colored halters and tight denim shorts. The stage came alive as the girls rocked their entrance.

"Let's treat this like warm-ups," said Danielle, goofing on stage.

"Ya mean sorta laid back?" asked Josephine.

"Yeah, yeah, y'know."

"Ladies and gentlemen, get ready. That's your cue girls. Are you with me?" asked the emcee. The girls flashed thumbs-up.

"And now, for our next competitors. Ladies and Gentlemen, get ready for Da Crew."

Da Crew attacked the stage in a frenzy. The baseline carried the chant, "Knock ya out."

"Take it easy," said Danielle.

"Fuck that. Let's wreck, yo."

The baseline dropped and Danielle moaned a Diana Ross classic, "Touch Me in the Morning." Danielle's a cappella chant reached a crescendo and another baseline riff brought Coco's raw rap to the forefront. With both hands holding the mike, she dazed the small audience. Josephine and Danielle made dance moves that astonished the crowd and dazzled the judges. Da Crew was destined for the finals. Busta and Eric viewed the girls' performance on a video screen in Busta's comfortable office, sipping champagne at the bar.

"Those girls are real good. You should bring 'em out," said Busta.

Eric smiled, his eyes still on the video. He arose and looked out at the audience of judges and performers. Now he got a true sense that Da Crew could perform well. But this is an amateur show, he thought. *Did they have the discipline to take it to the next level?*

"I could work with them." The words tumbled out of Eric Ascot's mouth, testimony to the girls' performance.

Out in the large room, Da Crew bowed amid cheering, each with a smile of accomplishment. Then they were off the stage.

"Damn, I got da munchies, y'all," said Josephine.

"Yeah let's go get sump'n to eat, yo," said Coco. She lit a cigarette.

A few minutes later, they were in a diner, enjoying spicy Buffalo wings between long gulps of soda. They laughed and smoked.

"Hey, thanks to reversible jackets and wigs we were able to perform in one piece," said Josephine.

"Word," Coco agreed.

"Just think about it. By the end of the night, a new star will be born," said Danielle.

"What, you've been pregnant this whole time?" asked Josephine.

"Stop bugging, girl. I'm talking about us. Da Crew. We're gonna get ours."

"Here, here," said Coco, finishing her soda. She lit another cigarette. Her mother's plight flashed through her mind. She smiled at the girls as a couple of boys waved and whistled.

"There they go, like packs of dogs looking to bone something," said Josephine. The girls laughed. They saw two cops tell the boys to move on.

"That's right, arrest 'em, officer," the girls yelled from the diner and laughed. Neither the police nor the boys heard.

"Yo, tonight let's rip up da stage," said Josephine.

"I think we could win it all. It's our chance at the big time. To the top," said Danielle.

"Yeah, yeah. I wouldn't be down otherwise, yo," said Coco.

The girls paid the tab and began the walk back to the club. They shared a cigarette as they envisioned victory. There were more cars in the parking lot now, more guests for the festivities. The moment they had been looking forward to moved closer.

"Yo, I'm telling you. Can't nobody stop us but us, so let's do this right, ah'ight, yo?"

"Amen. I'm feeling it!" said Josephine.

"Yeah, yeah, this is the big pot of gold. We've truly got to believe in ourselves. We know what we want, right?" said Danielle.

"Yeah," shouted the girls. They laughed, already

triumphant.

"Well, let's go take it," said Danielle. They formed a circle, exchanging high-fives.

The girls saw the trio approach: Lil' Long, Vulcha and a beautiful, statuesque woman. Kamilla's strapless suede dress made even Danielle breathless. Vulcha held her at his side like a prize. It was obvious from her body language that she didn't want to be with him, or perhaps to be here. Perhaps this scene was not sophisticated enough? Da Crew remained in their circle. The trio was standing next to them.

"Hey, Coco, Danielle and Jo, what're y'all doing out here? Flipping, smoking that weed? Try some o' this. This da shizit," said Lil' Long. He offered a rolled cigarette.

"Go ahead, spark it," said Danielle.

"Oh, yeah. You know Vulcha, and that's his new thing, know wha' I'm saying?"

"Hi. I'm Kamilla."

"I'm Jo."

"I'm Coco."

"Hi. Did you take classes at the Ninety-second Street Y? No, no, your face ... Well, hi, I'm Danielle."

"Your face seems a bit familiar. Sixteenth Street dance classes?"

"Yeah, that's it. You taught there?" asked Danielle, elated.

"Well, I was a student. Not for long." Kamilla's voice faded. She seemed uncomfortable.

"Here you go," said Lil' Long, passing the joint to Danielle. She puffed and passed it to Josephine, who choked and quickly passed it to Coco. Coco declined and the joint found its way to Vulcha.

"What will y'all be doing after you win?" The question hung momentarily in the air.

"Oh, it's open," said Danielle.

"Well, why don't y'all hang wit' us. Let me show y'all a mackadacious time," said Lil' Long. He winked at Danielle.

"Maybe," answered Josephine.

"That's peace," said Lil' Long. He pulled Danielle away from the group and spoke to her one-on-one. She returned to the girls.

"Who he think he be, trying to be on some kinda smooth talk?" asked Danielle.

"Why don't y'all chill wit' me so I can show y'all a mackadacious time? Mackadacious! Lil' Long can't even spell Mack," said Josephine. The girls giggled.

"Now he's macking, yo."

"Look at them wit' that big, shapely woman. Who did they jack for her?" asked Josephine.

"Let's go get ready to tear this shit up, yo."

"Yeah. Do what we came here for," said the lively Josephine.

The girls walked into the club. Guests filled most of the seats now. Lil' Long and his party sat next to the stage. The beautiful Kamilla showcased like a captured bird. Da Crew went backstage and took their position.

"Yo, that's one of da Chop Shop Crew. That's Wise. Oh shit, and there goes Silky Black," said Josephine.

"Shush," cautioned Coco and Danielle.

"Stop acting all bugged out," said Danielle. "You've been going all day. It's irritating."

"Ah'ight, yo. Chop Shop niggas getting ready to ketch wreck," said Coco.

"Yo, they da bomb," said Josephine, high-fiving both Danielle and Coco. The emcee's voice came through clearly and sent chills down the girls' spines.

"From da B.X., Edenwald, here are Da Chop Shop Crew. Ladies and Gentlemen, put your hands together and let's turn da party out."

The walls shook with the reverberating bass. As the quartet took the stage, sending the club wild, club-goers stood and screamed. Silky Black rolled with the crew from B.X.

"If you want some, step up an' get some now. If you want some..." went the hook. The audience participated unselfishly. The Chop Shop Crew was in charge. No one came close.

"Yo, they are *so* nasty," said Danielle.

"We got to rock shit out like them. They ain't front'n," said Josephine.

Coco stared intently as the performers stole the audience's soul and kept it throughout every song. They forced the audience to participate until they gave in to the tempestuous sin and lost their souls altogether. At the close of their performance, the Chop Shop Crew walked away with more hearts and more fans. The coup was complete.

Who could follow that? wondered Coco.

"Them niggas rocked this shit, yo," she said.

"They coming on later, at the end," cried Josephine.

As the group emerged from the stage, Silky Black wished all the competitors luck.

"You notice he was smiling when he looked at us?" asked Danielle.

"Niggas feel da real when they see it," said Josephine.

"There are about seven songs to go before we're Numero Uno," said Danielle.

"Ah'ight, so let's sit and chill. Draw on our power," said Josephine.

"You're still bugging, girl. *Stop*," yelled Danielle.

"Yo, yo, y'all chill. Let's sit over here, yo, cuz the both of you's bugging," said Coco, moving clear of the stage. The other girls joined her.

"There's no smoking back here, miss," said a voice. Danielle turned around to attack, but she saw the source of the voice and she smiled, putting the cigarette out.

"No doubt, my nigga. I'll put out for you, Silky," said Danielle and threw him a kiss.

"You've got to take care of your instrument, baby. Knock 'em speechless," said Silk. He watched Danielle's hips as she walked away. "Damn!"

They trembled as each contestant was announced. Even though they'd performed before, they felt butterflies in their stomachs. Their breaths came in short gasps as they watched other acts qualify for the finals. They jumped around together as the emcee began their introduction with short biographies. Then their turn came.

"Here we go, Ladies and Gentlemen. Our final finalists for you are Da Crew."

They ran to the center of the stage and were met by the lights. There they stayed, marking their territory like cats, making it difficult for anyone else to follow. Danielle sang and moaned her way into everyone's heart, while Coco rapped soul to go, words flowing from her mouth like no ordinary lead singer. She was vicious in her lyrical assault, took no prisoners. Josephine provided background vocals and hammered out a rap. She made steps that deceived the naked eye.

The audience had been caught napping. They had slept through six lullabies. The seventh rocked them awake. The club kids jumped to their feet, moving with the beat. They clapped their hands, even while they sought refuge from the heat of Da Crew. But there was no shelter from this storm. Coco shouted into the microphone.

"An old lady told me to knock out da competition, leave 'em dead, blood oozing from their fucking heads, rolling off with da lyrics. I kick like Bruce. My vocabulary is like a fist of fury when I come to say me an' Da Crew ain't fucking here to play. Tell you something. All y'all want mo'? Well, let me give ya Jo." And so it went, big with a pop for Da Crew. They renewed the onslaught of the Chop Shop Crew, whose members took notice and began discussing the girls' performance.

"Yo, dem honeys could open for us."

"No question, they could do a li'l sump'n."

"Yo, we should find out who managing them girls. They're nice."

"Muthafucking right."

"An' they got all those moves, too."

Upstairs in a booth, watching the video re-play was Busta, Eric Ascot, Sophia and Deedee. They watched Da Crew, re-run after re-run.

"They were without question the best," said Eric.

"I told ya they're butters," said Busta. The judges are gonna have to give those six other acts honorable mentions or something. Let me go see how they're doing. C'mon, maybe I could get ya rocking on da mike or doing a li'l sump'n on da turntables."

"Don't think so. My days like that are over, B.," said Eric.

An elevator took them down to where the finalists waited nervously. Deedee walked to Da Crew and hugged the girls. Eric, Busta and Sophia shook each finalist's hand, wishing all good luck.

Josephine noticed the gesture. "Everyone is so cool tonight," she said. "I'm so tired, but it feels great, like this should go on forever. This is really cool." The four girls continued hugging. Eric and Busta kissed each girl on the cheek.

"You were the best. Your show was great," said Eric.

"Yeah, you were the best," said Busta. "I can't dispute da truth."

Deedee and Sophia chatted with Da Crew. Eric and Busta wandered off to meet the other guests and judges.

"I'm saying, yeah, I would love to work with them," said Eric.

"Yeah, well then that's it. You know they won. You've seen the response. Let's check what the judges say," said Busta. There was a burst of music, then the boom of the emcee's voice.

"We've got Eric Ascot in da house tonight."

"And we've got his niece, Deedee," said Deedee.

"And don't forget his woman, cuz she is up in da house, too, y-o-o." Sophia had caught the mood. Da Crew laughed along. Even Coco chuckled.

The girls began pacing around, forming their usual circle, accompanied now by Deedee and Sophia.

"Wonder what's taking so long, yo?"

"Yeah, it was only seven acts to choose from."

"M-m-m, I don't like all this waiting around. For what?"

Coco lit another cigarette and sat on the floor. The wall supported her back. She seemed tired. Deedee noticed and went off to get two sodas. She sat next to Coco and gave her one. The pair watched Josephine and Danielle, who were roaming the club, attracting males.

"Ya know who we haven't seen in a minute?" asked Josephine.

"I knew you would be bringing that shit up again. That's just like you, Ms. Nosy Josephine..." said Danielle.

"But I'm right."

"Yeah. Yep, you're dead on the money. Anyway, I know that nigga wouldn't dare face up."

"You wanna make another bet?"

"What?"

"Look who's walking over."

"What da fuck! He's a bold muthafucker," said Danielle. Cory approached them. Josephine looked on with keen interest.

"Hi," said Cory, smiling. He gave Josephine a kiss, hugged Danielle and gave Coco the thumbs-up sign. Coco looked at Deedee, shrugged her shoulders and smiled.

"Aw, y'all are champs. You've got this in a bag," said Deedee.

"Well," said Coco.

"Well, what?" asked Deedee.

"Well, yo, they busted Cory wit' some other bitch in his ride earlier today, an' they claim that he saw them and busted an illegal U, tryin'a duck 'em, yo," said Coco. She inhaled the smoke with confidence.

"Oh no. What a dis," said Deedee.

"Yeah, but let's peep da show, cuz Danielle don't like to be dis, yo." They chuckled, high-fived and fixed their attention on Cory.

"Danielle, we hanging later?" asked Cory.

"I'm talking 'bout today, Cory."

"Today?" asked Cory. Josephine smiled. "Can you excuse us Josephine, uh, please?" asked Cory.

"My friends are not the ones unwelcome around me," said Danielle. Josephine high-fived her. Sophia walked away, both embarrassed and amused.

"I don't know what you're talking about, Danielle."

"You know what Cory? You're fulla shit. I know you had some bicth in your car today. Didn't you?"

"I was moving with different peoples at different times," said Cory.

"Were you riding around with a bitch today, Cory?" insisted Danielle.

"What're you talking about?" said Cory. "Come on, you know I'll never even try to play ya, baby. You're the one and only."

Danielle listened to his excuse. She wanted to believe him. Cory made good use of his opportunity.

"Yeah, and maybe you saw a ride which looked like mine. I wouldn't be dissing you like that! Have I ever?"

She had only known him a few months. *Maybe he's telling the truth.* Danielle looked deep into Cory's eyes. He was standing close and his presence overcame her recollection. She reached out and hugged him. Danielle heard and felt the vibration as Cory's beeper claimed his attention. She hugged him tighter and kissed his mouth.

"Aren't ya gonna answer the call?"

"Yeah, later. Right now it's ... it's not that important."

"Oh, that's how you be ignoring my beeps when you're with her ass?" Danielle asked.

"I don't be ignoring any beeps. Sometimes my beeper be off."

"Well, go answer it," said Danielle. Cory hesitated.

"Go," said Danielle. "It could be important." Danielle turned to Josephine, who was fascinated.

"It's close to that time," said Danielle.

"What time is that?" asked Josephine.

"Oh ..." they high-fived, laughed and yelled.

"The booty-call hour."

"Y'all made up quick-fast, yo," said Coco.

"I mean, I don't know," said Danielle.

"Where'd he go?" asked Deedee.

"To return a call," said Danielle. "And he ignores my beeps."

"Tell him he can use my phone," said Deedee. She pulled out her phone as if it were a dagger and handed it to Danielle.

"Cory," called Danielle, "you can use this phone,

Hon." Danielle shouted.

Cory came back to Danielle and took the phone. He dialed and spoke in hushed tones, then returned the phone.

"Thanks," he smiled.

"...and the *top three* finalists are ..." came the booming voice of the emcee, behind a thunderous drum-roll. Da Crew heard the names of other finalists, then suddenly everyone was kissing and hugging them. The crowd converged on them, mobbing them. Coco spotted Deedee and Danielle hugging. She rushed through the crowd, and past the screaming Josephine, to Deedee.

"Lemme use your phone. I wanna call this old lady to let her know, yo," she said breathlessly.

Deedee hugged her and handed over the phone. Coco who was not familiar with the phone, fumbled with it. She hit the talk button and got an immediate response. A female voice crooned, "Cory, is that you baby? Cory?"

"No this ain't no damn cory bitch," said Coco. She stared at the phone with a cunfused look until Danielle snatched the phone out her hand. The line was dead. Danielle, no stranger to cellular phones, checked the recent call button. Then asked Coco the number she had called. Danielle pressed the send button next to the number Cory had called. A girl's voice answered.

"Cory, you better stop playin' around. I ain't got time for this shit. I can seethis the sam number you just called from."

"This ain't Cory, bitch. He just happened to use my phone to call ya ugly ass."

"Who you calling a 'bitch'? And I am far from ugly."

"All Cory's girls are bitches, and when I finish with your ass you gonna be more than ugly," Danielle said.

"Hey, can I make my call, yo? I mean, I was da one..." said Coco.

"Gotta go, bitch," said Danielle. She pressed the end button and handed the phone to Coco. She strode over to Cory, who was unaware of what had occurred. Danielle delivered a stinging slap to his cheek, kissed him and walked away. Cory was stunned. He lunged after her. Vulcha stood in his way and Lil' Long escorted Danielle to their table.

"Go home, big boy," warned Vulcha, "Things could get crazy up in here." Cory saw Lil' Long hug Danielle, pulling her body against his. He turned and walked away, angry.

"From the frying pan into da fire," said Josephine, showing open palms. Coco slapped her hand. Together, they watched the Chop Shop Crew raid the stage and charge the atmosphere with their hyper rap blast. The audience jumped up in delight and stayed on its feet throughout the verbal assault.

****

"Yeah, I love me some Alize," said Danielle as she sipped the drink. She was with Lil' Long, Kamilla and Vulcha in a booth at the club Kazabo, expensive and fast.

"A little too sweet for my palate," said Kamilla, with a smile for Danielle. "But you probably need it to soften up your throat. I mean, y'all were doing that rapping and singing and dancing."

"It's a lot, but we really rehearsed our butts off," said Danielle.

"Yep, I know. I remember how those can get," said Kamilla.

"Remember, right? Rehearsals, sometimes they pay off," said Danielle. Kamilla now appeared calmer. The two beautiful ladies laughed together. Lil' Long and Vulcha looked on contented as they sipped gin and juice.

"I'ma hit that bitch wit' this thug-passion dick." Lil' Long leered at Vulcha. The two laughed loudly and raised their glasses in a toast.

Meanwhile, Coco, Josephine, Deedee, Sophia and Eric sat in a restaurant and feasted on a late supper. Busta stood and raised his glass.

"To Da Crew, who ran right through the competition," said Busta, "and now they're on to the bigger and better."

"Yeah, yeah," shouted Deedee and Sophia. Eric applauded.

"Well, I'm certainly looking forward to working with these talented young ladies. I think they have something," said Eric, drinking from his glass.

"Well, I think I speak for the whole group when I say thanks. And we're looking forward to working with you," said Josephine. Coco nodded.

The alliance had been made, Da Crew had achieved the attention it craved. Coco, Josephine and Danielle seemed destined to succeed. They were about to sign with a famous producer. It was a dream finally realized. Coco and Josephine hugged while the others cheered.

"Danielle would have eaten this shit up," said Josephine.

"I know what ya mean," Coco smiled.

"Yo, but we in deh," they both said and laughed.

****

Vulcha paid the handsome tab, and when Kamilla and Danielle returned from the restroom, they left. Lil' Long and Vulcha walked in the rear.

"Damn, damn, double damn!" said Lil' Long. He stared forward at Kamilla and Danielle's backsides.

"They got that shit goin' on in a ruff way," said Vulcha.

"Yo, nigga, I'm fucking that bitch raw," said Lil' Long.

Vulcha and Kamilla sat in the front seat of the Jeep and drank champagne. In the back, Danielle allowed Lil' Long's groping hands to roam her body.

"You want this, don't you?" she asked, teasing. They kissed, his tongue licking her throat. They drank more champagne and Danielle loosened up quickly. Before she knew it, she was on the hood of the Jeep, dancing and singing wildly.

Cory had been following them since they left Kazabo. With a forty-ounce beer in his hand, he stood in the night air, leaning against the parked car. He watched as Danielle performed. She looked down and saw him.

"What are you doing here?"

"Yo, boo, get down off the hood and let's go," said Cory.

"Go? Go where?"

"I gotta talk to ya." Cory's tone was harsh.

Lil' Long stepped out of the Jeep. He walked away and showered the side of the road. He turned to Cory, still holding his appendage.

"Big man, why d'ya wanna disturb da funky performance?" He stowed his penis and tugged at his zipper.

"Yeah, da funky show," said Danielle.

"Let's go. You're drunk," said Cory.

"This is da way ya like me? All gassed-up and ready to roll?" Danielle was slurring her words now. She jumped, falling against Cory, and he held her. Lil' Long moved toward them. Cory swung the bottle and smashed it against Lil' Long's head. The blow opened a gash under his hairline. Lil' Long winced. Vulcha leaped out the Jeep, gun ready. Lil' Long held up a hand to stop him.

"You're ah'ight, son?" asked Vulcha.

"Yeah. Yeah."

Kamilla held Danielle, who was regaining her composure.

"It's like everyone wants to dis me. Know wha' I'm saying?" Lil' Long wiped his forehead. Blood dripped slowly from his brow.

"He didn't mean to do it," said Danielle.

"Bitch, in my quest for immortality, weak niggas must fall."

He pushed the gun in Cory's face and squeezed the trigger. The bullet exploded and wiped Cory's face from his body. Kamilla grabbed the lunging Danielle, preventing her from running to the faceless Cory, now laying in a sea of red on the damp street.

"You killed him," screamed Danielle. "Just like that, you killed him. You're a murderer, a fucking..."

Lil' Long looked at the screaming Danielle, bemused. She was on her knees, face in the asphalt vomiting, her tears rolling.

"Bitch, it was self defense," he said.

"Hey, yo, son, let's be out," said Vulcha. He started the engine.

Kamilla tried to touch her, but Danielle wouldn't let her get close enough. She continued screaming. Lil' Long approached.

"Get away! Get away! You're a murderer," screamed Danielle.

Lil' Long put the weapon to her head. She grabbed the zipper of his jeans and pulled it.

"What da fuck? Ya gone loco, bitch?" Lil' Long tried to evade the grip on his penis. But she had it.

"Let's go back to da ride wit' this, Babe," he said.

"I don't want to go into da ride. I want it here and now," said Danielle, still in tears.

"Yo, Lil' Long, man. Let's be da fuck out," yelled Vulcha.

Lil' Long tore loose from Danielle and grabbed her collar. He pulled her to the Jeep and pushed her inside. Vulcha quickly drove away.

"Yo, nigga, drop us off at the Mo."

"Ah'ight," said Vulcha. He quizzed Lil' Long in the rear-view mirror.

"Nigga got a little insane. You know wha' I'm saying?" said Lil' Long.

"Yeah, yeah. Couldn't unnerstan' da shit ma'self," said Vulcha.

Vulcha stopped at a motel. Lil' Long got a room, and he and Danielle went in. She was barely through the door when she pulled the gun from Lil' Long's waist.

"What'cha do that for, bitch?"

Danielle pointed the gun at his head and moved closer.

"Strip," she ordered. But she had come too close. Lil' Long pounced. He knocked the weapon from her weak grip. She screamed, collapsing into a chair, crying. Lil' Long lit a coolie and offered it. Sniffling, but passive now, Danielle took the cigarette and puffed wildly. She coughed several times as she inhaled. The high calmed her.

Lil' Long had regained control of the situation. He made her dance for him and he gave her another coke and weed cigarette mix. He knew he had her when he ordered her to dance naked and she complied without hesitation.

"Yeah, c'mon bitch. Putty on me. Putty all on pappy," he chanted. Danielle's naked body swirled in motion. Her excitement grew with every move. Finally, fearing explosion, he reached up and grabbed her. He entered her brutally and continued his chant.

"Putty on me, bitch. C'mon, putty on me. C'mon."

Then he exploded in her, raw, just like he had wished. Danielle moaned and twisted. Lil' Long stared. He couldn't read her feelings. She had a crooked smile on her face. Her eyes stared, with no focus. She reached for his penis.

"More, more." Her lips formed the words, but she made no sound. He rolled her over and entered her with anger and pleasure. When he tired, he rolled away, gun at his side.

"I want another coolie. Keep your dick," said Danielle. Lil' Long gave her the coolie and stared.

"Yer ca-ray-zee, bitch," he said, eyes wide. He was tantalized in a way he couldn't believe. He wanted that body He was on her like a wild boar, savagely entering her ass. Then he lay, spent. He drifted into a short, deep sleep. He awoke suddenly.

"Bitch, where are ya?" he yelled. Her clothes were on the floor, but she was gone. He was frantic as he got dressed. His gun was missing.

"Oh, fuck. That bugged-out bitch," he hissed. He grabbed the phone and quickly dialed.

"Vulcha! Come get me, nigga," he yelled. He hung up and ran to the tiny office.

"A dollar twenty for the call," came the greeting. Lil' Long scanned the office for signs of Danielle and gave the attendant the keys and five dollars. He went into the cool evening air in search of Danielle. She could be anywhere, naked, with his loaded gun. Lil' Long heard tires screech behind him. He stepped out of the path and saw Vulcha.

"Muthafucka, learn how to drive."

"Yo, hurry up and get in. What's up?"

"Yo, I don' know. We came here. We fucked. Da bitch bugged out started singing an' actin' wild an' shit. Then we fucked again. Bitch wanted more coolie, so I kept hitting her off. Feel me? Then da bitch bugged out--curled up in a corner an' all. So I took a nap. I thought da bitch finally went out. Woke up, da bitch was gone, an' my muthafucking gun, too."

"Yo...yo, son," said Vulcha. He stomped hard on the brake, barely avoiding another car.

"What da?" said Lil' Long as his head jerked back.

"Yo, it was on da radio. Some unidentified naked bitch blew her fucking brains out."

CHAPTER 22

"What da fuck? You for real?" shouted Lil' Long.

"I'm telling ya, roots. See all da traffic backed up? She was found somewhere round here an' shit," said Vulcha. Lil' Long gazed at the slow-moving traffic.

"Da bitch wuz akkin' up all evening."

"Yep, but ya had to do it, didn't ya?" asked Vulcha.

"What ya tryin' to say? I killed her? Nah, wasn't me. I didn't hit her like that, kid," said Lil' Long.

"Yeah, but ..."

"But what?"

"You wanted to hit that bitch hard. I mean, kapow," said Vulcha. He extended his right fist and laughed.

"Just watch da fuck wha' your ass is doin', nigga, 'fore you cause a accident," said Lil' Long.

"What did you hit her wit'? A drunken dick? A suicide knob? Bitch couldn't stand it. She went crazy. Had to go shoot herself," said Vulcha, belching a violent laugh. "Since you love giving advice, why didn't you try talking da bitch outta killing herself?"

"I'm telling you, kid, I wuz hitting da bitch. Hitting da bitch. An' da bitch got freaky on me, kid. I crashed for awhile. Da bitch was all curled up in a corner, smoking coolies. I woke up. Da bitch an' my gat missing. I'm running all over da fucking place trying to find her. An' now your ass come telling me this bullshit about some naked bitch found shot."

"That's why traffic was backed up, I'm telling you, Star."

The flow of traffic became easy. Vulcha turned for the downtown lanes.

"That's some real crazy shit, Vulcha," said Lil' Long.

"Yeah, hit that bitch. She couldn't stand it. Had to

fucking shoot herself. If it wasn't da dick, then what did ya put in them coolies?"

"Same as always, man: dust and fucking coke. Yo, but I'm telling ya, da bitch wuz cr-cr-cra-zee way before I hit it, kid."

"Yeah, yeah. Seen how da bitch be moanin' an' grindin' on da stage an' shit, Roots."

"I'm telling ya, kid."

"Word," said Vulcha.

"Word up."

"Da bitch wuz one bad, crazy bitch," said Vulcha. Lil' Long joined in chorus at the end. They squirmed wildly and chuckled at the revelation.

"See how she wuz dancing on cars an' shit?"

"Yeah, well, that's da long and short of it."

"Yeah, yeah. Look at honey wit' them lips, in da next car, kid. Over on this side, nigga."

"Oh, oh yeah. Hmm," said Vulcha.

"I would love to put my dick right between your lips. Have a nice day, too." Lil' Long waved and smiled at the woman.

The woman held her gun ready, out of sight. She allowed them to overtake her. Then she waved as they went by.

"Assholes," she muttered. She could hear the music and laughter echoing from the Jeep.

"Bitch," they yelled as Vulcha swerved in front, awkwardly cutting her off and accelerated.

You don't stop. You don't stop. The lyrics blasted in the Jeep.

"I ain't fucking wit' no more dancing ca-razee chicken heads for a while, kid. I'm leaving 'em alone. Might kill a nigga. Crazy bitch!" shouted Lil' Long above the blare of the sound system. Vulcha drove and laughed.

CHAPTER 23

"So, it was all good, huh?" Miss Katie was at her post by the window. "Look at them hustle for their fixes. Man, oh man. Well, at least we don't have to worry 'bout where your mother is, huh Coco?"

"Yep, that's right, Miss Katie." Coco joined her at the window. She watched the street people wander about, sharing cigarettes and bottles. Every so often two or three would find their fix and hurriedly depart. "My mother couldn't survive out there," she said. "It'll eat her up, Miss Katie. She's better off staying inside. I mean, she'll die out there."

"Well, we better start working out a strategy to convince her to stay there, Coco."

"Maybe we--I--should just talk to her, y'know?"

"She's been there before, Coco. This isn't her first time. She knows what she's got to do, but that stubborn woman won't do it."

"Maybe she's just scared. People can be scared, right?"

"Yes. I am scared every day, every night. Do you see me put a crack pipe to my lips? People make their own choices. She could do better."

"Well, I'm gonna try an' help her get better. She's my mother."

"I know, Coco. I know, and I'll be your assistant in that matter. I, too, want to see her free and getting her life back on track."

They watched the skirmishes in the street. Members of different crack cliques attacked one another. Coco envisioned her mother in her clique. *What role did she play?* wondered Coco. The scene below brought a surge of anger. Coco clenched her fists tightly as the evils of crack were on display. Her mother played a lead role as she conjured up the possibilities.

"Isn't that one of your friends coming up the block?"

"Yeah. Wow Miss Katie, your eyes be working."

"Open the window, 'cause she won't find you in this mess."

Coco raised the window and yelled to Josephine. "Hey, Jo."

Josephine waved. She seemed anxious.

"Well, invite her up, Coco," said Miss Katie.

"Come on up. Third floor," yelled Coco.

"We're in three-D," yelled Miss Katie.

Josephine ran into the building and up the stairs. Coco met her in the doorway.

"Hi," said Josephine, breathlessly. "Coco, have you heard anything from Danielle? Her mother called me at about twelve today."

"No I haven't, yo."

"Why don't you come inside?" called Miss Katie.

"Oh, oh, I'm sorry," said Coco. "Miss Katie, this is Josephine, a member of Da Crew and a good friend."

"You're prettier in person. Coco showed me the group's pictures. Nice to meet you," said Miss Katie. "You were saying someone is missing?"

"Yeah, ah, Danielle. Another member of Da Crew. Well, her mother is worried."

Coco grabbed her jacket. She and Josephine were quickly out the door and racing out of the building. They ran down the block.

"Be careful," called Miss Katie from the window.

The girls waved back. They hailed a cab, which stopped.

"Where we going?"

"Well, let's go to Cory, see if he's seen her. Maybe--"

"Cory? Where does he live, yo?"

"Don't worry, I've got his address."

"Are you girls getting in or what?" asked the cab driver. They got in and Josephine gave him Cory's address. There was little talk during the twenty minute ride to Cory's house. The girls jumped out of the cab and ran into the house. The driver pursued them.

"Fucking pay the fare," he yelled. He wasn't worried; there were two police cars outside the house.

A few minutes later, Josephine ran out of the house, screaming. The cabby was unimpressed.

"My fare, Miss," he said. Then he saw the policemen approached, talking to Coco.

"She--They haven't paid their fare," he yelled.

"We're trying to conduct an investigation."

"But, but, they haven't paid."

Josephine sat on the curb. She sobbed deep and loud. Coco shook her head in disbelief. The cab driver shouted for his fare. Altogether, it was noisy.

"Hey, hey," said the police sergeant. "How much is the fare?"

"Five dollars."

"Five dollars?"

"Yes, five."

"Here," said the officer. "Now get out of here."

"What's going on? What, are they in trouble?" asked the driver.

"Get out of here before I give you a summons," barked the officer. The driver scampered to his cab and drove off.

"My name is Sergeant Wilder. If you girls remember anything, please feel free to call. Call collect, if necessary. Someone was brutally murdered last night. It could've happened to any of you."

"Ah'ight. Yeah, yeah, yo."

"His girlfriend is missing. I mean, they didn't leave at the same time. But you know, they used to get together, an' they sorta had a fight," said Josephine.

"A fight?" asked the officer. "What type?"

"No, I'm not talkin' like that. Y'know, they just weren't speaking to each other anymore. Not a physical fight."

Another officer joined them. "Hey, Sarge, their stories

checked out. Danielle, that's his girlfriend's name, is missing. According to witnesses they did have a lover's tiff but that amounts to nothing."

"Let me determine if that's nothing. Everything counts right now."

"Okay, they didn't leave at the same time. But they were seen arguing before he left."

"Who did your friend leave the club with?" asked the sergeant.

The other policemen got into a patrol car and spoke on the radio. Josephine and Coco faced the sergeant.

"Who did your friend leave the club with? Who?" The sergeant's question took on a new urgency. The officer terminated his call and approached.

"Hey, Sarge, I think you may wanna hear this," he said. The sergeant went to the car, picked up the microphone and spoke, then he listened to the radio. He returned slowly to the girls, a troubled look on his face. Josephine trembled. She reached out for Coco's hand. They waited fearfully.

"I don't feel well," said Josephine. Coco lit a cigarette.

"Okay," said the sergeant. This is not a game. If you're withholding information we'll find out. We're taking both of you in for questioning. And put that damn cigarette out." He rushed Coco and Josephine into the backseat of the patrol car.

"What da fuck is going down?" asked Coco.

"Somebody tell us sump'n. I want to talk to my parents," said Josephine.

"Your parents were already notified. They will meet us at the precinct.

The policemen got in the car and drove away, siren wailing, lights flashing. The car turned the corner violently and screeched to a halt at the precinct. The officers hustled them in the building and up the stairs to face two men in suits.

"Have a seat," said one of the men. They all sat. Coco and Josephine were close together, facing a detective over a battered desk.

"May I smoke?" asked Coco. She placed a cigarette in her mouth, looking at no one particularly.

"Sure you can. I'm Detective Carter and this is my partner, Detective Sazlowski. Did anyone tell you why you were being brought here?"

"Yeah, they told us to answer more questions," said Josephine.

"We already told 'em everything," said Coco, with a stream of smoke.

The detectives exchanged looks. Then Carter pulled an envelope from his breast pocket. He spread the contents on the table; black and white photographs.

"You told the officers that your friend was missing," said Detective Carter. Coco and Josephine looked down at the pictures. They saw it was a girl, naked and horribly dead.

"I feel faint," said Josephine.

"Get her some water, Saz. Are you okay?" Carter asked Coco. She was scrabbling through the pictures. Josephine rose and drank readily from the paper cup.

"Let me help you," said Carter. He turned the pictures so the girls could easily see them. "Did you know this person?" Josephine examined a picture closely. She saw that half of Danielle's face was gone. Her tattoo was visible. Josephine started to sit down, but missed the chair. She fell to the floor.

"Oh, my God. Oh, my God. It's not--it couldn't be," she said. She lay silent. Carter knelt, cradling her head in his arms. He held a white tab of smelling salt to her nose and squeezed it.

Coco selected a photograph and scrutinized it. The tattoo was Danielle's. All three had had hearts tattooed on their breasts, as tokens of friendship. Now she saw that the face in the picture was a distorted likeness of Danielle. Coco clutched her throat and lay the picture down. She shut her eyes and felt the swirling as her mind spun, rewinding memories of Danielle. The rush of her retrospection hurled Coco into vertigo. She grabbed the table to balance herself.

"Here, drink this," said Sazlowski. He handed Coco a paper cup. She gulped the fluid. He handed a second cup to Carter, still tending to Josephine. Coco breathed hard and lit another cigarette.

"I guess you guys know the person in the photo. She's been Jane Doe to us. Who is she to you?" asked Sazlowski.

"She was a friend," said Coco.

"Her name's Danielle Richards. She's..." Josephine sobbed uncontrollably. She could not continue. She grabbed her face and screamed. Her tears brought Carter back to his knees as he offered her more water.

"I'm sorry, Miss," he said.

"She's done nothing at all, 'cept hung wit' assholes," said Coco.

"Can you identify these assholes?" asked Sazlowski.

"Yeah, yeah, of course." Coco sat at the table and sifted through the pictures. Tears stung her eyes and splattered the photographs. Sazlowski went out and returned with what appeared to be two photo albums. He pulled up a chair and sat next to Coco.

"Look at these photos. Maybe your friend's killer left the club with her."

"I don't need pictures. She left the club with Lil' Long and his man Vulcha," said Coco. Tears ran into the creases at the corners of her mouth. She wiped her eyes with the back of her hands. She watched Detective Carter help Josephine from the room.

"I'm gonna check on my parents. To see where they are," said Josephine, looking forlornly back at Coco.

Sazlowski flipped through the pages of mug shots. He stopped searching and showed Coco two pictures. The first was captioned Michael Lowe, a.k.a. Lil' Long. The next was tagged Yves Velucien, a.k.a. Vulcha.

"Are these the men your friend Danielle left the club with?" Sazlowski pointed to the pictures.

"Yes, that's them," said Coco, meek now.

"Is this all you know about it?" The detective

pounced on Coco's weakness.

"Yeah, yeah. That's it," she answered, robot-like. She stared silently at the pictures, searching for answers. Sazlowski studied her expression for a few minutes.

"If you think of anything else, here's my card. Give me a call."

"Yeah, uh-huh, sure."

"I'll be right back," said Sazlowski. He retrieved the pictures of Danielle and closed the book of mug shots. "If you wanna call anyone, you can use the phone over there."

He shut the door behind him. Coco was alone. She looked around the empty room, trying to blot out the gruesome pictures that had lay on this desk. Danielle's face was etched in her mind. Coco rose and wiped her eyes. She heard footsteps. The door swung open. The detectives returned.

"You're free to leave any time. That is unless you've got something else you'ld like to share."

Coco walked past Josephine and her folks. They all wept. They looked at Coco as if she had done something wrong. Coco did not know what to say. She waved as she passed them and went out the front door.

The air struck her face and she swabbed at renewed tears. Coco struggled against the wind, halting to smoke cigarettes. She blew smoke into the face of dusk as thoughts of Da Crew crept into her daze. *Danielle had been alright*, thought Coco, waiting at a bus stop. *She was a bitch sometimes, but isn't everyone, one time or another? What had happened after she left the club with those thugs? Those muthafucking fake ass hoods* She started to board the bus.

"No smoking," said the driver. "Please get off, Miss."

She stepped off and threw the cigarette to the ground. The driver closed the door and drove away.

"Fuck you, too," yelled Coco, her middle finger raised at the departing bus. She cried again and resumed walking.

This is better, anyway. At least no one will stare an' fucking try to be nosy," she told herself. Coco set a steady pace, crying and walking, then settled into her bop when she neared the hospital.

She signed the visitor's log and went up to her mother's room. Mrs. Harvey sat on the edge of the bed, staring at the wall. Coco knocked.

"Come in." Mrs. Harvey was happy to see her.

"Coco, come in, come in. Come give Mommy a hug," she said, arms open. Coco raced forward and fell into her sobered mother's arms. They hugged and cried together.

CHAPTER 24

"Oh, Mommy, you're looking good. Real good."

"Well, they've certainly kept me ."

"Really, you weren't looking this good. I mean you...I was really scared. Please, no more, no more. Promise me."

"Now Coco, you know I've learned my lesson. I'm not gonna do that shit no more."

"Mommy, you said that before. I mean..."

"You sound just like that nosy Miss Katie."

"Mommy, Miss Katie has nothing to do wit' this. It's between us, you an' me got to work it out. I wanna support you."

"Support me with what? How an' what are you gonna support me wit', huh?"

"I'll be there for you. You won't need drugs, Mommy."

"Listen, girl, you don't know what'cha talking 'bout. Sometimes you start out slow an' suddenly crack takes over your mind and body. You *become* cracked, smoked. I know I'm not gonna let it beat me. I'm gonna get over it like I got over everything else. You know that my mother put me out when I was pregnant. I was sixteen years old, pregnant and it was cold. Your father took me to his mother and lied to her. He told her we were married and that I was eighteen. One night she caught a heart attack and died. Your father was nowhere to be found. Never came back. Friends told me he went down south. He left me with a whole lot of bills and you."

"Ma, he never really married you?"

"Getting someone pregnant don't mean you're married."

"I always thought you were..." Coco's voice trailed off. She stared at her mother and rekindled the same dreaded thoughts of her friend's death. Tears came.

"That's why I know you're so hard on yourself. You probably blame yourself for him leaving. You think you have to prove sump'n. You ain't got to. You're gonna survive like I'm gonna survive. This is just sump'n else I've gotta learn to deal wit', that's all."

"Mommy, I know you can do it. You can survive without cocaine, without crack..."

"I know. I've gotta give up drinking. I hate the running here and there for treatment. Staying all cooped up in ma own place, scared as hell. For what? All that has got to change."

"Only you can do it, Mommy."

"I will. I know I don't need any more of that. I can do it on my own. I'll do better. I ain't gotta stay locked up to do it, though."

Coco stared at her mother and listened intently as she mumbled the words she thought Coco wanted to hear.

"Mommy, I love you, and I don't want to see you down like this. But staying inside is the best thing. Look, you're even looking a lot better already. Everyone thinks you should stay inside an' get the treatment. I mean, I could stay with Miss Katie. There wouldn't be any problems, you know. I mean, it'll be tough sometimes."

"Tough? What you know 'bout tough?"

"I know, Mom. Believe that. Well, at least continue the treatment. See how good you're looking already? And it hasn't been that long. In like a month..."

"A month? Girl, you're bugging out. I'll think about it, okay? Ah'ight. How's life treating you?"

"It's kinda hectic, Mommy, but I'm surviving."

"I know you are, baby girl. I'll survive, too. If I could have a lil' nip of sump'n..."

"Mommy! See, you can't even think of nothing else but to get high or drunk."

"Who's talking 'bout getting high or drunk? All I'm saying is, sneak me a little bottle of sump'n. I'll use it at my discretion."

"Mommy, I..." A knock at the door interrupted them.

"Hi, excuse, me but I want you to know that there is

a meeting in ten minutes, okay."

Coco watched her mother straighten the linen on the single bed.

"Things look like they could work out at Miss Katie's. I don't have to ask. She's been here to see me. Tell her I really appreciate all of her help."

"She knows, Mommy."

"Well, tell her anyway."

"Okay, okay. I will."

"I'm sure you will."

"Mommy, I ..." Coco faced her mother. There was still so much to say. They looked at each other's faces, smiling for a second. Reaching out at the same instant, mother and daughter hugged.

"You're just a rambling, singin', spittin' resemblance of your father," said Mrs. Harvey. Tears fell quickly from her clouded eyes. Coco held her tightly.

"Mommy, another person I cared about was killed," she said. "I can't ..." She was surprised that the words slipped out, "afford to lose you."

"Who? Who got killed now?"

"Danielle," Coco's voice cracked with emotion. Mrs. Harvey held her daughter's heavy shoulders and she cried, too.

"Who? Wha' happened, Coco? Gunfight? She got shot at a damn rap show? Coco, that's the reason I don't want you involved in too much of da damn street's shit."

"Ma," gasped Coco, "nobody knows what happened, ah'ight? She didn't get shot at a rap show, so please save it. She went hanging out wit' these imitation hoods and next thing she's missing. We thought she wuz at...we thought she with a friend of hers. When we got there, we found the cops. They said she was shot point-blank in the head. Then they took us to da precinct and showed us these pictures of her."

"Coco, see, I don't want you to be running wit' them wild-ass girls, Da Crews or whatever, 'cause they gonna get you hurt, killed. That's why you want me to stay in, so you could be wild."

"That's not it. You're just better off on the inside. Anyway, one ain't really got nothing to do with the other. I mean..."

"You mean, you mean, you mean. Listen, you better start paying attention to what's popping off around you before you wind up shot or killed. See, this is just the thing."

"Ma, I told you she was hanging wit' these fake-ass gangstas."

"Excuse me, young lady. Just watch your mouth. You ain't talking to your buddies on the damn street."

"Sorry, but you keep going on about..."

"I know wha' I'm saying. People dropping around you like flies. What makes you think you're so special? Now that girl Danielle, wasn't she part of the group from your school?"

"Yeah."

"Well, just imagine. Her parents, they probably tried to talk to her before, but no. Young people, they know what's right cause they've been parents before."

"Look, Mommy. You're gonna be late for your meeting."

"I know there was another reason for all this staying inside shit. But I'm gonna be out watching what you're doing."

"Ma, I'll be back to see you, cause you're bugging."

"Yeah, I'm bugging. Right. We'll see."

"I don't mean it that way. All I'm saying is, nobody knows for sure, ah'ight?"

"Well I suggest you start taking shit a little more serious, Miss Coco. Everything happening to everyone else and not to Coco is not the way to look at things."

"Okay already, Mommy. Don't beat me over the head wit' that."

"And I'll be sure to let Miss Katie know, so she can keep tighter control. She'll love that part."

"Yeah Mommy, sure, ah'ight."

"What if..."

"Mommy, you're gonna be late for your meeting. I'll come and see you again. Take care of yourself and think about staying for the residential treatment."

"Residential program. Yeah, so you can run the streets..."

"I told you it's not like that."

"Alright, alright already. I said I'd think about this residential thing. Now you better get straight home. Do you have carfare?"

"Yeah, Mommy, I do."

"Take care of yourself, Coco," said Mrs. Harvey. She patted her daughter's sagging shoulders.

Coco turned and hugged the recovering shell of her mother.

"Mommy, please..." Coco's last attempt was cut off by another knock.

"Time," said the voice.

"Okay, " called Mrs. Harvey. She squeezed Coco's hand. "I gotta go, baby."

"See ya, Mom." Coco whirled into the hallway. The meeting was at the end of the corridor. Coco had the opportunity to observe a number of recovering addicts. They appeared to gain strength as they got closer to the meeting place.

Outside, Coco eased into her bop again as she made her way down the darkened streets. Danielle stayed on her mind, her death recorded in snapshots. Coco searched for answers. Coco halted as she recognized Rightchus.

"Whuz-zup?" asked Coco. The greeting came like a demand, but she couldn't take it back.

"Chill, Coco, I ain't trying to rush you or nothing. I'm just chilling. You know wha' I'm saying?"

"Yeah, yeah. Sure mo'fucka. You weren't trying to rush me, huh, yo?"

"Nah, Coco, that ain't my style. Coco, I'm sayin', I saw you, so I'm stepping to you like a brother to a sister.

You know wha' I'm saying?"

"A brother, huh? A brother? Then, brother you better start cleaning up your shit. Know wha' I'm saying?"

"I'm a righteous black man," yelled Rightchus, placing the palm of his right hand on his chest.

"Save it, yo. I ain't got time for da B.S.," said Coco. She extended her arm, her palm blocking Rightchus' mug.

"Why you wanna play me like that?"

"Because you're a crackhead. Is that reason enough, yo?" asked Coco as she made a move to leave. "I ain't got time for front'n ass niggas like you. I'm bouncin'."

"Coco, before you step, I got sump'n to say. Hear me out," said Rightchus. Coco hesitated. She saw the plea in Rigtchus' eyes and she waited.

"Ah'ight, yo. Kick da shit. Then step da fuck off."

"Ah'ight. Remember da shootin' a week or so ago?"

"What shooting? Every day people getting' popped, yo."

"Yeah, but I'm saying da shooting wit' Deja and da honey from your buildin'."

"You mean Bebop?"

"Honey wuz in da wrong place at da wrong time. See, them mo'fuckas were out to smoke Deja."

"Whoa! Hold up. Who's them mo'fuckas, yo?"

"Cool. I'ma tell ya soon enough. Someone put out a contract for a hit on Deja. Some shit that he raped a girl an' jacked her ride an' shit. You wuz supposed to be involved an' all."

"Wait up, yo. Deja was killed because he raped a girl?"

"Yeah. Her uncle is, um, what's his name, uh..."

"You mean Eric Ascot?"

"Word, that's da one."

"Wait up. You ain't nothing but a crackhead. Why da fuck should I believe your ass, huh?" Coco thought, *He might be right. Maybe Deja's killing was a hit.* Coco stared at Rightchus and thought about what he had told her.

"I'm sayin', if you don't believe me, check da stats. Check da stats, baby. Someone set up Deja to be killed, 'cause you and I know he didn't rape the girl. Them wuz two niggas sent by the devil."

"You bugging out or what?"

"I'm sayin'."

"I'm saying you da crackhead. Why you wanna stress?"

"Stress? Coco, da muthafucka killed my man, my nigga, my ace boom."

"Yeah, yeah, an' all that. So what? What did you do? Smoke some crack, yo?"

"I'm sayin' them niggas. Them's da one responsible for your friend's death. An' you know they hit that Spanish girl an' da big dude she was wit'. Them's Lil' Long an' Vulcha. Coco, it's gonna take a nation to hold them mo'fuckas back."

"You're sayin' that Lil' Long wit' da 'fro and that guy wit' da trunk-of-funk Jeep, always partyin', they been shooting up da town like that, yo? Why don't you go to the cops, then?"

"C'mon! An' sell da brothers out like that? Be real, Coco. I'd rather see shit stay da same. Gotta stay real. Know wha' I'm sayin'?"

"So why you choose to stop me an' try to feed all this bullshit to my ass, huh?"

"Yo, Coco, listen up. I ain't tryin'a run a game on you or nothing, but them niggas get picked up by the cops and come back wit' bags of muthafucking dough. I'm talkin' G's an' triple G's. Now, is them niggas workin' fo' da cops, or what? I'm serious!" yelled Rightchus. Coco doubled over in laughter.

"You're saying...ha, ha, ha...Lil' Long and Vulcha, them false hoods, they working for da police? How deep is their cover?" Coco howled. Rightchus stared, amazed at Coco's reaction. She seemed to choke with laughter.

"I know you think I'm only a crackhead, but I'm a street person who has knowledge of what's goin' down an' so on. When you check da stats you'll see. Boom! Rightchus was right. You gonna say, 'yo, Coco, boom.' Can I get five dollars? Yo. Help a brother out. You a top celebrity an' all that."

"Muthafucka, now you clocking my papers, too? How you living? Here's a buck to start the scramble." Coco handed Rightchus a dollar bill. He clasped it in both hands. Rightchus was gone as quickly as he had come. Coco continued her walk home. When she reached the building, Coco stopped and opened the door to her mother's place. She paused and turned on the lights. The one bedroom glowed with a putrid scent. She went to the window and gazed out. Coco saw the street people, once more, scrambling around like laboratory rats.

She wondered if any of them bothered to clean their apartments, or if they even had places to live. She cleaned the dirty kitchen first, and finished in the living room in the wee hours of the morning. She was exhausted. She took a shower and passed out in front of the television.

****

A knock at the door awoke her. She opened the door for Miss Katie.

"Hey, Coco, I heard you coming in last night. What happened? You didn't even stop by."

"I uh..."

"What a neat place. How'd you manage to keep it like this?"

Coco was not prepared for this barrage. She yawned and rubbed her reddened eyes.

"Oh, once you get the hang of it, it's kinda easy to keep it going, you know?"

"It looks real good," said Miss Katie. She walked around the apartment, inspecting like a doting mother.

"I would offer you sump'n to drink, but I haven't gone shopping."

"Oh, don't worry. Stop by when you're dressed, before you go to school. You *are* going to school, right, Coco?"

"Yeah, yeah, sure. I'll stop by, Miss Katie.

"So, will I see you later, Coco?"

"Sure. Okay Miss Katie. I'll see you."

Coco glanced around the apartment proudly. She knew there were still things to do, but right now, she needed an education. Shrugging, she made her way to the bathroom to get ready for school.

Coco walked out to the moist feel of the morning's air. Pausing, she lit a cigarette. She watched as people hustled back and forth through the building, not really going anywhere. Miss Katie, also the keen observer, watched the scene.

At school, people stared at Coco, asking insinuating questions. Teachers offered sympathy in obvious attempts to get the latest nasty rumors about Danielle. Coco searched for Josephine or Deedee, but neither were in school. She spotted the notice of Danielle's death displayed on the same bulletin board with announcements of parties. She left the building feeling disgusted.

Coco wandered through the streets. *Who could be next*, she thought, walking aimlessly. The cigarette dangling from her dried lips made the frown she wore even more pronounced. For the tenth time, she tried to call Josephine from a public phone. She got no answer and slammed the receiver into its cradle. She had left messages earlier, but there were no return calls. She decided not to leave any more messages. *Where was Josephine? Damn! Where are friends when you need them?*

Coco went up on the roof of her building and wept for Danielle and Bebop. Danielle had seemed so happy, Bebop so hopeful. Both happiness and hope were vanquished by the itch on someone's index finger. She remembered the Polaroid shots of Danielle's once vibrant body. They didn't even try to cover her face--or lack of a face. Coco gasped for air. She touched the spot where the fist had struck her a few weeks earlier. *Deedee had also been raped.* These incidents bore new friendships, but there were so many old ones gone forever. Coco rummaged through the pockets of her sagging blue jeans, in search of Deedee's phone number. She found the number and dialed quickly. Deedee answered.

"So how're you handling it?" asked Deedee. The question hung in the air.

"Ah, as best as I can. But you're gonna be at the wake, right, yo?

"Well, we'll...I'll see you there. Take care."

"Okay. Listen, if you feel like talking, feel free."

"Okay, see ya."

"Alright, bye."

Coco wanted to say more, but the words never made it pass the barrier of her throat. She inhaled deeply on her cigarette, filling her mouth with smoke, and blew it into the receiver.

Coco no longer felt alone. Her bop became brisk as she headed to a corner store for cigarettes, gum and a soda. She placed a cigarette to her lips. As she reached for her lighter, someone flicked a light to her cigarette.

"Thanks, yo," said Coco.

"Let me get one o' those stogies, kid," said the intruder.

"Now because you gave me a light, you gonna jack me for a smoke, huh, yo?"

"I'm sorry to hear 'bout Danielle dying, y'know, Coco."

"Yeah, that's peace. Have the stogie."

CHAPTER 25

Eric drove slowly and joined the traffic entering the city. His cellular phone rang.

"Whassup?" It was Busta. *I hope he doesn't want to hang out*, Eric thought. *I've got to pick up my girl.*

"Yeah, so how're you doin', B.?"

"E., we gotta talk."

"Ah'ight. Yeah, let's. When? If it's about Da Crew, I've got 'em booked for two weeks in the studio."

"Nah, nah. That's another story, E. I've gotta talk to you now."

"Now? Busta, I'm on my way to get my girl. We have a date. I've got to check you back on that tip..."

"E., hear me out. We hit da wrong fucking nigga, homey."

"Whoa. What?" stuttered Eric.

He swerved to a stop, almost side-swiping a car.

"Hey, asshole, get da fuck off the phone before it get your ass killed," yelled the other driver.

Eric pulled over to the curb and stopped.

"Meet me uptown at Mr. Gee's, Eric." The click followed.

Eric floored the gas, rejoining the traffic. *What had gone wrong?* he wondered to himself. Deedee said it was Deja. He quickly dialed home. No answer. He checked his watch. It was seven-fifteen. He dialed Sophia's number.

"Hi, Baby..."

"Where are you?" asked Sophia.

"Baby, what time does this thing start?"

"My partnership banquet, which I deserve, starts at eight-thirty, sharp. We should be there by nine, Sugar Plum.

And your niece says 'hi.' And no meetings, Sugar. Are you there?"

"Yeah, I'm here. I've gotta meet with Busta."

"Oh, no. No more auditions." This came out scathingly. Sophia was not holding back. "When you guys get together, it's like you get lost in some type of childhood business and I get left out. No!"

"Listen, Babe, I'll meet you there by nine-thirty at the latest."

"You're only saying that. Eric, your niece would like to speak to you."

" Put her on, Babe... So what's the deal?"

"Don't be trying to play out my good buddy for nobody else, Uncle E. Tonight is her night. Do you follow that, Uncle?"

"Yeah, I do, but where do you get off talking that kinda talk to your uncle? You're supposed to be looking out," said Eric.

"Well, I'm looking out for the best for both of you," said Deedee.

"Appreciate it. Now put your buddy back on. Talk to ya later."

"Listen, Mr. E., be there, okay? I mean it," said Sophia.

"Honey, I'll call if…"

"Don't call. Just be there, Eric... Are you there? Damn, I think I lost him. Well, he knows the place, time, where, how and why." Sophia pressed the end button.

Eric gazed at the flashing low-battery signal. "Shit," he yelled and then concentrated on the traffic. Within minutes he was at Gee's club. He went through the heavy red wooden door, past the beefy security. Inside, Busta beckoned to him. Eric felt a trickle of sweat down his spine. He smiled uneasily and made his way to Busta.

"Hey E., what's up?" Busta gave him a hearty hug and a closed-fist shake.

"What's poppin', Busta? You better cut down on your visits to the kitchen."

"No, see, when I get nervous I eat a whole lot more fried foods. Chicken? Send us a bucket over to the booth, honey." Busta gave the order to a passing waitress.

"A bucket?" echoed Eric.

"Yeah, yeah, man. A mo'fucking bucket. They have some good stuff up in here. Why, you have a problem?" Busta sounded husky, threatening. He continued to sip from a glass of beer. He held his tongue. Eric had to do the talking.

"Okay, okay Busta. What's going on?"

"We buried the wrong man. You know wha' I'm sayin'?" said Busta.

"No, I don't know what you're saying. So please tell me what da fuck you're talking about, Busta."

"I'm talking 'bout that hit, E. We...that guy, Deja. He wasn't da one who raped your niece. He was just a well-connected, small-time drug dealer," said Busta, his voice lowered to a raspy whisper.

The mellow sound of a clarinet, in the form of a jazz riff, came through the speakers. It collided head-on with Busta's heart-stopping message. Eric sat back and glanced around at the other patrons, as if waiting for someone to read him his rights. *Had he done something wrong?* He tugged at his nose, where sweat had suddenly formed. Busta noticed, as did the waitress who brought Busta's chicken.

"May I get you anything else, gentlemen?"

"E., don't sweat that shit. Yeah, couple o' beers and extra napkins. Shit happens daily, man. I mean ..."

"Busta, Deedee was calling this guy's name in her sleep," said Eric. He raised his brows. "She was saying, 'get off me ... get off me ... stay away from me, Deja.' She told me he was trying to rape her again. I'm sure it was this fucking drug-dealing Deja. It had to be him or his peoples. Either way, somebody had to pay."

"E., let me tell you, man. I got da word. I mean..."

"What word, B.?"

"E., I got da fucking word," repeated Busta.

Eric Ascot's attention drifted back to the music piped into the nightclub. He wanted silence. For once, the music haunted him. It sent chills down his back and he broke out in a sweat. Patrons laughed and drank. He thought of his brother. *The police had done nothing.*

"So what?" Eric asked.

"So what?" asked Busta. He was attacking a piece of chicken.

"Well, we got to do da right mo'fucking thing. Know wha' I mean, E.?" asked Busta, still grubbing as if his life depended on every bite.

"What are we gonna do?"

"Well, we gotta break da right mo'fuckas off a piece." Busta waved the chicken leg. "I mean, niggas can't be running free, raping, unsafe sex, spreading all kinda shit. They're out there, E. and your niece might not be their only vick. We got to make those mo'fuckers pay." Busta burped. The music from the club masked the guttural interruption. "Listen E.," he continued. "I'ma show you somebody with the knowledge on all that shit, like, why your niece was raped and all that. He might even tell you who did your brother. Believe it, E., I'm telling you, right now, I could bring him to see ya."

"Are you serious, Busta?"

"Eric, when do you know me to be joking?"

Before Eric could answer, Busta was on his cellular, chicken-stained fingers pressing buttons. Then he yelled into the phone, "Pick up that kid Shorty-Wop. Yeah, yeah, Rightchus, or whatever da fuck he wants to call himself. An' bring him downtown to Mr. Gee's, ah'ight." He clicked off. Busta gave Eric a long look, and ripped into a piece of chicken breast. Eric stared back, lit a cigarette and sipped a beer. He took a deep drag and exhaled to the accompaniment of a jazz riff. Busta finished all the chicken.

"Let's go," Busta finally said as he placed a large bill on the table and rose. Eric rose as if he was about to greet a bad verdict. A decision made by him was set to imprison his mind. His steps came tentatively. Eric felt like he did not want to move, but did anyway. Like a prison guard leading the walk to the chair, Busta led Eric to a parked van. There were two men inside, and the pair joined them.

"Give us a minute," Busta said to the driver. He wandered off to smoke a cigarette.

"Shorty-Wop, this is...," said Busta. The door slammed behind the driver.

"I know who this is, man. You don't have to tell Shorty nada, know wha' I'm sayin'? This da hottest brother out there mixing down R&B tracks, kicking Hip-Hop shit all over da place. Just blowing shit up, know wha' I'm sayin'? Shorty-Wop be keeping up. Know wha' I mean?"

"Yeah, yeah, no doubt about that. But Shorty, I want you to tell him sump'n. Shed some light on da scenario you kicked to me earlier."

"Eric Ascot! You all this an' you all that. Da beats, da drums, da music. That shit is on. An' if you need a new emcee, up an' coming, like maself included...shit, I'll be your man. Not even who... Silky Black...can do it like I can. What! I'm saying I'll rock the mike at the drop of a dime. An' R&B? Yo, yo, yo, that's me, that's me. Sang all the way through high school. Now I'm old school. Shit, but let me do my thing, even R. Kelly be listening. You wanna hear me bust a few rhymes or break it down? R&B style, even Reggae."

"Yeah, yeah," said Busta, calming the hyper Shorty-Wop. "But we wanna hear 'bout that rape thing, ya know wha' I mean?" Busta showed annoyance now.

"Shorty-Wop ain't gonna front. Eric, as God is my witness, da wrong man went down, see? It was these knuckleheads that should be dead an' stinking."

Eric lit another cigarette. He offered one to Shorty-Wop.

"Them niggas kill you at the drop of your jaw. You mouth off to any of them niggas an' that's it. Kapow." Shorty-Wop pointed two fingers. "I can't afford that, Mr. Ascot, you know wha' I'm sayin'? I got a family. Seeds, ya know. So I'ma tell y'all this. Hit me wit' some dough, record contract, whatever. Put me on, 'cuz I'm an aspiring rap star. I know it. I can feel all that."

"Shorty..." said Busta, running out of patience, "just tell us what da fuck you know an' you'll get hit wit' some dough, ah'ight?"

"Eric, your niece was gang-banged by two knuckleheads, Lil' Long and Vulcha. Them's da mo'fuckers. Two, not one," said Shorty- Wop, a.k.a. Rightchus.

Eric cringed. His lips uncurled as he snuffed out the cigarette. He stared at the street character, almost hating him.

"I don't mean to be so blunt, but that's wha' happened. Deja was tryin' to fuck wit' her in da club, but when she and Coco--"

"Coco?" asked Eric.

"Yeah, Coco, da dancer. Now she got a lil' sump'n going on, I'm sorta like her advisor. I be showing her moves that helps her when she be performing, know wha' I'm sayin'. So your niece rolls up wit' Coco and her girls in this bad- ass car...a Mercedes, a black one. With the whole kit, ya know. An' when they went outside, boom! Them niggas gun-butt Coco, knocked her out. Da bitch lay on da street, nose bleeding, swollen up like Santa's reindeer. They took your niece an' da ride. Them mo'fuckers were wrong.

"And they's da ones who hit your brother, know wha' I'm sayin'? He was payin' off someone. He was fucking 'round wit' Xtriggaphan. Fake-ass gangsta rappers, wannabes. Them niggas had beef wit' everybody. They owed Lil' Long dough, see.

"When Lil' Long went to get his dough...boom...he sees your brother wit' them niggas. He and Vulcha start beatin' down the Xtriggaphan niggas. Your brother, may he rest in peace. Your brother steps up to them, an', it's like, don't fuck wit' Lil' Long `n' Vulcha. Your brother did, an' just like that, he was killed. Just like fucking that." Lil' Long snapped his fingers.

"What about the musicians? Xtriggaphan? The drugs? All that shit the police ignored. Why didn't you say anything before?" asked Eric.

"Them niggas, Xtriggaphan, they s'ppose to be out in Cali or Cleveland. Lil' Long hit them niggas wit' some dough. Your brother was strapped and they killed him, right? Nobody cross Lil' Long or Vulcha. They not havin' it. But see, they did ma boo Deja, see, an' that was dead wrong. All he was doin' was a lil' scramblin', try to get a lil' swerve. But them niggas, they ain't no joke. Da police don't even fuck wit' them."

"Ah'ight, ah'ight Shorty-Wop. Hold this." Busta slipped a fifty-dollar bill into Shorty-Wop's hand.

Eric stumbled out of the van. He searched his pocket. He found a cigarette and quickly lit it. He needed satisfaction, but nicotine was not the cure.

"Shit! Fuck it!" He threw the smoke away. "We hired them niggas to..."

"Remember, if anything comes up..." yelled Shorty-Wop from the car as it sped away. Eric waved and dismissed any thoughts of Shorty-Wop, except for his message. He now knew the men who had murdered his brother and raped his niece; father and daughter, victims of the same people. Yet, they still walked around free as the wind.

Anger boiled in Eric Ascot. The sound of retching distracted him as he raised his chin and prepared for some sort of action. He noticed Busta leaning over the curb, vomiting. He rushed over to him.

"You ah'ight, patner?"

"Yeah, I'm ah'ight. Fucking chicken bones." Busta's eyes were teary as he coughed.

"We got to get rid of those mo'fuckers, Busta."

"That's how I feel, too, buddy. I'm wit' you on that."

"How much?"

"I can't say right now, but I know their fucking days are numbered."

"Fuck it. Let's end their shit now," gritted Eric as he hugged Busta's neck. 'I can't believe we paid the motherfucking rapists to kill someone else…"

"Ease up E. Chill, chill. Grab a hold of yourself. Cool out." Busta gingerly removed his neck from Eric's grip. He coughed and spit out a chicken bone.

"Fucking chicken bones. Word is…ugh, ugh," said Busta, holding himself steady, careful not to lean on a still angry Eric Ascot. "Word is Lil' Long and Vulcha or Vulture, or whatever da fuck his name is--them mo'fuckers down wit' da law; some sorta informant-type shit, know wha' I'm sayin', E.? Them mo'fuckers you got to be careful wit'. Da nigga Vulcha used to be down wit' me back in da days, nah mean. I know da motherfucka. It's da Li'l Long, he's a grimy motherfucka. It's gonna take a lotta dough. But they can be reached. They ain't da fucking untouchables, hiding out wit' 'em fucking tin badges."

"Let's do it, Busta. Just set that shit up. Set it up right now," said Eric. He swung his arms, swiping at the air, slapped Busta's chest, then his own. Busta nodded solemnly. Their right hands slammed together. The deal was sealed.

"Where you parked?" Busta asked as they crossed the street to the oversized brown doors of Mr. Gee's, where notoriety was the valid I.D. card. "I'm gonna go back inside for a minute. Chit-chat. How's Sophia?"

"Sophia…Oh, shit, I have to do something with her tonight. She's ah'ight, Busta. Go ahead, B. I've got this thing, some kinda dress-up party to attend. I really just wanna fucking get drunk, just tore up, assed-out, like ol' times and shit."

"Yeah, yeah. I hear you, E. But you got things to deal wit'. I got some business to take care of, myself. We'll do this some other time, know wha' I'm sayin'?"

"Cool. Call me, B. Set it, then call."

"Ah'ight, I'll do that, E. I'll see ya, man."

Eric ran to his car. Busta disappeared through the oversized red doors of the club. He headed straight to the bar. There he ordered a drink and stared ahead as he sipped. He winked at three women close by. Energy seeped into his groin area and alerted his scrotum.

"Ah-h-h," he said. "I'd love to be hittin' those panties tonight."

****

Eric raced home and dialed quickly. Sophia's soft voice answered, "Go ahead and speak."

"Babe, how much time do I have?"

"You're out of time, Mister. If you are not by my side looking sharp in thirty seconds..."

"Seconds? Seconds, babe?"

"Yeah, 'cause that's all the patience I have with your cloak and dagger business. Eric, just be here. Bye-bye."

Eric searched for shoes to match his black, double-breasted tuxedo, and the black bow tie with the stiff white shirt. *Well*, he thought, *if you're gonna be late, you might as well look good.*

Deedee appraised him. "Well, you look really good, but you're late. Sophia's gonna be mad. You'd better get stepping." She walked him to the door.

"Dee," said Eric. He wanted to ask her about the rape. Who was responsible for it and so on. There was never a right time. "Dee."

"Uncle E., is there something wrong? You wanna ask me something? You smell real good."

"Dee, how many guys? One or two?"

"One or two what?" Deedee was surprised by his nervousness, his awkwardness. Then she realized the importance of the question. She blinked, and felt the need to run and hide. Here was Uncle E., dressed his best and asking about the worst night of her life. She raised her head and looked him in the eye.

"If you mean the night I was raped, yeah, it was two. Those bastards will pay." Tears welled in Deedee's eyes. She could say no more. Eric held her close.

The comfort that Deedee found in her uncle's gentle hug was short-lived. The doorbell rang.

"Saved by the bell," said Deedee.

"Yeah. Who is it?" asked Eric.

"It's probably Coco and some other friends. I thought we'd sit around and watch videos. We...Uncle, tomorrow is the wake for Danielle, okay? Please don't forget. Pick me up at the church at fifty-sixth and Park."

"Remind me again."

"I will, I will. Trust me."

Eric met Coco at the door.

"Coco, how are you?"

"I'm cool, Mr. Ascot. Ah, you're looking kinda flava. Hot date?"

"Very hot."

"And very late," Deedee reminded him.

CHAPTER 26

"Hi, Coco. What's up, girl?"

"Whassup, yo? I'm chilling, trying to maintain. Your uncle looking kinda sharp. He's getting married or sump'n?"

"Uncle E. should be at some award banquet with Sophia. You met her before. She's a lawyer an' all. Her firm is throwing this big function tonight. So, did you hear from Josephine?"

"Nope. It's like the girl stepped off to another planet, yo."

"That shit is so fucked up."

"This is a phat crib!"

"Thanks. This is your first time here, right? Let me show you around. You know my uncle bought the two apartments on either side of us and the three apartments below us. And he converted them into this," said Deedee, both arms circling her head.

"That's hot. Oh, see when you got dough you can do anything, yo. Like my place will fit in one of your bathrooms. Can I smoke?"

"Smoke? Smoke what?"

"Cigarette, fool. I'll go outside if I wanna get weeded."

"That's cool. But if it's weed, then we gotta go to the next level. My uncle's in da house studio. It always smells like weed in there. He don't be knowing that I know what weed be smelling like or sump'n. But I swear da downstairs stays lit up," Deedee pointed. "Up here is where the living room area and the den is. And over there are the bedrooms. Mine is to the left."

"This shit is da fattest," said Coco. Her voice rose with her enjoyment. Deedee, too, was delighted. They hadn't seen each other since the night of Danielle's death.

"So shit happens there," said Deedee, pointing to the bathroom.

"Thirsty? We have mad drinks here. What are you drinking?" she asked as they headed for the kitchen.

"Ah, beer?"

"Let me see." She searched the refrigerator. "Beer. Okay, you're on. There's some. I'm having Chivas and Coke," said Deedee.

"Well, don't expect a lecture from me," said Coco. "Just go for yours. Just don't fuck wit' mine."

The girls slapped hands mid-air and Deedee poured her drink after handing Coco a cold glass of beer. They were happy to be in each other's company. Deedee was now feeling much more confident after the brief session with her uncle, culminating with an evening spent with someone she admired. The girls touched glasses. Then they both sipped.

"What else y'all got up here?"

"Just about everything. Wine. Probably champagne in the refrigerator. Just ask."

"Music! Y'all got that new Silky Black joint? Or that new Meff. They kinda hot. Put that on, yo, or that new Fat Joe."

"No doubt we do, and they're all mad flavas."

"I heard nigga, Silky Black might be going solo."

"Nah, he just broke out to make this one album. But he still digging in da crates wit' them Chop Shop niggas." Deedee moved to a panel, pressed a control, and the sound of Silky Black poured through concealed speakers.

"Oh, that shit is dope, yo. Da controls are like that? Where are the speakers?" Coco looked around in wonder.

"This crib is da shits. I've never seen anything like this, not even close."

"Wait. Let's check out da studio."

"You mean we're gonna get weeded?"

"Yeah, you might get a contact high from all that shit circling down in there."

The girls headed down spiral steps. Coco was a little clumsy on the stairs, preoccupied with the reverberating sound of Silky Black. The music got louder as they walked further down. They approached a mirrored wall. Coco peered around.

"Yep, this is the studio my uncle and my father built."

"This shit is all that. Peanut butter in a jar," marveled Coco.

"Wanna go inside?"

"Sure, yo."

Deedee opened the door and they entered. Deedee flicked switches and the lights came on. Coco picked up a microphone.

"One, two. One, two. `N' I say, whatcha gonna do? A one-two, microphone check!" she shouted. "It's phat. It's all this `n' that, yo. Lemme tell you sump'n about this thing." Coco began a lyrical game with the microphone. She turned to Deedee, mesmerized by her action. "Wow, you can make a demo up in this piece. You know how to run all this?"

"Not entirely, but I've been taking notes, mixing beats, sampling--all that kinda stuff. Just trying to learn some stuff."

"Do you have any of your shit, yo?"

"Yeah, I do, but ya know they're not all that high powered flava yet, so..." Deedee smiled nervously. "Well this is the control booth," said Deedee. She noticed Coco turn her attention to the studio's interior. The walls were lined with enough huge tape recorders, equalizers and amplifiers to stock any electronics store. Eric and Deedee's father had built a solid recording studio, and Deedee was a proud tour-guide.

"Yeah, yeah. It's nice," said Deedee, her nervous smile lingering.

Coco gazed and moved, delicately touching pieces of equipment. She rocked her body at different angles to check aspects of each piece. She was like a gardener, tending her plots.

"And that's the recording booth to your left, through the glass," said Deedee. Coco twirled. "That's where you would be toiling at your craft, girl." continued Deedee. She knew she had struck the right chord with Coco. Coco had been through a lot lately and even though Deedee wanted to discuss what Coco had been through, she did not push the issue.

"Yeah, yeah. Got to bust your ass to make it in da biz," Coco tried to sound like an experienced performer. "But it's all good, cause only da real serious mo'fuckas can take it to another level. Know wha' I mean?"

"I know," said Deedee, nodding her head.

"'Cause, like, your uncle, I ain't got to tell you nothing. He's all that. Why? 'Cause he's able to take da biz to that other level, see?" Coco said, raising her right hand to her lips.

"Yeah, yeah," said Deedee, "fire it up."

Coco pulled the long brown tobacco-wrapped joint from her shirt pocket and meticulously smoothed it out with her fingers.

"Lemme get it right," said Coco. She continued the action. Deedee came closer and offered a light.

"No. Oh, no, this is your house. You spark da shit, yo." Deedee tried to light the rolled blunt, but there was no smoke. "No, no, spark the other end."

She made another attempt to light it and the blunt blazed when the flame touched its tip. Deedee pulled harder and the smoke entered her lungs. She passed the blunt to Coco.

"Some good shit," said Coco. She coughed.

"Do you want another drink?" asked Deedee. Coco's coughing had intensified.

"Yeah, most definitely. I can see you wanna get me blow-ass," coughed Coco.

When Deedee headed up the stairs, Coco's mind turned again to the sound equipment. "Wow," said Coco, her thoughts exploding into the syllable. "Wow. Some pops gots it an' somes don't," she remarked. When Deedee returned, she said, "I know this shit cost mad lootchie. I know, I know."

Deedee passed Coco a glass of Harvey's.

"Josephine called a minute ago, left a message on the machine."

"She coming through?"

"Nah, I don't think so." Deedee hesitated.

"Oh, this is da bomb." Coco sipped again and again from the glass, and quickly finished the drink. "Harvey's and weed. That's some killing shit for your ass, I'm sayin'." Coco cleared her throat. Deedee averted her gaze. "Wanna get really booted, yo?" Coco fished in her pockets for something to smoke.

"Ah," breathed Coco as she snatched another 'blunt' from her shirt pocket. In one swift motion, she had the blunt between her lips. Coco made a sucking motion with her mouth and the blunt went ablaze. Deedee stood in awe. She decided to let Coco get high. Then she might open up.

"Yeah, let's get booted, Coco," she said. Her plan took the shape of the lit blunt.

"Pass that shit, girl," Coco demanded.

"You know, you know, it's really funny. I mean, Josephine, she said she..."

"I ain't trying to hear her funny-acting ass. Just puff an' pass da shit."

"Have you spoken to her since ... since the incident?" asked Deedee.

"I tried, yo. Called her house, left messages and all that. She ain't trying to get wit' me, see? Yo, I'm sayin', I've reached out. What da fuck did I do? We used to be girls, like, really down." Coco held up her middle and index fingers together. Deedee misunderstood and handed Coco the blunt.

"Like this," Coco repeated now with the blunt between the fingers. "Yeah, but I'm sayin' when da ship goes down, yo..."

"Yeah, I know what you're sayin'." Deedee took the smoldering weed. "When da ship goes down. But I thought being friends and all, if sump'n goes bad, you know, we would all stick together." Deedee reached for her drink.

"Yeah, I thought da same shit, yo, but it ain't like that. Ya know? I think no matter what group, no matter what field the group belongs to, there is always these external forces pulling it back from fully developing. If that group is ready, da members will come together an' put a check to the negativity." Coco paused. Deedee's face looked as if it were being smacked by the one-two combination of alcohol and marijuana. Coco wondered if Deedee understood anything that she had said.

"You look blow-assed, girl. Fucked up, yo." They both laughed giddily. "But that's da real, you know? People front. They try to make you feel that they wit' you when you know all the time they just wanna bounce, do their own thing. Danielle ... I mean, we had our differences, but we were cool like that. May her soul rest in peace." Coco sipped gently from her glass. Deedee noticed tears coming from Coco's eyes. She felt the sting as her own tears welled.

"It must be this weed," said Deedee, wiping at her eyes.

"It's not only the chronic, yo. You're dealing wit' da real, see wha' I'm saying?"

"What about Josephine? You think she's dealing with what's real?"

"I couldn't answer for her, Dee. She would have to."

"But she was hanging out with y'all. I mean..."

"I don't know. I haven't spoken directly to her. But I spoke to her mother an' she was acting kinda funny, know wha' I'm sayin'?"

"Like how?"

"When I called, her mother would pick up da phone an' be like, 'Coco, Josephine is not available at the moment,'" Coco mimicked Josephine's mother's voice. "Like I did her sump'n, like I'm looking for a job."

"Yeah," said Deedee. "I know what you mean." The blunt had gone out. It lay in the ash tray as a reminder of her plan. She had wanted Coco to get high, relax and maybe talk. Deedee reached for the blunt, lit it, and resumed her plan of action.

"Aw, shit. You getting open on da weed, yo. I don't know if I can handle it. I'm tore-up as it is right now," said Coco.

"C'mon, Coco, you can't front. You know you could handle this." Deedee passed the blunt to Coco. Coco yielded to temptation and as Deedee had hoped, Coco became more talkative.

"I, I know certain things that I'm checking before I even act on, you know wha' I'm saying? You know that kid Rightchus?"

"Ah," Deedee struggled to link a face with the name. "Rightchus?" she repeated.

"Yeah, yeah. Rightchus, that real black, short mofucka who be hangin' out by da clubs. Yo, he be out by da school late in da evenings. Always begging for money and cigarettes." Deedee jogged through her memory bank, but it was cloudy now from the smoke and the drinks.

"Naw, can't say. The name sounds familiar, I mean ..."

"Well, he was at da club da night that shit wit' you went down. Yo, dat nigga is pointin' fingers at Lil' Long and Vulcha."

"Word?" asked Deedee.

"Word up. He be knowing some shit."

"Them niggas," muttered Deedee under her breath. "Coco," said Deedee in a louder tone. "You're sayin' that, that this guy, ah, Rightchus is saying they--Lil' Long and Vulcha-- raped me?" Deedee rose from the soft chair where she'd been sitting. Coco glanced around at the mass of recording equipment. Then she heard fury coming through in Deedee's rushing voice.

"Them mothafuckas!" she yelled. "They deserve to fucking die."

"If they are really da ones, yo. They asses should be dead. Over wit', yo."

"But, but I think I'm sure. I mean, you're saying Rightchus is front'n'?" Deedee paced from one side of the room to the other.

"I'm not sure, cause Rightchus, he be cracking. He always front'n' like he's got knowledge of self, but he smokes da rock. I just don't know."

"Is there anyone else? Someone whose word is really bond? Then again, maybe it should just die, go away," said Deedee. Her saunter had now ceased.

"You an' I know it will never leave, yo. It's like luggage you have to carry forever to the grave," said Coco as she turned and looked at Deedee. The halting of her nervous walk was only temporary. Coco's words immediately proved to be the catalyst of a dreaded thought as she began a slow gait.

"We should go to the cops."

"Da tin badges? Are you for real?"

"I mean, they would investigate. I mean..."

"Da cops never look out for people like us," said Coco. She rubbed her soft brown cheek. "Plus, if Rightchus is telling da truth, then them niggas must be well connected."

"Why so?"

"'Cause every time they get picked up by da police, they be coming right back looking paid. Word, that's what Rightchus said, yo."

"They get paid by the cops?"

"I'm sayin' I'm not da one making da shit up. Don't be looking at me like I'm crazy. I'm just repeating sump'n I heard from a fucking crackhead. I mean, da shit might not mean nothing."

"So, how are we gonna find out if it's the truth or not?"

"I'm gonna approach them niggas, yo. I'm gonna be like, what. I don't give a fuck. Them niggas killed ma girl Bebop when they shot up Deja's place, an' they responsible for Danielle's death. You know wha' I'm sayin', Deedee? Them niggas are the ones who raped you. Da cops don't give a fuck. We got to take matters in our own hands. I'm saying, we got to take care of our business!"

"How are we gonna do this?"

"I really don't know."

"Listen, Coco, my uncle has some guns hidden. He doesn't know that I know where they are."

"What kinda guns?"

"Forty-fives, nines."

"Yo, we could do some damage. Forty-fives, yo?"

"Yep. Put some caps in them niggas' ass. End the whole shit." She pointed her index finger. "Pow!" she said. Deedee felt the surge of power that a gun gives. "Let's find out where they live, dress like prostitutes, real ho-ish. They pick us up—boom! We kill both of them."

"Nah, everybody's packing, yo. It ain't gonna be that easy."

"Coco, you think I should tell my uncle?"

"Tell your uncle what? I'm sayin, this is just speculation right now. You can't get da toasts without telling him anything, yo?"

"Da toasts?"

"Yeah, da guns, yo."

"I mean, I could get da guns. We...Me an' him haven't really discussed the whole incident. I don't know. Maybe he really blames me. Why didn't I just crash an' die?" Tears flowed down Deedee's cheeks. Coco rushed over and they embraced. Now they both were connected by a common cause, like kids in a playground. From the hug came a new bond.

"We'll get 'em, yo. I best be out. You'll be at the wake, right? So I'll see you tomorrow." Coco looked at her watch. "Damn, it's almost tomorrow already." They headed upstairs.

"Think Josephine is gonna show?" asked Deedee.

"I won't go there," said Coco.

"We'll see, won't we," said Deedee. "Let me call you a cab."

"Cool. Thanks, yo."

"Where are you going?"

"Home," Coco smiled.

"Alright. But where is home?" Deedee saw that Coco was trying to hold back tears. *She's a fighter,* thought Deedee as she dialed the taxi.

"Hell," Coco whispered.

Deedee kissed Coco's cheek. Coco patted Deedee's shoulder. They watched for the cab together, and Deedee looked on as Coco ran for the cab. She savored the growing camaraderie between her and Coco. The thought of breaking the information from Rightchus to her uncle overwhelmed her. *How would Coco handle that?* she wondered.

Coco too, was thinking as her cab rushed through the light rain. *I wasn't supposed to get this close, but she's cool people. I wonder how Mom is doing. I should go and see her. Maybe after the wake.* Oh shit! Coco almost screamed but the words never came. She saw Lil' Long and Vulcha parked at a diner, and Rightchus was standing next to their Jeep.

"Let me out right here! Thank you." Coco hurried down the block, her bop slowing down as she approached them. The thought of these three together stung her mind. Once again, her eyes welled as she strained to hear the conversation. The talk of revenge circled the heaven and brought a damp cloud to the new day.

CHAPTER 27

"You know, I don't know your biz like that, God, an' furthermore, if I did happen to know your biz, I wouldn't blow up your spot," said Rightchus.

"I ought to use some duct tape an' some gasoline on your ass," said Li'l Long.

"Let me shoot da muthafucka in his fucking mouth, Star. I'm telling you, Li'l Long, this muthafucka been snitching around," said Vulcha. He reached for his weapon of choice, a nine millimeter.

"I'm telling y'all. That ain't me, Blackman. Much respect an' all that, you know."

"Respect! Respect this." Vulcha raised the silver muzzle of the Desert Eagle to Rightchus' chest and nervously toyed with the trigger.

"No rounds? No corns?" asked Lil' Long "Now, see, you pissed me off. You done pissed ma man off. Money, if you don't give us da real jewels, my man's gonna cap you done."

"Ah'ight. Word. Listen, let me build wit' y'all like this: They trying to test y'all."

"Who is they? Give us names. Well, muthafucka?" asked Lil' Long.

"I don't really know them like that. I mean Eric, uh, Eric Ascot. He just wanted to check out my rappin', you know wha' I'm sayin'? He wanted to see what kinda comp is really out there," said Rightchus, giving his best con artist performance. "Busta, you've seen da guy, da scout who brought me to him. They was lookin' for a hit, know wha' I'm sayin'?"

"Don't play wit' us, you non-rapping mo'-fucka. They want a hit, huh? Well, tell them we have a demo we wanna let them hear, know wha' I'm sayin'?" asked Lil' Long, his eyes taking deadly aim at the nervous Rightchus.

"Hey man, I'm not giving y'all up, cuz y'all can make some demos, I know."

Lil' Long reached into his pockets and pulled out about a dozen tiny redcap vials filled with cheap, yellow-stained cocaine rocks. He poured them in Rightchus' outstretched hands.

"Now, you remember who really feeds you, muthafucka. Go on and enjoy. It's on da house," said Lil' Long. Horns blared as Vulcha pulled the Jeep abruptly into the traffic. They departed, leaving Rightchus standing on the corner. Coco ran over. She slapped his hands. The vials of crack littered the pavement.

"Bitch!" yelled Rightchus. "What da fuck you think you're doing, girl?"

"Saving your muthafucking, no good life. Your ass best tell me da truth about this whole shit or you ain't smokin' none of these goddamn rocks." Coco scrambled on the sidewalk, picking up as many of the small vials as she could.

"What truth? What da fuck you talkin' 'bout?"

"You know what da fuck I'm talkin' 'bout, nigga. Hello, da real fuckin' truth. You better start yakkin' away or everyone in da 'hood will know you is nuthin' but a fuckin' crackhead."

"I don't give a fuck 'bout no muthafuckas from da 'hood knowin'. Everybody got a nasty habit. Mine's crack. What's yours? Drinkin', smokin' dust? Cuz that's why your Spanish friend died. Too much fuckin' dust an' coke. So don't step to Rightchus wit' that bullshit."

"Bullshit! You fuckin' crackhead."

"Coco, you best keep your ass out of this an' stay in school, ah'ight. I'm tellin' you, if you keep followin' this shit up, yo' ass will be ended. I'm warnin' you."

"Well, you give it to me straight an' I'll let you smoke your rocks. And I'll handle my fuckin' business, ah'ight?"

"Can't you handle business without my fuckin' involvement?"

"No, yo."

"Why?"

"Cuz you started this whole shit. So now you've got to come straight, muthafucka."

"You seen their guns?"

"I have guns, too, yo."

"Guns? Guns? Listen up. You gonna need more than just guns to do battle wit' them niggas. Drug dealas an' cops. Fuckin' cops be scared, an' *you* wanna do battle? Coco, you stick to singin' an' doin' your thing. Get your swerve that way. Let da big boys handle that type shit.

"Coco, I told you 'bout da time I auditioned for Eric Ascot. He loves ma shit, ma shit. He love da way I put it down. See, I was standin' there, he comes along in a limo, pulls up and start checkin' me doin' my thing. At the end, he was like 'oh shit, we need you in a da studio right away.' He told me, I was all this 'n' that an' he would love to work wit' my ass soon. Soon as ya'll shit drops, he gonna work wit' ma shit. Ma shit be out there on your radio, in stere-ereo. Off the hook, baby," said Rightchus, singing and stomping his feet in rhythm.

Coco gazed at Rightchus with eyes reddened from staying up too late. They glowed crimson red with anger at Rightchus' comedic repertoire. Under the wrath of Coco's stare, the stirring of Shorty-Wop, a.k.a. Rightchus, ceased. She opened her fists, exposing small red and white topped vials with yellow rocks inside. He read her intentions and opened his lips to plead.

"No, Coco. No, Coco, don't."

"Nigga, please," said Coco. She hurled the vials at Rightchus. He failed miserably to catch all the vials. Most of them scattered in the street. Rightchus scrambled to retrieve them.

"Bitch, you best stay outta that shit. Leave peoples bidness alone or you'll be toe-tagged."

"Fuck you, you crackhead lowlife." Coco entered the park, ready to walk home. She turned back to see Rightchus being joined by a congregation of emaciated people in dirty clothes. They prepared to sacrifice their lives in the worship of the contents of the vials.

"Crackheads," Coco whispered. Her bop came off a little shaky.

"Stay out of it, Coco. You ain't much. Just a regular girl," Rightchus called.

Then he addressed his crowd. "Y'all muthafuckas come on an' collect your poison. It ain't free, it's gonna cost three." Business was brisk. Rightchus now concentrated on his growing flock.

CHAPTER 28

"I'm sorry, babe, but it just couldn't wait. I mean, I--I wasn't really late. I was there when you received your award, and I was very proud of you. So now you're full-time, huh?" asked Eric. He had managed to reach the awards banquet, but, as expected, he had arrived late.

"Don't you try to weasel out of this, and stop trying to be my friend. I worked for it and furthermore, Mr. Lateness, I was always full-time." Sophia laid the box of *Romeo y Juliet* on the table, and knowing Eric disapproved, removed a cigar and lit it. She gagged on the smoke. Eric reacted in alarm. The waiter rushed to the table with water.

"I'm sorry, madame, but there's no smoking allowed. May I get you something to drink?"

"I'm sorry too," said Sophia. "May I have a double martini? And I don't know what Mr. Lateness here wants." She stared coldly at Eric.

"I'll have what the lady's having, thank you," said Eric.

"Please hurry or I may be tempted to light up again," said Sophia. The waiter departed.

"Now, see, I told you not to light that cigar. What..."

"Yeah, you told me, but I'm not in the mood to hear your late butt, 'cause when I talk to you, you don't try to hear me."

"C'mon, babe, you're not still running that shit."

"That shit? That shit happens to be my bread and butter and your lateness made me look sorta bad."

"Sorta bad. I mean, I apologized already."

"I don't give a damn if you apologized ten times already. If I want to have the eleventh, you will give it up, baby. And furthermore, my smoking brought a waiter running to our table, thank you. Otherwise, we would've been sitting here waiting. Oh, but I'm good at waiting. I've been practicing all night. Eric, you don't even want to start with me."

"I'm sorry."

"Unh-uh. I did not ask for it yet."

The waiter arrived with the drinks. Eric glanced around the cafe. *She's right,* he thought as he studied the stage. An elderly man with a long white beard sat at a piano, center stage. The lights dimmed. *Good,* thought Eric. *I wouldn't want everyone else to see me grovel.* He smiled as he turned to Sophia, sipping her martini. Eric heard the pleasant note of the piano just as he met Sophia's hostile glare.

"Baby," Eric said softly, "you know I wouldn't do anything intentionally to hurt you, so please, please forgive me."

"But Eric, I asked you nicely..."

"Baby, I know you did."

"Well, if you dance with me ..."

"Dance? Babe you can't dance to--well, err, I guess you could. May I have this dance?" Eric stood in supplication.

"Yes, thanks," said Sophia.

Eric guided her out on the floor. He smiled and embraced her petite frame. She was beautiful in her simple black dress, which revealed more now than Eric had noticed earlier. *She's stunning,* he thought. He held her tighter.

"Hmm" she murmured. He grabbed her hand and swept her off her feet. He was floating on the cloud provided by the pianist. Sophia held to him firmly, not caring where the ride would end.

"Your place or mine?" asked Eric.

Sophia said nothing, but molded herself to Eric's body.

"Well, you are well-dressed. My place, mister. Hurry and don't be late." She disengaged from Eric and headed for the exit. Eric sprinted to the table, paid the tab and hurried out of the cafe. She smiled when he got in the car. Eric challenged the smile with a hard kiss. Sophia resisted at first, then gave in. His hands met the silky black barrier around her soft flesh.

"Alright, alright. Let's go. But is Deedee okay?" Sophia caught her breath. "Eric, let's go to your place. We..."

"Call the house."

"And risk waking her?"

"You know Deedee doesn't hear nothing when she goes to sleep."

"So why call?"

"When I left home, one of her friends, Coco, had stopped over."

"Oh, the call is for Coco?" Sophia dialed the number. "No answer."

"No answer means Coco's gone. Deedee's probably in bed."

"Good. Just the way we planned this, Mr. Lateness."

"I won't be late now." Eric massaged Sophia's thigh. The fabric felt supple in his hand, her flesh warmed to his touch. She put the car in gear and zoomed out of the parking lot.

Eric and Sophia, a little drunk from the evening's activity, crept up the stairs like kids who had broken curfew. They dashed into the bedroom, where Eric's hands quickly encountered the silk panties covering Sophia's ass.

"Take it easy," whispered Sophia.

"I'm just trying to be on time."

"You don't have to try. The loving ain't goin' nowhere. It's right here, waitin' for you," said Sophia in a throaty whisper. She turned to face Eric, her dress clinging to a toned, five-foot-eight, curves-in-the-right-places body.

He watched with fascination as she reached up and made the black dress disappear with her arm movements. Eric kissed her gently, biting Sophia's earlobes while his hands moved smoothly all over her buttocks.

"Ooh. Oh my, are we the impatient one..." sighed Sophia as her body clung to Eric's and her heartbeat galloped, her breath coming in gasps.

"Ahh," she moaned as their bodies fell entangled on the huge waterbed. The bed swayed slightly. Sophia rolled on top. She peeled off the rest of her clothing. Eric kissed and sucked at her nipples. Sophia's naked body came in contact with the wool covering his erection.

"You're not out of your clothes yet, good looking? Late again, huh?" whispered Sophia. She straddled Eric. He could feel her soft skin. His hands roamed, kneading her taut hot brown body. His touch made her skin burn. Her tension uncoiled into mush. The heat ignited Sophia, raising her temperature to dizzying heights.

"Ah, uh, I can't wait on you, honey. I want you inside of me now," she whispered as she pulled Eric's zipper down and unleashed his erection. She easily slid the condom over its head then she mounted and began rocking back and forth.

"Ahh, yeah, baby," said Eric.

"Shh, ah," whispered Sophia, kissing Eric's face, her arms wrapped around his neck. The cheeks of her buttocks were cupped in his large strong hands. Her gentle rocking brought him to the gates of ecstasy.

CHAPTER 29

Lil' Long held his finger on the Glock's trigger. He stood watch in this position until Vulcha was a step away from him.

"Five thou," said Vulcha as he approached. It was the password. Lil' Long relaxed.

"Five G's," said Lil' Long. "They drug dealin' asses be gettin' over from da cheap protection we be providing their asses wit' Vulcha." He placed the gun in his waistband. They got back in the Jeep.

"So whatcha sayin', kid?" Vulcha jerkily pulled the Jeep into the traffic.

"I'm sayin' they should be hittin' us wit' mo' dough, see? They gettin' protection from da cops. I mean, when was da last time a bust went down?"

"True."

"That's worth a couple G's. An' mo'fuckas able to operate safely. Nobody, I mean nobody, runs up on nobody. We're like operation safety net, see?"

"True dat, kid. So what you sayin'?"

"I'm sayin', nigga, we need a muthafuckin' pay raise."

"Yeah, now you talkin'. It ain't no lie, nigga," said Vulcha, his eyes steadfast on the road.

"I'm sayin', Vulcha, you got a new chumpy an' all. How's what's her name doing?"

"Who that, Kamilla?"

"Yeah, that big-titty bitch."

"Don't be callin' my bitch no bitch, mo'fucka. That's ma woman."

"Don't be runnin' that 'who's callin' who bitch', Vulcha. We go way back, but that don't mean I won't break you off sump'n," said Lil' Long, caressing the black handle of his gun.

"I ain't da enemy, kid. Let's you an' me go have a drink an' discuss this matter like gentlemen."

"Good idea, sir," said Lil' Long in a mocking tone. They both laughed. "But I mean it," said Lil' Long.

"Mean what, nigga? Get a raise?"

"Yeah, and the other question, too. How's your woman?"

"Hit her wit' dough. Hit that phat ass often. She's always smilin', know wha' I'm sayin'? No stress."

"Yeah, yeah, nigga. Talkin' 'bout hittin', we should pay mofuckin' Busta a visit."

"But how do we know? That nigga Rightchus might be makin' up da shit to strum up some biz for himself."

"Nah, nah. That nigga, he'll be doin' much shit, but Rightchus is never, ever wrong, Vulcha."

"So let's talk to Busta. Lemme talk to him, kid."

"Vulcha, I know he's your man from way back an' all, but check da stats. Rightchus has never been wrong. We should be takin' duct tape an' baseball bats to that fat, mo'fuckin' Busta-ass nigga."

"I put in a lot o' work for that nigga, before he went legit. Lemme build wit' him, see what he got to say, know wha' I'm sayin'?"

"I'm saying da nigga is da enemy. Da nigga is tryin' to get us. We got to get him first. Pull up. Pull up right here. They got some good southern fried chicken in this spot."

"Let me see him first, ah'ight?" asked Vulcha, looking at Lil' Long. Their gaze was held together by Lil' Long's bitten lips.

"Ah'ight," said Lil' Long, "for old school's sake. Getting soft, nigga? Don't get weak on me." Li'l Long winked as he spoke. Vulcha knew that Busta's days were numbered. He pulled the vehicle into the lot. They headed toward the all night diner. Circulating thoughts of Busta were disturbed by a voice. A man appeared out of nowhere, his hand outstretched.

"You must leave the keys, sir," said the attendant. Vulcha kept walking and threw the keys over his shoulder. They landed next to the attendant's feet.

"You're careless, Vulcha."

"Let's get drunk, ah'ight? I ain't getting careless, either. I know your ass is thinkin' because Vulcha have da piece of ass at home that he soft. But I'm not, nigga." By now Vulcha was sitting across from Li'l Long, sipping an Alabama Slammer.

"Well, you know my motto, mo'fucka: All weak niggas must die in order for me to be immortal." Li'l Long raised his drink. Vulcha stared at Li'l Long and considered talking with Busta without Li'l Long knowing. He contemplated if, and why, Busta wanted to kill them. Vulcha knew he had to see Busta before Li'l Long did. Li'l Long had never like Busta. He gave him props only because Vulcha had asked him to do so. Li'l Long would kill Busta on sight. That's just how he was. He downed his drink and ordered another.

CHAPTER 30

The day was cloudy and it dragged. By ten thirty, most of the kids had gathered in the huge hall of the funeral home. The entire school, including faculty and staff, were gathered there. The hall was frozen silent as everyone filed passed the gold and white casket. Some stopped briefly, others broke the silence with sobbing outbursts. Danielle's family was there, all dressed in black, their faces solemn and their eyes red. Josephine stared at the casket then touched it. She wanted to ask *why?* But only sobs came. Josephine saw Coco next to the window and approached her. Coco was staring longingly out the window. She watched the kids outside, forming groups and engaging in gabfests.

"What's up, Coco?" Josephine startled Coco, who whirled to face the girl she had considered a friend.

"Yeah, what's popping, Josephine?"

"A lot o' people showed up, huh?" asked Josephine. Coco noticed her eyes swollen from crying.

"Yeah. How have you been?"

"I been better. Look, you probably don't understand, but my parents..."

"We better go outside, yo."

Both girls walked hastily out of the building. The gray skies hung delicately, as if the slightest interruption would cause them to come crashing down to earth. The girls stood amidst their peers and briefly hugged. Then Josephine resumed her explanation.

"My parents, they think I could be next, so they didn't want me out of the home for a minute. I'm lucky they let me come here. Listen, she was my friend, too. I'm still expecting the phone to ring and she'll be on the other end. I miss her," said Josephine, tears streaming down her face. Coco hugged her and they both cried together. Their sobbing drew the attention of other mourners. Grief stricken kid's came to Coco and Josephine, shared the sorrow and moved on.

"My parents want to send me to some school down south. I don't really wanna go, but I don't have much choice. After all, they're still my parents. I mean..."

"You got to do what's right, yo."

"I don't know what's right. I mean, Danielle...I got to go, Coco. Listen, take care," said Josephine, who was still crying.

Coco stared at her and realized she wanted to know what Josephine had meant, but didn't ask. Before she knew it, Josephine had rejoined her parents. They waved at Coco, hugged Josephine and walked away. *What about the group?* Coco almost shouted. *What about our friendship?* She dug her hands through her pockets found a pack of cigarettes and quickly lit one.

"May I have one of those?"

"Hey whassup,Deedee? Creeping on me, huh? Yeah, sure yo, you can have one." She offered Deedee the cigarette. "Having a rough ass day."

"Oh yeah." Deedee puffed along with Coco.

"This place. Damn, there's so much sadness. I spoke to Josephine."

"Josephine? How's she doing?"

"Well, she's pretty caught up wit' the death and all. Her parents tryin'a ship her outta town."

"Where? Did she say?"

"Down south somewhere. I don't know, yo."

"So what's gonna happen with y'all and the singing?"

"Well, damn, I don't really know for sure. I guess right about now everything will be on hold."

"Coco, you shouldn't. You aren't gonna quit now. I mean, you've got to do sump'n for Danielle, you know."

"Yeah, right now, da shit's too sad and I miss her too much, yo," said Coco. Tears formed in her sad eyes, her throat exploded in a choking sob. Deedee hugged her. Coco's body shuddered from the emotion. Deedee's body swayed with Coco's. The clouds continued to stain the sky, leaving it hopelessly gray.

****

The phone rang once, then again and again. Eric reached up to get the call, but he was pulled back onto the bed by Sophia.

"Oh, aren't we in a rush to get this call," she said with mock severity.

"Rush? I only rush for you and business. Oh baby, don't do that."

"Let the machine pick this one up, babe," said Sophia, toying with Eric's semi-erect penis, her hands busy making designs in his pubic hair. The phone continued to ring until the machine picked up. It was Busta. Eric grabbed the receiver.

"Hello."

Sophia watched Eric for a moment and then jumped out of the bed. She threw a pillow at him before she went downstairs.

"It's' done, E. I'll meet up with you later."

"Yeah, alright. I'll talk to you later. At the bar? Cool."

****

Busta put the receiver down. Lips traced kisses all over his body. He smiled and stroked the hair of the woman sucking his erection. The lip service brought him the relief he sought, but he had failed to notice the listener standing at the door of his apartment.

"Fat fuck," whispered Vulcha as he left his listening post for the streets.

****

Eric peered out the window and saw the clouds. *It must be raining on Busta's end in the city,* he thought as he ran down the stairs in search of Sophia. He found her in the kitchen drinking orange juice. He embraced her and stroked her body.

"Let's go back and roll in my big water bed," he suggested as he rubbed his hands over Sophia's breasts. Her nipples hardened to his touch and her knees weakened as she felt his manhood thrust against her.

"Why are you and Busta playing cloak and dagger?"

"Business, babe."

"Your niece left you a reminder," said Sophia, handing Eric a piece of paper. He read it quickly.

"Oh, I forgot. Today's the wake for that girl, ah, Danielle."

"Well?"

"Well, I told Deedee I would, we would be there..."

"Let's go, then."

"You mean at this moment, babe? We could still get sump'n in. I mean we got time. It's perfect weather for staying in"

"I wasn't the one who told Deedee that we would be there." She kissed his lips and attempted to pull away, but he held her. He ground his body into hers and pressed his mouth against hers. She fell back against the kitchen sink, uttering soft phrases of protest.

"Come on honey, you know you don't have time for anything thing like this. Ahh... You're always in rush." Eric continued with the business at hand; Undressing and tasting Sophia's passion on her skin.

She held Eric's arms tightly as he gently hoisted her to the edge of the sink. The tongue lashing commenced.

"Hmm," Sophia moaned. Eric's lips now pressed against her exposed upper thigh, his tongue crept to an already wet spot. Sophia thrashed her legs, her moans grew louder and her breath came in gasps. She smiled at Eric and closed her eyes.

CHAPTER 31

"Why didn't you just end that mo'fucka's life right there, Vulcha? You should've killed him and his bitch," yelled Lil' Long into the receiver.

"Yeah, yeah, I should have, but I wanted you to know. That mo'fuckin' Rightchus was on point again, Star."

"Th-th-those m-mo-mo'fuckas go-got con-contract on us? Who they th-think they d-dealin wit', huh? Mo'fuckin' fools? Vulcha, come get me now, ni-nigga." Li'l Long slammed the phone into the cradle.

"Yo baby, I gotta to take care of business, ah'ight? So I'll call you later," said Vulcha, glancing at Kamilla.

"Leave me some money," she said.

"What do you do wit' all this money?" Vulcha took out five one-hundred dollar bills and set them on the night stand. He had called Lil' Long from Kamilla's place and he was upset. He felt Busta had done the wrong thing. He had known Busta since he was a little boy running the streets and Busta was a big-time drug dealer. Now he had gone legit. But why had he put a contract on Vulcha and Li'l Long?

Vulcha paused and watched as the rain sprinkled the Jeep's roof. The droplets formed tiny puddles. *It's not coming down so hard,* he thought and quickly walked to the vehicle. Vulcha opened the door, got in and drove to meet Li'l Long.

****

Kamilla dressed and left immediately. *I have to see those girls,* she thought as she hurried from the apartment. She hailed a cab and headed for the high school. At the school, she learned of Danielle's wake. She quickly found another cab and headed for the funeral home.

****

Lil' Long and Vulcha rode to the sound of weapons being cocked and uncocked, magazines being loaded then unloaded. Vulcha parked the vehicle in front of Busta's apartment.

"You wanna do this alone, kid?" asked Lil' Long.

"Why?" asked Vulcha.

"Cuz he was your man, know wha' I'm sayin'?"

"Yeah, I hear you, nig. But this strictly 'bout biz, see? Ain't no mo' friendship bullshit, see? It ain't goin' down like that. Da nigga crossed us."

"Word is bond, and a mo'fucka who does that, has to be dealt wit'. Know wha' I'm sayin'? He was your man. You wanna handle da biz?"

"That's peace," said Vulcha

"Ah'ight, let's do this."

"What? Man it's been on," said Vulcha with a grimace, which spoke of vengeance. But his tone dripped of sarcasm as he continued. "Yeah, let me give this fat muthafucka the big payback."

"Yeah, yeah, handle your biz, son," said Lil' Long, offering his right fist for encouragement. They walked away from the Jeep. Both were decked out in black leather jackets over black T-shirts and black jeans. Li'l Long's Afro was neatly braided. Vulcha walked a step in front, collar up, with a black beret to shield his bald pate. Killing without fear was the thing these urban angels of death performed. Vulcha flaunted a pair of nine-millimeter Glocks, cocked and ready. Behind him, Li'l Long had a Desert Eagle strapped to his right side. They got off the elevator and found Busta's apartment.

Vulcha rang the doorbell. Li'l Long stood guard next to the stairs. He swayed as if drunk. Vulcha rang a second time. He heard sounds within the apartment, but the door did not open.

"Busta, whassup? Got some biz to see you on, big man," he called through the door. He rang the bell for the third time, nodding to Lil' Long. The rattling of the door caught his attention. Vulcha stood and waited. He was uneasy now. Just as nervous as on that cold morning when he was released on parole after serving nine months of a one-year bid. Back then, it seemed like every day was cold. He was trying to survive on the streets. Snatching chains was all he knew--a street specialty that yielded long ropes of gold but was short on cash.

Busta had owned and operated many weed spots back then. He hired Vulcha immediately when he saw the young Vulcha stalking his victims.

"You gonna have to keep getting up after getting your swerve, kid. Doeth unto others, know-wha'-I'm-sayin'? Why take his shit in violence? Take it in peace, see? You don't have to hurt the brother. Come, I'll show you," Busta had told him. Vulcha listened. His eyes grew wider as Busta peeled a crisp hundred-dollar bill from a thick wad of bills.

Busta continued, "Brothers will pay for all types of entertainment, cuz we love that type o' shit. Nobody else love that shit like we do. We wait on long lines in the coldest of night, searching through our pockets trying to get into a nightclub." Busta placed the clean bill on top of a public phone, damaged by an angry user. Vulcha had taken the bill and several more.

Vulcha ran one of Busta's weed spots. It kept him indoors, out of the cold, but it landed him another stretch in jail for parole violation. He had never repaid Busta for his kindness, Vulcha remembered as he waited.

"Who dat? Who is it? Ooh, aah, agh. Shit."

Vulcha heard the hiss of passing bullets. He turned in time to see smoke departing the silenced, shiny muzzle of the Desert Eagle held in Lil' Long's left hand. He turned and stared at the space carved by the bullets. They had ripped the upper half of the door nearly to shreds and mutilated Busta's heavy body with holes the size of baseballs.

"These rhino shits are really bad, kid. I'm tellin' you, da rhino rounds will penetrate anything.   Don't sleep. Damn!" said Li'l Long.

Vulcha realized what had transpired. He pushed, and the door swung open.   He stood back as if to admire the handiwork, awed by the damage done by the bullets.

Vulcha walked slowly into the apartment without speaking. He glanced around, guns clenched tightly in each hand as if he expected Busta to rise. Busta's bleeding body moved in slow convulsions. Thick red blood flowed, staining the soft, plush, earth-hued rug.

Vulcha ambled over to Busta's jerking body.   He dropped a one-hundred dollar bill in the spreading blood stain. He fired twice and Busta's body jerked for the final time. Vulcha slowly shook his head as Lil' Long spewed his venom.

"All weak mothafuckas must die in order for me to achieve immortality. Niggas must perish. That's why we still here, kid. I don't joke when I go to smoke a mo'fucka." Lil' Long held his Desert Eagle high. Vulcha gaped, grasping for words. They came in an uncontrollable outburst.

"I--I thought...I thought I was da one to take care of this fuckin' problem. It was my problem. He was my man, remember? We go way back. What--What, you don't trust me or sump'n?" he asked.

"You're heated, nigga. I saved your fuckin' life an' you don't even..." Li'l Long began his search, lifting long gold chains with heavy medallions, rummaging through drawers.

"Let's go, Vulcha. This fat mothafucka kept everything in da fuckin' bank. Let's get his producer friend. You can shoot his ass. But are you gettin' soft, nigga?"

Vulcha looked at his old friend's apartment. He fired one of his nine-millimeters twice into Busta's head. Then he leaned down and removed a diamond encrusted ring from Busta's twitching left pinky.

"I knew your ass would want that shit, yo. Let's go before po-po start hitting the doors."

"Yeah," said Vulcha. "Let's use da fuckin' stairs."

They were quickly down the stairs and out of the apartment building. The rain was now a slight drizzle. They ran to the Jeep.

"Let's find us a music producer, kid," said Lil' Long. He pounded his fist against Vulcha's.

****

The taxi pulled-up outside the funeral home. Kamilla rushed up the steps. She wanted to warn Coco and Deedee. Kamilla was sickened when she saw the mourning family members. She avoided the casket, asking other mourners about Coco's whereabouts.

She followed the route she was given in search of Deedee and Coco. On her way, she was startled by a strange voice.

"You used to be one of Big Hank's girls. Now you're Vulcha's pet."

"Who are you?" asked Kamilla, startled.

"My name is Rightchus, but you can call me Shorty-Wop. It's all good. So what's your game, lady?"

"Well, how about this. I'm tryin' to find some friends."

"Li'l Long and Vulcha?"

"No," said Kamilla. Her frown showed complete scorn. "Now, how do you have all this info, Shorty?" Kamilla looked down at the diminutive street informant.

"Oh, those names irritate you, huh? Coco and her friend's location for twenty. Shorty has to make a livin'. Woppin' shit ain't that easy, know wha' I'm sayin'? Although, I wouldn't turn down a night wit' you, baby."

"Here." Kamilla handed Rightchus a twenty. "I wouldn't go out with you if they paid me a million."

"They're over there, in the diner. They're probably lookin' for you, too." Rightchus was a little upset by Kamilla's last remark. "Why wouldn't you go out with me? I'm not the right stature?" Rightchus raised his index and middle fingers of both hands. Kamilla ignored him and hurried to the diner.

"Cuz I can get that way. I'm gonna blow up soon. I'm workin' on different angles, you know."

"Work on gettin' yourself a shower, my brother," said Kamilla over her shoulder.

"Why you wanna dis a brother? See, it's women like you that cause a brother to shoot a bitch."

Kamilla didn't hear or see any of Rightchus' gestures. She was in the diner, where she spotted Coco and Deedee.

"May I join y'all?" asked Kamilla. "We have to go see Eric Ascot."

"That's my uncle. What is it about?" asked Deedee. She was startled and impatient. Coco stared at the intruder.

"I overheard Vulcha this morning. He was on the phone. Something about being set up and paying back the person who did it. He mentioned Busta and the music producer, Eric. I will not let them kill anybody else."

"Why? You were there when they did Danielle."

"When I last saw Danielle, she was alive. Vulcha said that Lil' Long gave her a suicide knob to slob."

"Bullshit. Them mo'fuckas killed her. As far as I know, y'all were together, know wha I'm sayin'?" said Coco. Her shrill voice attracted the attention of the other patrons.

"What y'all staring at?" asked Deedee. "Let's go. My uncle should be home. They acting like they ain't never seen people have a discussion before." They headed for the exit.

"Ladies, ladies, you haven't paid," called a disturbed waiter.

"How much? Will this cover it?" Kamilla slipped the waiter two twenty- dollar bills.

"Yes. Wait for your change."

The trio caught a taxi and the car sped away. Rightchus ran toward it.

"Stay out of it. It's bigger than y'all," he shouted. "Y'all are not listening. All right then, fuck it. Y'all handle your BI and I'll handle mine." He pulled out a cellular phone and dialed. "Can I speak to Inspector Dawson?"

"Dawson here. Who is this?"

"Rightchus. Some shots ready to pop. Those girls…"

CHAPTER 32

"Oh shit, we're gettin' pulled over? Them mo'fuckas crazy, kid? Whassup? Your insurance expired or sump'n?" Li'l Long joked at the police sirens. Vulcha drove on.

"They better recognize these plates. Niggas know not to fuck wit' me."

"Nigga, you are a non-driving mo'fucka. That's why da mo'fucka pullin' us da fuck over."

"Them niggas been on our tail for awhile."

"Ain't you gonna stop, son? You need to stop an' ask da officer where fuckin' Eric Ascot lives, cuz you akkin' like you lost, nig."

"Stop?" asked Vulcha incredulously. "Ah'ight. I'll stop, but if this mothafucka keeps me too long, I'm smokin' his ass." He pulled over to the side of the road.

"Here they come, walking over like two fucking faggots," said Vulcha.

"What I do? I ain't done nuthin' illegal, so why da fuck are you stoppin me?"

"Hello gentlemen," said the officer as he came to a stop next to Vulcha's side of the vehicle. "You seem to have a broken tail light."

"That shit was fine earlier. Now it's broken? C'mon, that's da reason for stoppin' a nigga?" asked Vulcha. Lil' Long eased the passenger chair back just as the second officer squeezed off three shots that swished by his head. One bullet grazed Lil' Long's neck and struck Vulcha in the head.

"It's a hit," yelled Lil' Long. But it was too late. Vulcha's body slumped in the driver's seat. His head fell on the steering wheel, causing a continuous blast of the horn. Lil' Long opened fire with both guns. He hit one officer twice in the face. The other ducked. Vulcha's limped body shifted and took several shots in the chest. Lil' Long returned fire, hitting the second officer. The officer dove for cover, dragging his wounded limbs in a bid to escape. But Lil' Long overtook him, the fury of the Desert Eagle ripped his face to shreds.

Lil' Long ran back to the Jeep. Vulcha's body was hanging out of the vehicle, his blood mixed with the rain, staining the asphalt.

"Vulcha, Vulcha. C'mon, kid. Talk to me. Fuck! You mo'fucka, don't die on me. Don't die on a nigga," he screamed, cradling Vulcha's head in his arms.

Vulcha's lifeless body had fallen completely from the seat now. Lil' Long tried blindly to revive him. He walked the body up and down the street, but Vulcha's legs just dragged and his blood flowed with the rain that was pelting down. Lil' Long sobbed. He screamed as he laid Vulcha's body on the street next to the other two bodies. Lil' Long checked their ID's. They were the police, all right: Detectives Carter and Sazlowski. On the front seat of the patrol car was a matchbook, inscribed 1-800 HIT-DEAD in red. Lil' Long threw it on the wet asphalt. For a moment he didn't know what to do. He listened to the police radio: "Please respond, Detective Sazlowski, Detective Carter. Respond, over. Did you make contact? What is your GTA? Is there a patrol in the sector?"

Lil' Long picked up the microphone.

"In order for me to be immortal, all weak mo'fuckas must die. Sazlowski and Carter are dead. Why was a hit put on me? You can't use me no more? Fuckin' cowards. Bitch-asses. You cant stop me either, bitches." He fired his weapon into the car's communication system. He looked once more at Vulcha's body. Then he was off, running like a man possessed.

Lil' Long rang Eric Ascot's doorbell. Sophia promptly answered the door, slightly opening it. Lil' Long kicked the door completely open and smacked Sophia with the butt of his gun. He stuck the nozzle in Eric Ascot's chest, while standing over Sophia's unconscious body.

The taxi arrived at the house with Coco, Deedee and Kamilla just in time to witnesse Lil' Long's dramatic entry.

"Is there a back way?" asked Kamilla.

"Yes," said Deedee.

"That's probably where Vulcha went," said Kamilla. "He gave me a twenty-two. I'm gonna go back there and surprise him."

"Let me go wit' you, yo."

"No, Coco, come with me," said Deedee. Let's go through the window and get the guns. Uncle E. keeps them in his bedroom."

"Ah'ight, yo," said Coco. She helped Deedee climb through the window. Meanwhile Kamilla entered the rear door. She heard Lil' Long yelling.

"They killed my man! For what? You mo'fuckas has got to pay."

Kamilla, not knowing what she was up against, entered the room and pointed her gun at Lil' Long. Before she could pull the trigger, Lil' Long's gun blasted twice. Kamilla fell in a heap. Her made-up face splattered on the wall like some grotesque artwork. Lil' Long turned the gun back to Eric. Eric's mouth gaped. He held his hands high.

"Put your mo-mo'fuckin' h-hands d-down, nigga, this ain't no fuckin' stick-up. See, it's like this; in order for me to be immortal, all weak motherfuckas must die," said Lil' Long. Then, without warning, an explosion filled the room. Lil' Long wobbled and staggered. He turned to see Coco holding a smoking shotgun, and Deedee, pointing a forty-five at him. Another outburst hit him and he slumped on his knees"

Take that, Mr. Immorality," said Deedee.

"Hello!" said Coco.

The Desert Eagle remained in Lil' Long's grip as the blood oozed profusely from his slumping body. Deedee took aim and squeezed off one more round. Lil' Long fell forward, his body twitching.

****

An unmarked police car pulled up and two officers jumped out.

"You better stay here and not move," said one of the officers.

"I ain't goin' nowhere. Think I'm stupid wit' all them guns going off?"

The officers ran to the house and then returned to the car. He keyed the radio.

"Confirmed killing of Michael Lowe, a.k.a. Lil' Long. Yeah, two girls took care of him. We have someone by the name of Rightchus, claims he knows both girls. He tipped us off that they would be coming here. Over."

"Rightchus. Ah, he's a good informant. Take care of him. He has given us some very useful tips. We may still be able to use his services." Rightchus gazed intensely at the police radio. Now he understood his role.

"You guys really can't be trusted, huh?" asked Rightchus. His eyes widened as he stared at the police officer, gun drawn and radio in hand. Rightchus never got the answer.

To be continued in:

Ghetto Girls II

Black Print Publishing
287 Livingston St
Brooklyn, NY 11217 (718) 875-1082

Thugs and the Women Who Love Them
by Wahida Clark

List Price: $14.95
Paperback: 209 pages ;
Publisher: Black Print Publishing
ISBN: 0-97227711-0
(October 2002)
Book Description
Meet kyra, an aspiring doctor, Jaz a third year law student and Roz pursuing a degree in chemistry, Three best Friends with one major thing in common. *They all love thugs.*

About the Author
Thugs and the women Who Love Them is the first book from Wahida Clark, an inmate in a United States Federal Prison. Clark Brings us into a world of sex, crime and brutality, all the more real because she lived it. Ms Clark is hard at work on her next book, *Every Thug Needs a Lady*

Order Form

Use this form to order additional copies of **Black Print's Publishing's** Titles as they become available

Name /Company:...
Address :..
City.................State.............Zip.....................................
Phone:..............................Fax......................................
E-mail ....

Item	Price	Qty
Thugs and The Women Who Love Them	$14.95	
Choices Men Make	$13.95	
Ghetto Girls	$14.95	
Mistrustful	$14.95	
You Are not Alone	$13.95	

Signature :..